Her response and the hint of superiority in her voice fanned his anger. And seeing the perfection of her throat, his lust as well. He resheathed his sword and took a step forward. She regarded him calmly. Sugiyama grabbed the lapels of her robe and tore them apart. He stood at arms length and admired the delicate pale body that was exposed to his gaze. She had just come from her bath and her skin was smooth and delicately scented. She tolerated his gaze for a moment, then turned to go. He held her forcefully and a grin appeared on his thin lips. Without a word he forced her down to her knees.

Also Published by BLUE MOON BOOKS

The Legendary Age

WOMEN
of
GION

AKAHIGE NAMBAN

BLUE MOON BOOKS, INC. NEW YORK

Women of Gion
ISBN 0-8216-5036-X
CIP data available from the Library of Congress

Manufactured in the United States of America
Published by Blue Moon Books, Inc.
61 Fourth Avenue
New York, NY 10003

Cover design by Steve Brower

CHAPTER 1

THE WIZENED MAN CAME OUT OF THE MISTY DRIZZLE, cringing towards the light. He slid onto the liquor-stand's bench and looked around as if frightened. The rain and mist obscured the pagodas and buildings of the city of Miyako. The area around the city's former Demon Gate was almost deserted, and the *shochu* seller was about to fold up and go home. "What'll it be?" he asked instead.

"Big cup. And some of the stew."

He drank the fiery sweet-potato liquor quickly, then licked his lips and ordered another.

"Pay for the first one," said the counterman. He had too much experience with customers drinking then refusing to pay. Particularly miserable looking ones like the skinny craftsman before him. "You can pay, can't you?" he asked, suddenly suspicious.

"Hee hee hee. Of course I can," the elderly man laughed, his unkempt topknot fluttering. "He he."

"Show your coppers then."

"Coppers? Hee hee hee. Coppers the man wants. How about this then?" He shoved a hand into his grimy blue-dyed under-apron and showed the contents to the seller.

The *shochu* man gulped. Resting in the cupped palm were several small pieces of silver, obviously cut from different squarish silver *momme* coins, and a tiny nugget of yellow gold.

"Got it honestly, did you?"

"What's it to you? Gimme another cup, and some of those cooked radishes."

The counterman complied as the elderly artisan shoved a piece of silver at him and hurriedly hid the rest, as if reminded of his fear. He gulped at his liquor and ordered another. The thin rain continued to fall, obscuring the

1

sounds and the sights of the night. Only his face was lit in sharp, tired angles by the single paper lampion on the *shochu* seller's cart.

The *shochu* man started closing down and after another drink the wizened craftsman slipped unsteadily into the night. The sound of the rain hid the quiet footsteps behind him. It also hid his gasp of surprise as strong arms held him briefly. When he was released he slumped easily to the pavestones. Two burly figured lifted him easily. Only the minnows heard the splash as he hit the waters of a small canal. The Imperial City of Miyako, home to the All Under Heaven, slept on through the rain.

† † †

Sugiyama Tamasaburo walked out of the clan elder's villa. His face was set in its normal scowl and expressed none of his feelings. He stood for a second, watching the eddies of dust raised by the wind. Finally he shrugged slightly and turned to go. The clan had no need of his skills, the elders had made that clear in the recent talk. A noted brawler and fencer in a clan that wanted no more trouble with the ruling Tokugawa was an anachronism. He had been told politely, but very firmly, that he would have to find employment elsewhere. His younger brother would eventually inherit his father's post. And the stipend that went with it. Sugiyama shrugged mentally. He did not care for financial security. Nor the boredom nor the staid life that went with it. But the affront—being thrown out of the clan—stung deeply. His shadow preceded him in the late afternoon. The small townlet had few pleasures to offer, but right now he needed at least one of them. He headed for a house he knew. There was a young wife there. She had been accommodating to him in the past. She was available, and he was in the mood for a woman right now. Unrelieved violence did that to him sometimes. Townsmen, seeing the thunder-visaged samurai, scurried out of Sugiyama's way. They knew that an expression such as Sugiyama bore on his face was an invitation to trouble. Moreover, his reputation as a brawler preceded him.

He stopped before the house. Wood had faded to grey, thatching straw was sticking out untidily. He bent under the straggling thatch and stomped inside. The plump woman looked up from the mortar. Sweat had beaded her brow and her sleeves were held back by a sash tied crosswise over her patched blue gown. Her face was pockmarked, but otherwise roundly open. She saw Sugiyama and alarm showed on her face.

"You must not be here at this time," she hissed, staring past the stocky samurai. "Not at this hour!" There was a hint of supplication in her voice.

He said nothing as he stepped onto the cracked wood of the house platform. He drew his sword, still in its sheath, from his sash and laid it beside him. She watched his actions as a rabbit does a snake's. Before she could say a thing he had her by the shoulders and she was being pulled backwards. She struggled fruitlessly. He pushed her down and flipped open her worn gown. She tried to fend him off with one hand while covering the triangle of fur at the juncture of her legs with the other. Without haste, using only a portion of his strength he forced her knees open and slapped away her hands, then knelt between her thighs.

His cock was thick, throbbing with impatient lust. He forced the crown at the entrance to her cunt.

"Let me prepare first," she begged.

Sugiyama ignored her and pushed strongly forward, embedding the tip in the dry hole. She sobbed and tried to relax and ignore the painful penetration. With one thrust he was up her channel. She protested weakly, pushing against him with her palms, to no avail. He rose on his hips, mashing down on her pubic bone to increase the penetration. His hands groped for her soft small breasts and his mouth searched for hers. She turned her face away and he nuzzled into her neck. His ass started bobbing and his long dark pole shuttled greasily into her cunt. She sobbed, now partly from awakening lust as her moisture started to rise. She knew he was always like this, and that if she wanted any pleasure, she had better get it before he came. He removed one hand from her breast and crushed one of her buns to him. She raised her legs to facilitate his entry and locked them over his heaving back. Her eyes were partly closed now as she allowed him freedom to do with her what he willed. Sugiyama was panting audibly now and his stones were slapping wetly against her raised ass. Both his hands were clutching at the soft buns, powerful fingers dimpling the skin deeply. She cried out and closed her eyes just as his own lust exploded, drenching her willing but far from satisfied insides. She heaved her hips up at him, hoping for some more, hoping for her own dew to descend. He endured her frantic motions for a minute, then pulled out of her and groped for something to wipe his cock. She looked at him reproachfully but did not dare complain.

"Hey! What the devil do you think you're doing!" The watchman's rough voice broke into his pleasure. Sugiyama acted reflexively. His short-sword, still sheathed, was out of his sash and, held reversed, hilt forward, blocked the blow of the staff at his head. He rose in one smooth motion. He unsheathed the *wakizashi* with his right hand, turned right and the short-sword cut across the man's belly. He twirled the hilt in his hand, then plunged the blade twice in a smooth motion into the heavyset man. The staff clattered to floor, followed by the hollow thump of the body.

Sugiyama ignored the frenzied screaming as he pulled his clothes together. Only a slight smile betrayed the pleasure he felt as he walked out of the house. Neighbors hovered uncertainly, waiting only for the sight of his back before they could rush inside. He walked out of the town. Passing the house of the ward headman he stopped and entered.

"I have killed the night firewatchman," he said formally.

The headman gulped, but did not rise from his bow.

"He was impertinent. Report that to the city magistrate. You know my name?"

The headman nodded fearfully. Sugiyama's reputation preceded him.

"Good. Don't forget to report."

He headed eastward, his shadow going before him. Behind, had he cared to notice, he would have heard the wailing of the new widow, and the gnashing of helpless townsmen's teeth.

† † †

4

Isei grunted as he rolled the last rock into place. He straightened his aching back and wiped his face. Then he picked up his gun, cast one last look at the small mountain clearing, and turned to go. Above and around him the tall pines whispered to the wind the sorrow he himself could not express. Only the slight tightening of his face muscles betrayed the pain of leaving, the hurt of the mound that hid the last of his children and his woman.

He descended the mountain. Before nightfall he stood at the fringes of the cultivated fields of the tiny hamlet from where his woman had come. He turned and bowed to the mountain. The peak, white with snow, still shone a reflected red as the last rays of the sun touched it. He did not think he would see it again. In the growing dark and cold Isei found a lair among the roots of an oak he knew well and curled up to sleep. He dreamt, terrifying dreams of pale-faced ghosts wailing at him from the dark. In the night, in the cold of his dreams, he finally wept for his family, taken from him by cold and disease. Behind the ghosts he could see the impassive face of someone-something that should have helped but didn't: that looked at the dying children impassively and studiously. Isei clutched his gun to him and his shivering turned to a burning desire to know: how? why? The cold iron stuck to his clutching hand, and he fell into a deep sleep, his decision, unknown to him, already made.

Isei woke with the dim memory of something calling to him out of a dream. He struggled with the memory. It was the face of his dead child that brought the dream back. Over his child loomed a massive face. Calm, peaceful, inhuman. It looked at him, a gnat-like human, and the bow-curved lips seemed to move with laughter. Rage seized Isei again as it had in his dream. He wanted to grab his child and run. He heard the child lisp ''Miyako, Miyako,'' and looking up again he knew that he was looking at the face of the Daibutsu. Very well, the omen was there, but what it meant, he had no idea. He walked down the slope, heading south and west. Eventually, the path he followed, as paths will, reached a destination. The small clearing was well planted with sweet potato and radish, greens and a few small apple trees. It was being well tended.

The farmwoman looked up from her work. She was

weeding a tiny plot of taro. The big leaves nodded above her. Isei studied her remotely for a moment, then stepped boldly forward. She looked up, startled, then straightened. She had a broad, red face half hidden by the kerchief she wore under her broad hat. Her torso was bare and she wore a ragged petticoat that might once have been red, but was now a faded and mud-stained brown. Her breasts were erect and firm, stained and streaked with the sweat of her labors under the sun. He smiled slightly. He liked women with broad shoulders, the broader the better. And broad hips for the bearing of children. She made no move to leave when she saw him approach, merely gripping her small hoe.

He stopped before her and smiled shyly. The smile, he knew, had won more than one heart before. At first she had seen only that he was a mountain man. His pants were coarse castoff weave, probably bartered from some farmwife like herself. He wore a doublet made from the skin of a black bear, the fur turned outwards. It displayed his bronzed muscular chest. Hung from the vine belt that held the doublet closed were a number of baskets cunningly woven from akebia vine. A heavy woodsman's *nata* hung at his side. Its plain wooden handle and sheath were well polished with use. On the other side hung a flask of black powder. In one hand he casually held a long matchlock. A length of extra slow-match was looped around the slim stock. He was bare-headed and notwithstanding the long hair bound at the back of his neck and his unshaven jaw, she saw before her a man of uncommon facial beauty. His features were regular, cheeks high and smooth. Piercing eyes under mulberry-shaped eyebrows complemented his hawk nose. Involuntarily almost, she smiled back.

"You have been working very hard," Isei said, stroking some of the sweat away from her breast.

She smiled but did not move. "There is plenty of work, and someone has to do it. My man is busy elsewhere."

He chose to interpret it in the way he fancied. "Two can do more than one." He unsheathed his *nata* and bent to help her weed. With his energetic help they were soon finished. She straightened up and smiled at him, wiping her sweaty forehead with the back of her hand.

"You are very sweaty," he said and deliberately, using

his palms like sponges, wiped the sweat down her body to her waist.

"Mr. *sanka*, let us go to the shade," she said pragmatically as he unloosed the ties of her petticoat.

"My name is Isei," he said, almost primly. He did not like to be called by the epithet the lowland people used for his kind.

They walked to the shade of the forest and she dropped her petticoat, then undid her hat and kerchief. He dropped his own clothes while looking at her. Her figure was firm and blocky. Her calves almost massive with muscle. She was slick with the sweat of labor and anticipation.

She lay down on the reddish cloth, her knees raised and her arms spread. For a brief moment he looked at her welcoming black thatch. It was bisected by a long pink slit bordered by thinnish lips. He dropped to his knees beside her, kicked his pants off and moved his loincloth out of the way. His cock, thick and a bit short, jutted out of a nest of fine black hairs. He laid himself prone upon her and pushed mightily with his mantool. The breath went out of the farmwoman as she received his weight and she smiled happily at the treetops as he rooted between her legs. The smell of their sweat mingled with the salty female perfume and was born away by the wind. The knob of his cock widened the dew-drenched orifice and Isei thrust in to his full length.

"That is good Isei, that is good!" Her mouth was fully open and her hips glued themselves firmly to his. Her full calves intertwined with his own. He rose somewhat and started jerking into her in a broken drumming rhythm which he knew women liked. She Ooooed frenziedly and clutched at his ass. The speed of his motions increased. She dug into him, biting at his sweaty shoulders frantically. Moaning incoherently he felt that her hips were triphammering back at him and his cock seemed to be swimming in a warm bath. He paused for a moment to savor the sensation.

"Go on, go on you beautiful cock, you mountain tree you. Fuck me, again, again," she cried, staring at him with eyes rounded with passion.

He obeyed and his cock triphammered at her, his nuts slapping against her moisture with a strange sticky sound.

7

At last he began to feel his sperm rising. He fell onto her, biting at her nipples and neck and clutching handfuls of her large and muscular behind. She urged him on inarticulately and clawed with blunt hard fingers at the muscles of his back. Isei's juices exploded and he flooded her interior with his milky essence. The odor of male sperm was added suddenly to the breeze.

Isei lay on her, his cock still jerking, and she started rubbing a finger between his buttocks, trying to stimulate him to another trial. She smiled as he raised his head.

"You fuck good," they said simultaneously, and she laughed broadly, pinching his behind fondly.

There was a growl behind them and Isei pulled out of the woman and spun around, groping unsuccessfully for his matchlock. The huge brown bear rose to its hind feet and sniffed expectantly, then charged forward. Whether they had disturbed the beast at its feeding, or whether the smell of the randy woman had excited it, Isei neither knew nor cared. He leaped sideways, groping now for his *nata,* the heavy square-ended knife-hatchet that all foresters wore as a matter of course.

The woman squealed and leaped for a tree. The bear passed Isei in his charge and the heavy blade sliced down. The shock of the blow was greeted by a bloodcurdling roar. The bear spun and raked at his tormentor. Isei danced out of the enraged animal's way and chopped again. The blade sliced through softer belly flesh as the bear reared up for a crushing blow. One of his paws hung limply. Isei backed, fumbling in his pouch. He found the tiny clay shell that held his fire first, then the larger fire egg. The egg hissed ominously as he lit the match. The bear roared and charged again. Isei slipped the bomb into the beast's maw and danced away again. A long talon raked his side, a mere scratch. Isei turned and ran, the bear turned, though slower, and set off in limping pursuit. Two steps and the obstruction in his throat grew into a painful volcano that blew his head off.

Isei looked for the woman, then looked at the scratch on his side. He could barely believe what had happened. Few men had faced a brown bear and come through it alive. Suddenly it was clear to him what he had to do. The capital of Miyako, where, as family legend had it, they had come from aeons before, would be his goal. There he would inquire of the Yakushi Nyorai daibutsu. His family dead, of such a tiny thing as a sickness, whereas he, facing death, was still alive. Why? Resolutely he turned his face to the south.

† † †

Momoe giggled nervously and tried to push Saburo's calloused hand away. His teeth nipped gently at her soft ear, and his hands stole again into the folds of her plain cotton robe. She sighed and relaxed against his muscular chest as his lips moved down to her shoulders. She shivered slightly as a stray hair from his topknot tickled her cheek.

"No Saburo, we must stop. I'm a good girl!"

"Very good indeed, darling Momoe, the best of all girls in Miyako." His hand did not cease its wandering and he now held her small plump breast. Her heart fluttered at the touch. He bent and parted the lapels of her summer-printed *yukata* robe. The tiny nipple slipped between his lips and involuntarily Momoe moved to urge more of the mound into the delightfully warm cavern. She was disappointed when he removed his lips only to recover as the other nipple was treated in the same way.

A flood of loving feeling rushed through her body. She felt her insides moisten as they did when she played with herself, delicately stroking the petals between her legs. His hand seemed to divine her thoughts and it wandered lower across her belly, stopped by her tightly wound *obi* sash.

Momoe made a token protest, even pretending to slap at his hand while wondering how he would overcome the barrier. He raised his head and looked into her eyes. His own were dark almonds, twinkling usually with humor, and now, with passion. His tongue flicked out and licked the tip of her nose, and then his mouth was upon hers and he was searching her tongue with his own. She responded lovingly, clutching his muscular body to her own, when she realized that his kiss, pleasurable as it was to both of them, had only been a diversion. His left hand had glided between the folds of her *yukata* and her red wraparound underskirt and up her legs. One of his fingers was gently teasing the soft hairs that grew at the base of her rounded belly.

"You must not do that . . ." she started to say, and then realized how foolish it was. They both knew what they were about, both were adults, she sixteen and he a newly-made craftsman of twenty. So instead of protesting, she relaxed trustingly against his broad shoulder and allowed Saburo the freedom of her person he craved.

Saburo found Momoe's sudden capitulation exhilarating. He kissed her lovingly again and his hand parted her thighs gently. His right hand went around her and stroked the small breast through the slit at the base of her *yukata* sleeve while he stroked the full length of her plump little cunt with his left.

The soft lips gradually moistened and Saburo inserted a questing finger between the lips, searching for her nubbin. A woman had taught him all about sex on her *goza* mat some years ago, and he fancied himself an expert. He twiddled the tiny button slowly and then faster. Another finger dipped in circular motions into the sweet tight hole while he nibbled at her neck and throat. Momoe clutched at him as he penetrated the initial narrow entrance of her vagina and encountered the thin skin barrier. He drew her moisture out gradually, until his finger was slick with her internal moisture. The faint hint of an enticing perfume came to his nose and he wondered what she would do if he were to raise his finger to his nose and sniff her essence. He put the thought from his mind till later.

Saburo let Momoe incline backwards on the soft moss. They had sneaked into the garden of one of the temples, intent on their affairs. Fortunately for the color of her clothes, Saburo had thoughtfully brought along a small *goza* mat. He slipped her thick linen sash off and opened her robe. In the summer moonlight she barely had time to see his muscular body as he stripped himself, then lay down between her legs. His fingers returned to playing with her juicy pussy and he reinserted the delightful finger up her channel, gradually widening the opening as much as he could.

Her shy hand stole down their bodies until it encountered a warm thick fleshy knob. She grasped it delicately, not really knowing how to go about it. He pressed forward and she noted the tip was slightly sticky and wet. Saburo rose and directed his prick to the tiny eagerly waiting hole. She spread her legs as far as she could and felt with her hand as the knob tip touched her lower lips.

"Hold my shoulders dear Momoe," he whispered. "It will hurt for only a moment."

She did as she was bid and he sank gradually into her sweet body. The work of his fingers had widened and softened the passageway. The head made its way up her channel, slowed only momentarily by the thin membrane at its throat. Then the shaft was through, coasting up to end nosing at her cervix. Momoe sighed and clutched Saburo to her body. The pleasure of having him in her was almost more than she could bear. Their tongues meshed and she pulled him on, hoping to increase the pleasure. He withdrew somewhat and she hauled back at him, terrified it was over. But then his weight came down again and he started a sweet motion with his fleshy shaft. She accommodated herself to his motions and the pleasure of his being filled her body. She was unconscious of the inarticulate cries that escaped her lips, stopped only when his mouth covered hers, resumed when he bent his neck to suck on her nipples.

Their joined motions became faster and faster. They rocked together in a panic, he trying to bury himself to her depths, as she urged him on frantically. Their pleasure rose steeply, like a bubble rising through oil, growing as it rose. Momoe found herself suddenly bursting, her pleasure overwhelming her and she bit his neck and twisted her hips hard to anchor Saburo to her. At the same time she was conscious that he was wriggling on top of her, his pole jerking frantically at her insides, which were being flooded by warm liquid.

The spurts from Saburo's organ gradually died down and he lay on her as if dead, barely moving. After a while the weight became uncomfortable, and she bit his neck lightly. "You liar," she said.

"What? What did . . ." He saw her laughing face and she bit his chest.

"You are a liar Master Saburo. You said it would hurt a bit. But it didn't, not at all." Momoe stretched languidly. "I have never felt such pleasure in all my life. Look at the moon. Oh!'' she suddenly remembered. ''I must rush home. It is late.''

They hurriedly dressed, though not so hurriedly that their fingers did not meet on one another's body.

''Tomorrow then?'' she asked, suddenly shy.

''Tomorrow I go to your father and tell him we are married. We will have the feast soon and you will move in with me,'' Saburo said firmly. Momoe rested her head on his chest, happy beyond words.

† † †

The fully armored warrior lay on the ground in a sea of red. A lance pinioned the figure to the ground. The sword lay far from the outstretched hand. Arrows transfixed various parts of the anatomy to the loamy earth. The warrior's face was hidden and the disarray of the gilded armor exposed the sprawled figure's back, where cords had been cut.

Ito Shinichi approached the sprawled figure and addressed it with the long poem from the most recent play about the Soga brothers. He was naked and just risen from the bath. He stopped his chant and bent, tugging at the warrior's bloodstained loincloth. Crouching, he spread the buttocks and gazed for a moment at the exposed anal button and the mossy cleft beneath it. His penis grew hard and strong from its nest of wiry hair. He moved his hips forwards, then stabbed into one of the holes, then the other. Out again, and repeat.

Under him, the young girl gritted her teeth. The first penetrations were painful, and the weight of her master's body made the fake armor cut into her skin. Gradually the heat of his body, and the slick feel of his long thin prick began to penetrate the pain. Her breathing quickened as the knobby stick caught gratingly at her entrances, penetrated, then withdrew again. She caught herself in time from responding to the thrusts, allowing herself to move just a tiny bit as her insides were flooded with his sticky come.

Before the mansion and lower in the bowl-shaped valley the lights of Miyako, formal capital of the Land of the Sun's Source, came gradually alight. The sun stroked the

12

hills in one last fond farewell. In distant Edo, capital in all but name, greatest city in the world, the Shogun conferred with his counselors. Beyond the seas mysterious pale barbarians moved about their own affairs, affairs that were not to affect Japan to any great degree for two centuries.

"My dear, may I interrupt?" The voice spoke over Ito's shoulder. He looked back at his wife with disfavor. "Do you want to have her?" he asked.

"No," she said pragmatically, barely looking at the concubine. "Mr. Uemura is here to see you. . . . Isn't this the armor you received from Abbot Saishiden of Saionji? Do you think it wise? It is probably very valuable, and the holy man could probably see you from here, you know." She pointed to the barely visible gables of the temple that rose above their garden wall to his left.

Ito looked at his wife patiently. She was much younger than himself. Her arms were slim and her heavily made-up face unlined. Moreover, she had no inhibitions and supported his personal sexual quirks with a devotion that was commendable. If she had a fault it was her coldness, which displayed itself, among other things, in excessive caution and a tremendous greed for money. "The estimable abbot can only see me if he climbs up onto the eaves of his temple. Besides, he and I are both men of the world. He is hardly likely to object to the use I make of his gift."

Ito's hips jerked and his tongue stuck out of the corner of his mouth as he felt his climax overtake him. He grasped the girl roughly, pulling the soft mounds of her ass back at him as the white milky fluid blended their pubic hair to a sopping mass. His eyes closed for a long moment of pleasure, then he turned back to look casually at the girl before him. Something attracted his attention and he peered at her back thoughtfully.

"Mr. Uemura is waiting," his wife reminded him. He rose and shook his penis absently while examining his wife's face sharply. Ito Haruko recoiled slightly at the unusual scrutiny he gave her.

"Uemura, you say? What does he want?"

"You know!" she said in exasperation.

"Do I now!?" He looked at her sharply as before, then looked at the armor again. An unusually sharp look stole over his face. He walked past her and into the house.

Exasperated, Haruko followed. Her face was a frozen mask underneath her makeup.

Uemura Sonzaemon was a fine young dilettante. He had been sent to Miyako by his family to study, and was nominally a ward of Ito's, who had known Uemura's father. He was dressed in the latest fashion. His hair was briskly brushed into a smooth topknot, his shaven pate glimmered. His clothes were all of fine silk and his sword furniture, though impractical, was decorated with gold leaf. Only the hard look in the eyes and around the mouth spoiled the impression of languid good looks.

"I wonder, Ito-sama," he said as soon as the polite preliminaries were over, "whether you could advance me some trifling sum . . ."

"My dear boy. Of course that is out of the question. Your father has entrusted you into my care and I would hardly dare exceed his instructions . . ."

Ito's unctuous old-fashioned phrases left no doubt in the young man's mind that there was no chance of squeezing extra money out of the old crow. He politely made his farewell. The effort was worth making, however slim the chances. He would have to fall back on a more certain resource, and possibly on another avenue altogether.

CHAPTER 2

"THERE WAS ALSO A DEAD BODY FISHED OUT OF A CANAL IN Shimogamo." Saga, the elderly counsellor, continued his litany of the night's events. "Craftsman. No positive ID. The local police officers are investigating. He died by violence: strangulation."

The governor and chief magistrate of the Imperial City of Miyako was only half listening to the litany of the night's events. His sharp, handsome face bore an unusually abstracted expression. The counsellor forced back a grin. The boy was developing well since his accession to his father's office. He was proving to be a prudent governor and an astute magistrate. The source of his distraction was a well-known secret. Mildly illegal, but then good administrators and chiefs were difficult to find and must be allowed their minor peccadillos.

Matsudaira Konnosuke was indeed thinking of his chief distraction. She had given him a hard time the previous night, refusing him her normal favors merely because he had been delayed several hours in the performance of one and then another of the onerous duties that were his occupation as well as privilege.

Matsudaira felt a tightening of his loins at the thought of his chief problem and delight. The memory of her golden hair, full white breasts, the rose tattooed between her thighs, and above all her enthusiasm and delight in all things erotic excited his imagination. He wished he could simply stand up, dismiss the clerks and counsellors, and storm into the inner rooms for a session with Rosamund: his prisoner and ruler. He forced himself to patience and concentrated on the night's murder.

"What about his effects?" Matsudaira asked.

"That's one problem," the bulky counsellor nodded.

He gestured behind him and one of the lower ranking samurai serving as a clerk crept forward and placed a tray on the golden tatami between the two men. Saga, the elderly counsellor who had served Matsudaira's father ably, lifted the plain cloth cover and slid the tray forward towards his lord.

Matsudaira examined the objects on the tray carefully. A nugget of gold, cut off from a larger piece, the chisel marks clear. Several pieces of silver, ditto. Some small steel burins used in the gilding and cabinetmaking trade for which the city was famous. A kerchief. He raised his brows.

"We're examining. Asking among the gilders to see who is missing."

"Let me know." Matsudaira said. They moved on to discussions of other matters.

A mile or so away across the city of Miyako a slim, slight-looking woman walked through the gate of an unpretentious warrior-class villa. Her kimono was inexpensive but well made and clean. Her hair was simply coiffed in a rather old-fashioned female topknot that had been slightly disarrayed. She walked with a confident stride rather than the normal pigeon-toed patter of a town woman.

Her plump maidservant greeted her from the *genkan* entryway and told her that the master was in the back, endlessly practicing with his sword as usual.

"Has the kimono material I ordered from the weavers arrived yet?"

"No, mistress Okiku. Momoe, the girl who usually delivers, has not been around today."

Okiku nodded in dismissal and made her way to the small bamboo grove in the back, carefully avoiding the puddles from the previous night's rain. She stopped, slightly hidden by the thick boles of the bamboo, to admire her man.

Miura Jiro was a giant by the standards of his day and place. His six-foot plus of muscle and bone moved with a liquid smoothness as he drew, sheathed, then redrew his large two-handed *katana* from its black lacquered sheath. He resheathed the blade, grunted doubtfully as if unsatisfied with his own performance, then saw Okiku between the bamboos. He walked towards her, admiring as usual her perfect poise, and the unconscious posture she had taken which hid her body behind the bole of a handsbreadth-thick bamboo.

"Did you find the teapot you wanted?" he asked in greeting.

"No. Only this new Satsuma stuff around, which I don't care for. And we're going to need the gardener to come around again . . ."

He nodded indifferently. Domestic matters were her own affair.

"Someone attacked me this morning," Okiku said casually.

Jiro turned to her in surprise. "Where?" he asked. Knowing her, he forebore asking if she had been injured. Odds were the other side were nursing more than bruises.

"I took a short-cut through the old Imaura villa lands. Three men stepped out behind me and tried to throw a sack over my head. Judging by their manner, I'd think they were interested in more than an hour's fun. White slavers. Looking for a woman for the brothels, I would imagine. I hurt all three of them, one badly, I think."

Jiro said nothing, waiting for her to elucidate.

"There have been a number of such incidents over the past year. I wonder if we should do something about it?"

"Maybe we should," Jiro rumbled. "Why didn't you kill them?" He was nominally a teacher: of fencing and of Western Barbarian knowledge. Unofficially he was also an *onmitsu:* a covert private agent of the shogun, ruler of the Japans. Kidnapped women could mean a number of things, all bad.

She grinned. "Very fast fellows. Except the one with the knife in him. Theirs, not mine. I left him there but the others were gone."

† † †

The thin-faced, middle-aged samurai looked at the bound figure before him and smiled tightly. The small windowless room was dark, the plaster walls of the storehouse giving off a smell of damp and disuse. He knelt by the bound young woman and slipped his hands inside her loose robe.

She cried out softly, trying to move out of his grip. The samurai rose and stepped to the door.

"What about the other one?" he asked quietly.

"Ah . . . We had an accident there. The woman fought back. Hirose was badly hurt."

"And?" said the samurai sharply.

"She got away. Didn't see us though. Sure of that. We took care of Hirose."

"Good. Go away. Try somewhere else. The area you worked must be all up in arms by now. I'll take care of the new flower."

"Right." There was a slight patter of vanishing footsteps and the samurai stepped back into the storehouse. He was always careful not to let his face be seen. Neither his suppliers nor the distributors knew his face or name. He lifted the masking scarf. The woman was blindfolded and would not see him anyway. No one would ever know that Hori Narimitsu, respected secretary to Counsellor Ito was anything but what he seemed. But luxuries are expensive, and he liked his comfort.

"Lie still," he whispered in a hoarse voice. "I will make you more comfortable, but you must not try to fight me."

He tested the silk scarves that tied the soft flesh carefully. Most of his customers did not like to have the merchandise bruised. They usually preferred to inflict the bruises themselves. Hori stroked her arms. The quilt he had spread on the floor was not for her comfort, but for the preservation of the delicate merchandise. He flipped up the skirts of her robe and of her cheap red underskirt exposing her thighs and the soft dark triangle at the bottom of her belly.

The woman tried to struggle, twisting her hips aside, but her jailor ignored her efforts. First he feasted his eyes on the captive. She ceased her struggles and peered fearfully into the dark of her blindfold. Smooth soft hands caressed the skin of her lower belly. A finger was inserted between her lower lips, then raised. She heard an audible sniff. The other hand continued stroking her as if soothing a wild animal. Notwithstanding her fear she gave in to the sensation and her trembling ceased. The hands spread her legs apart and a finger was inserted even deeper into her body.

Again she tried to resist, to no avail. This time she felt two knees kneeling between her thighs. The hands stroked upwards, caressing her breasts. They lay like low hills, tipped with wide brown patches against her heaving chest. The fingers played with them, causing her nipples to come erect. The nipples were briefly touched by cool moist lips. Then she felt the tip of his cock worming its way between her lower lips. Knowing there was nothing to be done the woman waited helplessly as the knob slowly penetrated into her vaginal tunnel. Though he had her at his mercy, she was grateful for his delicate touch. Involuntarily she began responding. Her hips rose to meet his, expecting a full thrust of his loins. Instead, her captor toyed with her, withdrawing the desired morsel from her, pulling himself in and out as she reacted. The breath hissed in her mouth as she panted, wanting and yet not wanting the violation of her body.

"Oh no, oh no, oh no," she muttered as she suddenly felt the climax come upon her. Her body jerked with her pleasure, for the first time in weeks. She subsided, thinking of her former husband and his hurried way with her body. If she were to be treated this way . . . well, things could be worse.

The cock was withdrawn from her cunt though she would have wished it in her longer. She felt it making its way up her body. The tip nudged into her belly button as the man crouched over her. Then to her breasts, touching each nipple in turn and leaving a trail of sticky fluid. She was conscious that he was crouching over her now—the tip of the cock smelling strongly of her insides—hovering over her face. The flesh sunk down until he touched her lips. She tried to move her head away, not comprehending, but found her ears were held by strong hands.

"Suck," the genteel voice said softly.

"No! I couldn't! How terrible," she responded in surprise and loathing.

"There will be much worse things," he said in a low commanding voice. "I, at least, am getting you used to it gradually."

She tried again to refuse but found the fleshy shaft forced between her teeth. So hypnotized by the sensation, she did not even think of biting. The thick shaft filled her mouth, was withdrawn, then descended again, almost causing her to gag, but removed each time at the last minute. The speed barely changed, but suddenly she felt the shaft pulsing against her tongue. She knew what was about to happen. Dreading the flood, she tried to withdraw. Her mouth filled with a stream of acrid creamy liquid which perforce she had to swallow. The spurt died into a stream of drops and the penis was withdrawn from her mouth. She tried to spit the stuff out, but a large cup of water was held to her lips instead and she drank gratefully.

"Let me give you some advice," the voice came at her out of the dark. "You are to be a gift to a great lord. One with powers of life and death. He will do with you what he wills. With any luck, you will have a much easier life than you otherwise would have had as a dweller in a poor neighborhood. But, you must learn to obey, without question, your master's every whim."

She nodded in the dark, knowing what he said to be the truth.

CHAPTER 3

PEERING THROUGH THE CRACK IN THE SLIDING DOORS ITO Shinichi huddled in the darkness of the bedding closet. He licked his lips while one hand fumbled at his crotch.

Before him, oblivious of his scrutiny, Ito Haruko was flat on her back. Both her thin legs were raised to the ceiling. Uemura crouched over her, topknot awry. He was sweating visibly. He looked down at the juncture of their legs, at his own thick and now bejuiced pole that was shuttling in and out of the black furry thicket at the base of Haruko's stomach. He pulled her legs apart as wide as he could and rested his entire weight on his long shaft that was sinking out of sight into her flesh. Her cunt hair was sparse and the grip of her cunt lips on his cock was visible every time he withdrew.

"Reluctant to let me go, eh, reluctant to let me go," he was muttering through clenched teeth. His perfect hairdo was undone and he was breathing stertorously.

Haruko clutched at her sharp small breasts, squeezing them roughly. "Deeper!" she commanded. "Dig that cock in deeper. Now, now!" She half raised herself, belly muscles ridging, in an effort to see how deep he was in her. She saw the pulsing of his organ. "Don't come, don't finish now!" she cried and grasped the root where it merged with the soft bag. The pulsing stopped though Uemura's face turned as purple as the tip of his prick. He let her legs down and she hurriedly motioned him onto his back. She knelt over his face and parted the long inner lips of her cunt. They stuck out over the outer ones and he parted the two flaps with his tongue. She bounced up and down, fucking herself with the tongue he held obligingly erect. One hand diddled her clitoris while the other snaked over his chest to his erect member. She teased the monster

21

for awhile, moving it to and fro over his belly, then set to work with her hand, exciting it to a red randiness. Uemura gripped her thigh, then inserted one hand between her buttocks. She raised her head with pleasure. He inserted a finger gradually to the portal of her anus. Haruko stopped her ministrations to his cock and moved the hand away. "I don't like that," she scolded.

He desisted, but his tongue tired and he started sucking the inner labia with his lips. Haruko moved away and raised herself over his erection. Guiding it with one hand, she sank down gradually until he was engulfed entirely in her warm soft cavern. Her fingers dug into his chest and she bit him painfully.

"Now I'm going to fuck you," she said crudely, and started bucking over his supine form. He tried to help her, raising and lowering her hips, but soon knew it was unnecessary. She was lost in a world of her own pleasure. Her hands squeezed her rather sharp breasts with almost painful intensity. A lock of black hair fell over her eyes from her elaborate hairdo. Uemura took the opportunity to please himself, touching and pinching her skin, drawing figures on it with his nails.

Her eyes flew open and she stared blindly at the clothing closet before them, then rammed her hips deeply onto his cock. Her sharp pubic bone dug into his and he raised his own hips, hoping to come as well. She rocked and raved above him, spittle splattering his chest. Her hair was wild and she held him down below her with a violent grip. Slowly the spasms subsided. She breathed deeply, then rose off him, searching for some paper to wipe herself. He looked at her retreating thin buttocks ruefully. Without embarrassment, he began stroking his slick staff, looking at Haruko all the while. Ignoring him completely, she prepared her toilet. "I really need a competent maid," she said to herself, peering into the polished silver mirror.

Ito could barely contain himself. The sight of the man masturbating himself to a climax, and the sudden fountain of milky fluid almost made him spurt in sympathy. He crept away hurriedly, tripping the slide behind the closet which allowed him access to his own quarters. He was breathing heavily. His eyes were slightly glazed and he knew he needed relief from the pressures that the scene he had just witnessed had raised. He rushed through the inner rooms to the outermost sliding door of his inner sanctum. His page knelt motionless before the door.

"Bring the girl to me. To the rear garden, as usual," Ito commanded breathlessly and stalked on. The page bowed to the floor and rose smoothly to call the young girl and help her make ready.

Ito strode into the garden in one of his favorite costumes. He was dressed as a footsoldier of the period when Miyako, then known as Heian, was the actual capital of the islands. A short leather hauberk covered him in front. His face was dotted with black to simulate unshaven jowls. His hair was undone and he wore a metal forehead protector. He waved a sword in the air ferociously. His legs were bare and his buttocks exposed underneath the armor. Beneath it he wore nothing but a loincloth.

The girl emerged from the mansion. She had been with the household a long time and knew what was expected of her. Ito regretted the absence of the other one: she had been fresher and still exhibited her emotions without artifice. She stood before him dressed in formal court hunting-clothes. Over it she wore golden armor that glittered in the sun. Her face was made up in pale pink and over it she wore a tall black sugarloaf hat: the sign of aristocracy. Ito raised his sword. The aristocrat quailed before the provincial warrior. The warrior advanced and the effete aristocrat retreated hurriedly. The warrior slashed wildly with his sword and the aristocrat turned and fled. The warrior, his sinews toughened by years of campaigning, was faster. Beside a small pond he caught up to the fleeing figure and tripped it. The aristocrat fell to the ground, tried to roll over, babbling promises and threats. The warrior laughed and sneered. He inserted the tip of his sword underneath the aristocrat's clothes and ripped them off in quick strokes. The brocade robes fell away, exposing the aristocrat's nakedness. The warrior grinned and began beating the smooth white limbs with the flat of his sword, making the other whimper and beg for mercy.

Ito fell onto the sprawled figure, the two sets of armor clashing together. He revelled in the discomfort of the metal and leather carapaces as his cock stabbed deeply into the waiting girl's overflowing cunt. He scowled. She was

23

not supposed to be so eager. Nonetheless he pumped away vigorously, mouthing curses as the girl pretended a reluctance at his embrace. The feel of violent lust overcame him and he felt again the power of the primitive wild warrior. His hands dug deeply into her ass and his breathing quickened. He felt the arrival of his climax and the woman beneath him urged him on, panting frantically. His body was beyond control now. A mass of unexpended come was boiling in his crotch.

"Now you die!" Ito cried triumphantly. He pulled himself from her soft cunt, scrabbled at her side and drew the gilt-hilted sword that the effete aristocrat had not even thought to draw. He raised the blade, poising it before him in *chudan kamae* for one delicious moment, then cut downwards as a spray of male liquid inundated the armor-clad woman resting on the ground.

She managed to catch his weight as he fell, and he lay on her as if dead, then raised his head and smiled off into the distance.

There was a step in the gravel walk behind them.

"Abbot Saishiden of Saionji temple is here to see you, my dear."

The voice of his wife broke into Ito's reverie and he slowly pulled himself off the girl. The armor was digging into his sides uncomfortably. It was a beautiful piece and he expected to use it frequently, at least for the present. Ito Haruko examined the girl with a raised eyebrow. Not too badly damaged this time. Her husband fancied himself a bold swordsman, but every once in a while he missed, and some of the women bore scars to show for it. At least he was properly apologetic afterwards. He really would not hurt a fly. Ito examined his wife at the same time. She appeared as cool and collected as ever. There was no trace of the recent past, of the way her legs had been spread, of the flush of passion that had inundated her interior. She knelt properly before him, wiping his moist cock with a soft tissue paper she had produced with wifely efficiency while he looked carefully and thoughtfully at the girl's back.

"You will have to change, dear. You cannot meet him informally."

Ito acquiesced and marched off to his quarters. She

peered after him doubtfully, chewing her lip in slight puzzlement.

The abbot was a jovial, plump-jowled cleric. His temple, now in the first stages of reconstruction after many years of neglect, was rising next door to Ito's villa. He and Ito had developed an odd friendship based partly on shared love of Chinese poetry, partly on the recognition that they were both men of the world, with tolerant views and passionate temperaments.

Ito bowed properly and the abbot bowed in return. They sipped tea. Ito motioned to his page and the latter brought forth a small, plain wooden box. It rested, half covered by a silk kerchief, on a black and red lacquered tray.

"I am so grateful for your gift," Ito said. "Please accept this trifle. It hardly makes up for the efforts you have gone to."

The abbot opened the plain wooden box and raised the small tea bowl inside. "O ho ho," he said coyly. "Modest gift indeed. Ito-san, you shame me. This is a gift fit for a prince, let alone a lowly cleric like me. A bowl from the table of Senno Rikyu, Master of Tea himself. Why, the armor was nothing."

"Not at all," said Ito. "You know my taste. Gilt armor. Such an extravagance. And practical too."

"Practical?" said the cleric, smiling faintly.

"Well yes . . . You see, I have peculiar tastes. And your armour fits one of my women so well. A wonder it is so light too: just perfect." He laughed heartily. The abbot, guessing at the import of his words, joined in. His eyes were thoughtful, hooded, while his full lips curved in amusement.

"May I disturb?" a cultured voice came from the other side of the *shoji*. It slid aside at Ito's murmured assent. A middle-aged, rather thin samurai knelt at the entrance.

"Ah, Hori-san. Come in," Ito said jovially. "Abbot, please met Hori Narimitsu, my secretary. You have much to talk about. He is exceptionally well versed in Chinese literature, and a great collector."

The two men bowed to one another. They drank their tea and chatted until the abbot made his leave. Ito signalled Hori to stay as he accompanied his guest to the entrance of the mansion.

"It is a great pleasure to have you as my neighbor. I am extremely pleased you are refurbishing the temple," Ito said.

The shaven-headed clergyman looked at his neighbor with an expression of benevolence. "There is nothing so important as supporting the temple to the one-and-only Daibosatsu Yakushi Nyorai."

Ito murmured quietly that there were many buddhas and kami just as illustrious, but that of course of them all . . .

"No," the abbot insisted somewhat rudely. "There is none but the Daibosatsu." He was obviously an enthusiast, and Ito was prepared to give much latitude to such. "I hope you will be able to contribute some trifle, to aid in the gaining of merit," the abbot added casually. He bowed and left, his train of monks falling in around him.

Ito watched him go, then chuckled. "So that is what it is all about. Oh well, perhaps I shall contribute a little something. Can't do any harm." He returned to the room where Hori still sat as before. Seating himself he motioned his secretary to make himself comfortable. They talked about various affairs until Ito, idly playing with a brush, asked abruptly, "Hori-san, that young woman? The one you recommended to my attention last week? Have you any idea what has become of her?"

"No, I have no idea, Ito-san. I merely noted that she was the type you seemed to like. As in other occasions before, I took the initiative of calling her to your attention."

"She seems to have disappeared. Left the mansion on some errand I'm told and has not come back. Pity. She was quite good. I'll need another such soon . . ."

Hori bowed respectfully. "If one such comes to my attention. . . ."

Behind the sliding paper *shoji* door, Ito Haruko listened on in growing puzzlement. The house, alive with the sound of servants and retainers moving about, darkened with the night. There was a look on her husband's face that presaged deep thought. She wondered what had crossed his mind.

CHAPTER 4

MOMOE CAME TO WITH COUGHS RACKING HER FRAME. THERE was something hard and slick under her chest. Something else was pushing at her back without pause, and two warm hairy pillars were bounding her on either side. She tried to rise and realized, from the rocking, that she was in a small boat. Smells gave her another clue: she was in a fishing boat. Her conscious feelings of her environment widened. She coughed some more and her chest ached. The hands stopped pummeling her. She felt something soft and heavy, rather pleasant, leave her back and a rough voice, trying to speak kindly, said "You are all right now?"

Weakly, she nodded, then became suddenly aware of her nudity. She sat up and the world swam before her. She was conscious of a hard arm and shoulder trying to support her, and a bottle was pressed to her lips. She drank, then coughed some more, but the fiery liquor spread warmth through her body and she relaxed somewhat, knowing by now that she was not dead. She leaned against the warmth and again, the consciousness of her nudity returned. She wondered why she had bothered taking off her clothes when she had jumped into the waters. She had looked for Saburo the following day, but no one had seen him at his small workshop. He had not returned that night, nor the day after. Despondency and the realization that she had been taken for a fool gnawed at her. She felt the eyes of her neighbors on her, as if they knew she had been a foolish girl, and an abandoned one at that. In a fit of despair she had wandered off, distancing herself from the city and the shame it held for her. Finally she had resolved to end her life, hoping for some happier existence in the afterlife. The smell of fish in a rocking boat was obviously not it.

27

Her eyes focused and she stared at her rescuer. He still held her patiently. She recoiled in shock. He was as naked as she.

Momoe covered her mouth, then her breasts. She flushed scarlet in her confusion, and he looked on amusedly.

"What's the matter, do you swim with your clothes?" She blushed and lowered her head. "I wasn't swimming . . ."

"I know," he laughed. "But I do. In an' out th'water the whole day. We get many like you: wanting to drown themselves. Changed your mind, I hope? No need to kill yourself is there? Sure got a nice body, shame to waste it." He said cheerfully. His hips jerked involuntarily.

Suddenly the awareness of what she was looking at impinged on her confusion. In lowering her face she found herself staring in incomprehension at a long dangling member between his thighs. It grew, long and thick, and she thought, thickening, from a hairy bush that covered his lower belly. For a moment she was just fascinated. She wondered why he had a wisp of straw tied to the end: aside from that and a similar one that held his topknot in place, he was naked. Then to her wonderment it started swelling, jerking upwards in irregular steps. The realization of what she was watching made her want to move her face, but she was held by the fascination of the new sight and by two warm hard palms at either side of her face.

Momoe watched incredulously as the massive member climbed to a full erection. It curved backwards in a mighty bow, exposing a smooth underside. The straw wisp constricted it near the tip where an angry red, one-eyed, heart-shaped knob stared back at her haughtily. Instinctively she turned to retreat. A smooth hand held her hip tight and another inserted itself between her buttocks to the hairy grotto where none but her own and Saburo's hand had ever been before. She looked at the bank in panic . . . reeds, bushes, trees, and in the far distance, mountains, but no people. The hand was demanding. It found the warmth of her two delicate lips and roughly inserted itself between them. To her surprise she found the sensation almost as pleasant as when Saburo had done the same to her. She was conscious of the male body kneeling behind her and of the warm hairy belly pressing against her own smooth ass. The hand was withdrawn as the monster reared itself between her legs. The straw scratched the delicate inner surface of her thighs. She stilled her fear and prepared herself for the pain of insertion. The broad knob bumped against her lips, then he found the sweet hole and began inserting the long member.

Instead of the expected pain Momoe found that the long shaft brought with it a feeling of relief. Her vagina opened expectantly at the passage of the massive pillar. She sighed in surprise. Inside her, strange wild sensations seemed to lead directly from her warm cavern to her spine. The roughness of the straw ring brought with it a piercing sensation of lust, something she had not felt so intensely with Saburo. She turned her mind from thinking of that faithless traitor and simply allowed her body to enjoy the new sensations.

As the man moved into her, the sensations increased. The boat rocked to and fro with their activities. The sun warmed her back and she could feel the hair on his legs and belly as he plunged his pole into her depths. Her cunt, barely used to the presence of a male member, registered a protesting twinge. But soon the pleasure of a male body on hers and a male member in her female channel erased the feelings of shame and all but the faintest memory of the treacherous Saburo.

Momoe melted in the hard fisherman's arms. She squirmed her ass backwards trying to feel as much of the man as she could. She felt she was a female eel, struggling to twine herself around a delicious male. The fisherman reciprocated. His hard body possessed hers with a certainty she had not felt with Saburo. One of his hands went around her belly, digging into her pussy mound while he stroked his own pumping staff. She lowered a hesitant hand and touched the soft, large hairy bag that was hammering below her. He urged her on with quiet grunts and murmurs and she supported the soft stones with the flat of her hand.

The rhythm of his movements became abrupt, the shaft of his cock barely moving in her cunt. The scratching of the straw raised her blood to a fever pitch. Involuntary cries and gasps escaped her lips. She bent her back far down into the boat, lying on her knees and chest. Both her

29

hands tried to hold the shaft, feeling its silky-slick length, even poking a questioning finger into herself to feel it buried in her. The fisherman seized her generous hips forcefully and pulled her roughly back and forth while he raked his stubbly chin across her unprotected back. She arched back at him, willing him to split her apart. Wild spasms began in her untutored cunt and she ground herself as well as she was able into the man behind her. He responded with a final lunge that sent her onto her face in bilge that smelled of fish. Warm liquid spurted, filling her insides, completing her own orgasm as she twitched wildly and rose to a precipice of feeling. He pulled his shaft out and rinsed it, and then Momoe's ass, with handfuls of water. She rose slowly to a seat, too shy to look him in the face. The fisherman grinned.

"Better to be alive, in't?" he asked. His accent was thick, almost incomprehensible. "Like t'do't agin, but gotta work," he said cheerfully, hauling at his nets. Dumbly she tried to be of use, glorying in the living feel of her body, in the play of her muscles, the sun on her skin. Above all she rejoiced in her newly awakened womanhood, in the discovery of the pleasure to be found between her legs.

"Eh Funacho, fine fish you've got!" The other fishermen were heaving their catches ashore on the beach near the tiny hamlet. Momoe was at first embarrassed by her nudity, then found that it was more common then clothes for both men and women, and in any case, for the fisherfolk, the fish were of importance, not her nude body. Most of the men wore nothing more than the wisp of straw around their cocks in the fashion of her rescuer.

"Found her in the water," the fisherman said.

Momoe bowed and said, "Thank you for your help."

"Help with the fish," he grunted.

'Help' in this context meant not only unloading them amidst a gaggle of naked brats, flat-dugged old crones and a few plump fishwives, all naked as the day they were born, but cleaning and racking the fish as well. They worked late into the night, gutting the small fish and threading them onto lengths of twig. Their work was lit by simple rush candles, which shed a glow on the bronze bodies. The smoke of the fire around which they huddled and of the smoking candles mingled with the smell of fish grease which eventually deadened the nose.

Momoe was working next to a youngish woman whose blunt fingers were amazingly agile at capturing the fish from their tubs and threading them on the gill-lines. She showed Momoe how to do it. They stopped towards evening for a meal consisting of cooked sweet potato, some of the fish, and a millet gruel, all of which Momoe found almost unpalatable.

The young woman smiled at Momoe. "Shozo fucked you did he?"

Momoe gulped a mouthful of scalding sweet potato in surprise. "Such smooth skin you've got. I shouldn't wonder," the woman continued.

The woman's country accent was almost incomprehensible to Momoe. But her tone was kindly and she obviously meant nothing offensive. Momoe nodded dumbly, a blush flooding her cheeks.

"Good lay, i'nt e?" asked the woman. "I like it when he gives me a bit. Every night too, most times."

"Are you a friend of his?" Momoe asked, still trying to digest the information.

"I's wive. 'Cho's m'name," the other woman chuckled. "Good fisherman. The best." That was obviously uppermost in her estimation. "Goin ta stay awhile?"

Momoe looked at her dumbly, not knowing what to say, or what to do. Tears started running silently down her cheeks.

"Don't cry, missy. You kin stay 'ere." The fishwife stroked Momoe's naked thigh. "So smooth y'are, an' so pale. Wish I 'ad skin like yourn." Her hands casually explored Momoe's thighs and back, and she rubbed at the knotted tired muscles. "Just a little bit more to go, then we kin rest."

A shadow fell over them when they finished the fish. Momoe and the other woman looked up. It was Momoe's rescuer. He motioned to the woman, who got to her feet with alacrity. Momoe watched them walk to a corner of the hut that was sheltered by a thin screen of reeds. Emulating the others, she simply lay back, feet to the fire, and drifted off. From the corner she could hear the rustling of straw and the sighs and liquid sounds of love. As she drifted off to sleep she wondered if what she felt was relief or envy.

She woke, confused for a moment, chased by nightmares. A hand was on her crotch. She stared through the dark and could barely make out 'Cho's thick form.

"I tried to get 'im to 'ave you too, but 'e's too tired. I'll do you then."

Momoe wanted to protest, but the warmth of the other woman's body against her cool skin was too good to refuse. 'Cho rolled Momoe flat on her back. She whispered fish-scented endearments as her lips stroked Momoe's tired skin. Then suddenly she was lying between Momoe's legs and their lips were pressed together. Momoe started to resist, then realized that the young woman was far more experienced than she, and that her touch was infinitely pleasing. She returned the kiss, mingling their saliva and exploring the fishwife's mouth. She touched the stocky muscular body that lay over hers, shyly at first, then with increasing boldness as 'Cho explored her as well. She touched 'Cho's full breasts first and the woman obliged her by bringing each teat to her mouth. Momoe licked them at first, then growing bold, sucked a fully erect nipple into her mouth. 'Cho encouraged her by sinking her chest down, covering Momoe's face with a warm pillow. Momoe's hands slid further down stroking 'Cho's hips and fondling her ass. The buns were large and muscular and between them, almost at the bottom, Momoe could feel long silky hair, sticky with the man's come.

'Cho was just as busy. She stroked the girl beneath her, marvelling at the smooth white skin, now only lightly tanned from a day's exposure. She felt Momoe's hesitant exploration of her ass and parted her legs widely to allow the new girl access to herself. "Stick it in my bung?!" she whispered.

"What?" Momoe could not understand.

'Cho gently moved a hand under Momoe's ass and raised her hips, then tickled the tight ring of muscle at Momoe's anus. Momoe did not object, except for clenching her muscles involuntarily. Soon however she relaxed, and was actually disappointed when 'Cho moved on, stroking forward now, dipping her fingers in Momoe's cunt. The town girl reciprocated, finding the sperm-gluey hole and inserting a crooked finger inside. 'Cho began panting, then she lay full length on Momoe and started rubbing her full mound against the other girl's. They wriggled together, Momoe finding the delightful friction a wonderful relief. She clutched at 'Cho's anatomy, muttering endearments and quiet cries as she reached a climax. 'Cho did not withdraw then, and Momoe found a delightful difference in making love to a woman: 'Cho continued the movements of her body without losing any of her enthusiasm. They came together several more times before the two girls fell asleep in one another's arms.

CHAPTER 5

SEVERAL DAYS WALKING FINALLY BROUGHT ISEI OUT OF THE mountains onto the lush plains. He came to a small town as dusk fell. A rainstorm was on its way and he felt the need for some shelter in this strange land of sleek keen men and rounded soft women. People shied away from him and occasionally small children threw stones, at which he growled and they fled.

He was hungry and tired and the strange place made him nervous. He left the town hurriedly. Shadows were gathering in the eaves and lanterns, glowing like the more familiar fireflies, were being lit. At the edge of the town he stopped. A wonderful smell was coming to his nostrils. He sniffed with appreciation, then again. It was coming from somewhere to his left, through a grove of pine trees. He left the roadway and padded silently into the forest. The smell increased. He came to what appeared to him to be a magnificent structure. The house was large, constructed of well-planked wood. The eaves were not thatched but tiled: an innovation he had never seen before. The smell was coming from a semi-detached cookhouse, connected to the main building by a covered walk. Isei slavered at the smell, and wondered at the effect it had on him. There were sounds of movement from the house. Male voices and obedient female ones. He knew he should move on, but the smell drove him frantic with hunger and he crept closer.

A woman was bent over the stove. A pot of rice was simmering on one pot hole, another pot on the other. As she stirred the second pot a blast of the magnificent smell overwhelmed Isei. He fell to his knees beside the open doorway, his gun, forgotten, almost slipping from his hand. The woman turned, startled at his movement. Her hand flew to her mouth and she suppressed a shriek. She had a pleasant, smoothly-rounded face and her hair was covered by a scarf. To Isei she was finely dressed, but he did not notice the patched condition of her kimono, her worn *geta* sandals, nor her simple hairdo.

She started to scream, then seeing his passive kneeling form she asked sharply, "What do you want?"

"Ah . . . ah . . ." he stuttered, overwhelmed by the scent.

"Yes? What is it? We want no beggars here!"

"Ah, Mistress . . ." Isei said miserably, "What . . . What is that thing?" he waved vaguely at the pot.

She looked at him then laughed, not bothering to hide her mouth politely. "A cooking pot, you fool. What are you that you don't know . . ."

"No, please. The food you are cooking."

"Hmf. A beggar. I thought so. And a dirty polluted *sanka* at that," she sneered. "Haven't you ever seen soup?"

"I am no beggar," Isei said proudly, rising from his knees. She retreated, and he fumbled behind him to produce the soft pelt of a fox. "I will pay!"

"For a bowl of soup? Of simple *miso-shiru* bean-paste soup? With a fox pelt!?" She laughed incredulously.

He nodded dumbly, bowing to the floor again then raising the pelt in both hands. She snatched it greedily from his hands.

"Have you a bowl?" she asked. He shook his head. She fumbled in the dark corners of the cooking hut until she found an old cracked wooden bowl and ladled the dark brown steaming soup into it. Isei watched with bright eyes as she held it out to him with one hand. He turned and squatted by the door, ignoring her completely. He peered into the depths of the warm liquid. A reddish cloud floated in the transparent steaming liquid. Vegetables, known and unknown, a tiny fish, and squares of some unknown substance floated in the soup. It looked like something his grandfather had once described to him, having heard it from *his* grandfather. Isei raised the bowl carefully to his lips and took a slow sip. His mouth was flooded with an exquisite sensation. He closed his eyes in appreciation, lost in the pleasure of the moment.

Heavy footsteps and the smell of cheap stale liquor overwhelmed him suddenly. A blow sent him and the bowl flying.

"We want no beggars here!!" a male voice broke into his pleasure. Furious, Isei rose to his knees and started groping in the dark for his matchlock. He faced a large dark man holding a big wooden mallet, the kind used for pounding rice.

"Get out of here you lousy beggar!" the man snarled. "This is an inn, not a beggars' home."

"Hey, what have we here innkeeper?" Three other male figures, reeking of cheap sake, staggered out of the inn's backdoor. One was in the act of exposing himself for a piss.

"Har, a mountain man, a *sanka*. What's the dirty one doing here? Class of the place going down, eh innkeeper?"

The innkeeper raised his stick and took a furious step towards Isei.

"Having it off with your wife, was he?" one of the men egged the innkeeper on.

The woman protested furiously, rebuking the man and cursing Isei in the same breath.

"Let's have some fun with the dirty beggar!" one of the men said. The five of them advanced on him in a group, and finding his matchlock, Isei took to his heels. The chase was short. Isei's pursuers would not venture into the trees, and his own woodcraft allowed him to speed silently into the welcoming darkness.

He peered at the dilapidated inn from his shelter. As the night wore on he brooded about the treatment meted to him. The sound of the drinkers at their cups came to him through the night and he mourned his lost soup, savoring the memory of the one sip he had gotten.

Finally Isei's rage overcame his caution. He crept down to the building unnoticed. A tilted lantern, its sides torn and bearing letters he could not read, announced the name of the inn. Furiously he struck at it. The lantern tilted further and the paper sides caught fire. The fire climbed to the wooden support. Isei opened his mouth to call out, then shut his mouth with a snap. His rage was fuelled by the laughter inside, and he watched curiously as the flames rose and started licking along the posts and lintels. He crept back into the woods, grinning like a wolf as screams suddenly erupted from the dilapidated building. More and more of the structure started glowing with the flames in the front. In the confusion, one of the drinkers must have dropped a candle, for suddenly there were flames bursting out of other corners of the inn. The handful of people inside fought their way out as best they could. Isei watched them, laughing. Then his eyes narrowed. One of the figures rushing out was trailed by a tail of sparks and a minor flame of its own. He hurried after the figure through the woods. The figure screamed in a high-pitched female voice: It had noticed the flame on its tail.

Rather then trying to take her clothes off and beat out the flame, the innkeeper's wife ran in panic through the woods. Isei caught up with her. He gripped the corner of her kimono and pulled it from her, stamping on the flames in the tail of her dress. She screamed mindlessly as he ripped it completely from her, leaving her in her red shift.

She cowered away from him, trying to cover her nakedness with her hands. "Are you going to rape me?"

Isei stood there dumbly, only raising the burnt kimono to show her what had happened.

"No, no. I'll not let you!" she cried out hysterically. Her crossed forearms covered her breasts and she glared wildly about. "Dirty *sanka*, I'll not let you. Rape! Help, rape!"

"Shut up woman," he said fiercely. When she did not stop, he reached for her and put a hand over her mouth. She struggled furiously and his patience broke. He bore her back on a convenient fallen trunk. The rough bark scratched at her back.

"Stop your screaming!" he hissed wildly, then released his hand. Perhaps misunderstanding his motives, perhaps not caring or scared out of her wits, she immediately started to scream again. Isei's hand was back on her mouth in a flash. Then he became conscious of their situation. And of the fact that he had a painful and taut erection. He held her down wordlessly and began undoing his homespun trousers. She struggled, silently now, and the smoothness of her body excited him further. He pushed her down on the log, straddling her thighs, then began biting—as softly as he could under the circumstances—at her nipples.

They were tight with the cool night air and his warm breath softened them somewhat. She peered at him fearfully over her breasts, her fears realized. He smiled back and she turned her eyes away, renewing her struggles. The motion of her hips on the log excited Isei further. Her pubic mound was raised high and he could feel its prominence rubbing against his stomach and chest. Lustful pictures filled his brain. He had never taken a woman against her will before, had never needed to. Mountain women welcomed male attentions, or simply ran off. But they were never as soft and as helpless as this female.

At last she was spread over the log. Isei straddled her, then pulled his rough pants and loincloth off completely. His thick stubby cock sprang into the cool night air. He lowered his bottom between her splayed legs and directed the top of his cock to her entrance. She struggled at the pain of his insertion into her dry cunt. Isei pulled out and groped at his belt. He poured a small handful of oil from the tiny flask and applied it to her dark bush, then rubbed it in furiously. The pepper and roots he had macerated in the oil started taking their toll. She struggled less, not only resigned to her fate but realizing suddenly that there was pleasure in it for her as well. Isei's thick blunt cudgel sank smoothly into her and the oil started lighting a fire in her loins. The position was uncomfortable, and their combined weight dug splinters into her back, but the fire roused by the oil was unquenchable now. She mewed with relief when their hairs meshed together and the mountain man began rising and sinking into her helpless body.

Isei explored as much of her upper torso as he could with his lips and tongue. This plains woman tasted different from any other woman he had ever had. But her cunt was the same slick avenue of all the others. His movements became abrupt and he felt his climax beginning to rise. Beneath him, her mouth still shut by his palm, he could see that the woman was pleading about something. She too had noticed the impending climax. Isei slowed down, allowing her time to catch up. Muffled cries came from beneath his palm. Her eyes closed to slits and the whites showed. She seemed gripped by a palsy and Isei knew she was about to join him. He let himself go and they rocked together on the rough wood. She finally managed to raise her legs high, and as the volcanoes of their passion exploded, throw them over his back. They rolled off the log together, onto a bed of ferns. Through the trees Isei could barely make out the glow of the fire and the calls and cries of people around it.

He stood up over her, his shrivelled member cool, tucking himself into his clothes.

"You raped me," she said wonderingly.

"Yes," he said gruffly. He felt obscurely guilty. "You were screaming so loud, so . . ." He threw his hands up.

"I've been raped before. By a samurai, before I was married. It was nothing like this." She was talking to herself, hadn't even heard him. She felt her cunt delicately with her fingers and a smile of bliss came to her. She looked up at him as he retied his belt. Hesitated a moment. "Will you come again? Sometime? I won't scream. . . ."

"Maybe," he said.

"We can meet here," she said eagerly. "I'll . . . I'll bring some soup!"

He grinned and turned to go.

She watched his shadow slip between the trees, then searched for her scorched robe and slipped it on. The mountain man had forced her and yet, . . . Yet it was the best fuck she had had. She puzzled over it, and over her lack of shame as Isei made his way into the wood and down the road, heading west and south.

CHAPTER 6

SUGIYAMA WAS RESTING ON THE VERANDA OF THE LAVISH inn, the only place he could find, when the courtesan entered with her train. She had an exquisite white face highlighted by the red on her lips. Her hair was built into the large hairdo that was becoming popular and there were gold pins stuck in the hair, attesting to her professional success. Her attendants included a muscular young man armed with a short-sword, a maid, and an elderly male who was obviously responsible for the baggage. They were all dressed in pilgrim's dress: white clothes and bloused pantaloons, leggings, and wide sedge hats. On the courtesan the plain pilgrim's garb looked a mockery: It was of the finest silk and she wore her clothes with an ineffable air of elegance.

Sugiyama idly wondered what she cost, then thrust the thought from his mind. The inn was taking the last of his money, and he could not be bothered with anything pecuniary: it was beneath his dignity. The courtesan sent her attendants hither and yon, attending to her needs, the young man she called Matsuo doing most of the running. Sugiyama sniffed in displeasure at the man's dog-like devotion to his mistress: Women were for serving men, not the reverse. He rose and sauntered off as dinner, in lavish lacquered trays, was brought from the inn's kitchens to the courtesan's room. The inn owner, who apparently knew the woman, begged an interview after dinner and expressed his appreciation to the famous Osatsuki for honoring his establishment.

The manservant came suddenly out of the dark, bent on an errand. He slammed full tilt into Sugiyama. Sugiyama slid back with the blow and his sword hissed from its sheath. All unknowing, muttering a perfunctory apology,

Matsuo hurried on to his mistress's apartment. Sugiyama raced after him on silent feet. He raised his two-handed sword and struck just as the manservant slid open the *shoji* door looking onto the garden.

The full cut slammed into the roof beam above Sugiyama's head. He cursed and tugged wildly at the hilt. The servant cast one horrified look over his shoulder and leaped into the room, fumbling for his own weapon.

"No, Matsuo! Run, run!" the prostitute cried, seeing Sugiyama's face. "He will kill you. Quick, through the back!"

Matsuo started to argue but the look on Sugiyama's face convinced him and he slipped rapidly through the door. Sugiyama, managing to release his sword, was about to give chase when the woman rose and threw the hem of her outer kimono high. The cloth sail checked Sugiyama's charge and obscured his intended victim from his sight. Matsuo promptly slipped out the back. Sugiyama glared at the woman, then at the *shoji* behind her. It would be useless to chase the base creature now. He turned on the mistress and raised his sword.

"You will die!" he called, angered.

"If I must," she said calmly. "I am Osatsuki."

He advanced a step.

"You do not even have the courtesy to introduce yourself?" she said coldly.

"To my equals, not mean people," he sneered.

"My former name was Gojo-no-Satsuki-hime of the *kuge* nobility, and *we* did not even *talk* to mere samurai," she answered formally.

Her response and the hint of superiority in her voice fanned his anger. And seeing the perfection of her throat, his lust as well. He resheathed his sword and took a step forward. She regarded him calmly. Sugiyama grabbed the lapels of her robe and tore them apart. He stood at arms' length and admired the delicate pale body that was exposed to his gaze. She had just come from her bath and her skin was smooth and delicately scented. She tolerated his gaze for a moment, then turned to go. He held her forcefully and a grin appeared on his thin lips. Without a word he forced her down to her knees.

Satsuki did not bother struggling against the lout. She

merely allowed herself to be forced down and sat on her knees passively. When he exposed himself she examined his cock with professional interest. It was erect and inflamed with lust and he jerked his hips at her as if to intimidate her with its size or the hint of violence it included.

A boor, she decided, and one who must needs be taught a lesson if possible. Let him think he was raping her. Her turn would come soon enough. She resisted his hand and he forced her head roughly to his cock.

"Bite me and I'll make you regret it!" he warned, and a thin steel *kozuka* appeared suddenly in his hand.

Satsuki shrugged mentally and applied her red-painted lips to the erect member. She licked at it rapidly, using only the tip of her tongue, then applying only her lips, finally absorbing the entire member into her trained mouth. He forced himself as deeply into her mouth as he could. Her throat muscles worked on the fleshy tip and there seemed to be no end to her depths. His hairs brushed roughly against her makeup and she regretted the need to remake her face before he could see her again. He tried to withdraw and with an exercise of will and muscle she managed to overcome his peak. His come erupted into her willing mouth. Gobs of hot fluid flooded her mouth and disappeared down her throat. She made a perfect oval of her lips to ensure that none of the milk dripped in an unseemly fashion down her chin.

Sugiyama withdrew from Osatsuki's mouth and pushed her down on the floor. She sighed in exasperation at his crudeness and did as he bid, trying to channel his energy in productive ways. His movements were more controlled this time, driven less by lust and more by pleasure. She touched him in the appropriate places, raising his pleasure gradually, offering him different parts of herself in a planned design. He nibbled at her breasts, then found his hands being directed to her ass, to the small of her back. She twisted in his arms, assuming different postures, never detaching his stem from her flower. Without knowing precisely how it had come about he found that she was controlling their movements and the speed of their love-making. It was easier to fall in with her directions than to perform as brutally as he normally did. Following her unspoken directions he explored her glorious body thoroughly. Nothing he did aroused opposition, everything he started ended as she wished it. As his lust was fanned, as it grew in his loins to a major explosion, he found that she was the most receptive female he had known, unconquerable.

His cock stabbed into her unplumbed depth for one final time. One of her feet was stroking his shoulder, the other supported them in a tangle of limbs. Her mouth was on his, sucking his life out just as her cuntal muscles were sipping delicately at his rampant cock. Sugiyama gave a groan of mixed defeat, relief, and satisfaction and flooded her interior with his sperm. He bucked heavily into her as her fingers stroked the last of his lust out and into her ever empty insides.

"Lie with me for a while," the courtesan said. Her hands stroked his brow and the small of his back, relieving the small muscular cramps. Unheard by him in the darkness she wiped his flaccid cock and her own sopping cunt with her special paper which always lay by her side for the purpose. One never knew, she had told Osei her junior partner, when one might need it.

Sugiyama lay staring at the ceiling, his smooth muscular breast rising and falling peacefully. For once, he realized, sex had given him some modicum of peace. And for once, too, he found that he had met a professional he could respect: One who in her own sphere of endeavor was as technically competent and as naturally gifted as he was with his sword.

Satsuki lay beside him contemplating his profile. He was a boor, granted, and vicious to boot, but there was a hint of promise in him. Perhaps, she thought, he needed a lesson in humility more than anything else. She felt something dig into her back and was about to move away when she realized what it was.

Her hairpins were scattered on the quilt beside her. She brushed idly through them until she found the one she wanted. It was enamelled and topped by a bunch of azalea blossoms: her namesake. But the shank was steel, sharp as a razor and pointed like a needle, made for her by her friend Okiku, a former ninja assassin. She grasped it carefully and moved to act.

CHAPTER 7

ITO CHEWED HIS LIP ABSTRACTEDLY. HE SAT ON A SOFT *zabuton* pillow in a room devoted to business, the bustle of his household about him. Though retired, he had retired with honor. He had no desire to end his days with his belly ripped out. And if the affair came to light, he might well be required to do so. His duty was to report things directly to the authorities. But fortunately the authority was somewhat unclear here, which gave him some grace. Formally the Imperial capital was governed by a governor responsible directly to the shogun—one Matsudaira Konnosuke currently held the post. Matsudaira had little control over clansmen, particularly senior clansmen of senior clans such as himself. On the other hand, throwing himself on the mercy of his own clan could be disastrous. One reason he had retired here, away from the clan lands in Mito, was to avoid the priggishness that was even now beginning to emerge in that domain. No, no. Far better to rely on the local governor, who, it was rumored, had certain things in common with himself. Ito sighed. It was going to be a difficult business. And costly, in both money and pride. He called for his secretary to make the preparations for his call upon the governor.

† † †

Osei had just finished entertaining a customer. He lay on her, his two swords tossed carelessly in a corner while his sword of flesh shrank into a morsel and was expelled from her tight hole. One of her legs was extended while the other was bent over his ass, the sole of her foot stroking his sweaty flesh. His mouth was occupied by her breasts as he sucked first one nipple then the other, his teeth painfully pleasing to the erect nubbly flesh.

He soon rose to go and she helped him dress, performing the appropriate functions and handing him his sword. He left reluctantly, and she knew that he would be back soon, as soon as his purse and balls were full again. Elder Sister Osatsuki would be pleased. Not at the profit, though that too was not negligible, but because steady customers were the best proof of a courtesan's worth.

There was a discreet scratching at the door to her room. The *shoji* panel was slid aside and the elderly woman who acted as maidservant, messenger, and occasionally procurer for Osei ushered herself in, knelt on the floor, closed the *shoji* again, then bowed to Osei.

"Osei-sama. There is a messenger for you."

Osei sighed. She was rather bored with business. Elder Sister Satsuki, her mentor and senior partner, had decided to go on pilgrimage to the shrine of Benten near Hiroshima, and here she was holding the fort with almost no one to talk to.

"He is from a good house," the maid whispered excitedly.

Osei rose as gracefully as she could—all of Satsuki's teachings had not yet penetrated—and swayed over to peek down at the entryway to the house. The man who had brought the message, though no samurai, was obviously the servant of an upper-class household. Excitement mingled with apprehension gripped her. She was more accustomed than before to going among the great and the rich, yet this was the first time she would have to do it on her own. . . .

"Do you know who he is from?" she whispered.

"No. He handed me this." The maid handed a small lacquered box to Osei. She opened it and her hand flew to her mouth in consternation.

"Send him away," she whispered urgently. "Say . . . say I'll be following immediately. Then get me a palanquin and come back to help me dress. Hurry!" The maid scuttled out of the room, and Osei started preparing herself to go out. Her whitened hands were trembling slightly as she applied the rice-flour powder to her face.

Osei's plain hired palanquin stopped in front of the gate of Miura's small house. She stepped out and paid the bearers hurriedly and rushed inside. Satsuki would not approve of the unseemly haste, a small inner voice cautioned her. "Excuse my interruption!" she called out in a timorous voice as she stepped into the *genkan,* the pounded-earth entryway to the house. There was no answer and she was so agitated that she paid no attention to courtesy. She slipped out of her lacquered clogs, stepped onto the polished house platform, and opened the *shoji* sliding door, then passed through the room to another *shoji* and threw it open. She squeaked with terror and dropped to her knees. The woman facing her relaxed and her hand dropped to her naked thigh. A small throwing *shaken* spike disappeared in the covers. Of the three swords the man under her was wielding, two were lowered. The third still thrust boldly into the damp thicket of heart-shaped black hairs between the woman's thighs.

"Why Midori, whatever is the matter?" Okiku made as if to rise to come to Osei's aid.

"Not now!" Okiku's mate's rumbling voice came from behind her and his large hands pulled at her muscular waist. "Not . . . now!" His back arched and from her position on the floor Osei could see the massive shaft ram deeply into her friend's cunt. The thick column jerked convulsively and a froth of white cream spread from the juncture of the diminutive woman's lower lips and the thick pillar of the man's erection. He fell back and his hands relaxed. "Why don't you come here instead?" He asked conversationally.

"Can't you see she's upset?" Okiku scolded.

"No. Not at all. Okiku-san, forgive me for intruding. I am embarrassed . . ."

Okiku laughed. "You've seen us at more than this. And joined us too. What is the matter, dear Midori? Or should I call you by your professional name?"

Osei-Midori crawled closer and began to sniff. Okiku wrapped her hands around her and rocked back and forth. She grinned over her shoulder at Jiro, who seemed to enjoy the movement. It was not entirely for Midori's benefit.

"I have been called to attend to the Matsudaira Konnosuke, the Governor!" she said in alarm.

Jiro laughed. "I knew he fancied you!"

Okiku took Midori's face in her hands and said seriously, "So why are you worried? You know him."

"Yes, but . . . but. But not as the Governor," Midori finally whispered. "It is . . . it is frightening. An official summons . . ."

"There is nothing to worry about." Okiku kissed Midori gently, and the courtesan responded hungrily. "Don't worry. He's not a different person. He merely wears different clothes . . ."

Jiro was sitting up and he leaned over his wife's smooth shoulder. "And you can always have him take them off you know. I'm sure he'll like that . . ."

Midori smiled through her tears. "It was rather foolish. But I am of the mean people and he is such an august personage . . . I am so sorry I interfered in your fun."

"Interfered?" Okiku asked, a glint in her eye. "I wouldn't say that."

Midori smiled shyly back. "May I be of assistance?" she asked softly.

"This time *I* will pay," Jiro joshed her, reminding her of their first meeting in the mountains of Yoshino.

"There is no need, Jiro-san. You have paid in full."

She knelt between their legs and applied her face to the soft fragrant bush of Okiku's pussy. Her tongue licked out and she touched the area of the clitoris, then lowered her face and laved the length of Jiro's sticky column.

Okiku leaned back full length on her man. His large root joined them at the loins. He jerked upwards as she forced her neat ass down on him. Midori rocked back on her heels and examined the view. The entire length of Okiku's cunt was exposed. The male root too, was visible for whatever part of it stuck out the slit. The delicate lips parted over the angry insertion and clasped the shaft as if reluctant to lose even the smallest morsel. Jiro and Okiku continued rocking while they waited for Midori to make up her mind. She took her time.

Finally she leaned forward again. She flattened her tongue and laved the length of the joined organs, collecting the dew off the ensemble. She matched her motions to those of the couple, and both of them started trembling with the pleasure of her busy tongue. She smiled and changed her tactics. Using her warm oral digit as a finger she touched the folds of Okiku's lovely cunt. Okiku started jerking wildly, her head tossing from side to side. Jiro assisted Midori by clutching at Okiku's little breasts, squeezing and moulding them with his large hands. Okiku yowled and jerked her hips in a frantic rhythm and her salty juices flooded Midori's tongue.

They rested to breath for a moment, then Okiku slipped off Jiro and urged Midori over to him. Midori replaced her. The sensation of Jiro's monster cock inside her was wonderful. He shafted her energetically and she could feel Okiku's mouth and hands working her up to an orgasm. She came delicately, her insides squeezing his cock, trying to maintain her decorum. Jiro's face was red and it was clear he was ready to explode. Okiku smiled and remounted the rampant prick and Midori applied her lips again to the beautiful combination of male and female parts. Jiro was rough and impatient this time. His teeth were clenched and he pulled Okiku to him, holding her hips in a painful grasp. At the right moment, as his cock started pulsing, Midori applied her mouth to his balls, sucking them into her mouth. One of her fingers dug deeply into Okiku's cunt, following the cock almost to its tip. Another dug delicately into the man's ass. Jiro jerked off the bedding and his balls constricted in rough and uncontrollable spasms. Midori sucked hard at the juncture of man and woman-flesh. The foam of white thick liquid was laved away by her attentive ministrations, and she felt her own insides wet with sympathy and pleasure with her friends.

They reached the governor's mansion in plain palan-quins and requested an audience. While they waited they knelt at the entrance to a room guarded by two fully-armed samurai. The guards knew both Miura Jiro and his lady by sight, but nonetheless subjected Jiro and Okiku to keen-eyed scrutiny. The other, the courtesan, they did not know and filed her face away for future reference.

The man and two women were bid enter and the samurai slid open the painted sliding *fusuma* doors and announced Jiro.

"Mr. Miura Jiro and escort."

Jiro bowed, then was bid enter. He rose and the two women rose with him. They entered the room and the *fusuma* was slid shut. They knelt again and bowed deeply.

Facing them, on a low *tatami*-matted dais, sat Matsudaira. His semi-formal clothes were of rich silk. His sharp face was topped by a knife-thin topknot that streaked across a shining shaven pate. His face—the high cheekbones, piercing eyes and hawk nose—hinted at intelligence mixed with a touch of sensuality.

"You are Miura Jiro, *ronin*."

Jiro rumbled an assent.

"And the women with you, Miura Okiku and the courtesan Osei?"

Jiro bowed again and gave the affirmative.

"Please follow me," Matsudaira Konnosuke, Governor of the Imperial City of Miyako rose smoothly to his feet, dismissed his page, and strode regally into the inner rooms behind his seat. The page slid the *fusuma* closed behind the last of the two women.

Matsudaira flopped down on a cushion, slipping off his silk *haori* coat as he did so. He moved his shoulders and reached for a large ceramic bottle of sake warming in the kettle over the firepit.

"I hate those formalities," he growled.

Jiro flopped down beside his friend and laughed softly. "*You* chose to be the governor. You should have stayed an itinerant doctor."

"Duty," the young governor shrugged.

Midori was hovering uncertainly in the corner of the room. Matsudaira smiled at her. "Do you still remember me?" he asked pleasantly.

She nodded dumbly. Matsudaira was struck by the unusual cast of her hair. It was brown and soft, almost wavy. So unlike that of most Japanese. He wondered how she had come by it. Perhaps she was the by-blow of some visiting Southern Barbarian. Jiro's father was one such, and the giant bore traces of his Barbarian ancestry in the shape of lighter hair and complexion.

"I won't bite you girl, . . ." he said gently.

"Maybe you should, Goeman. I think she'd like that," Okiku said.

Matsudaira laughed. As Goemon, a wandering doctor, he had bitten Midori quite often. "I think I should. . . ."

"Absolutely," a new voice joined the conversation from behind a *shoji* screen. "As a matter of fact, I will too . . ."

Midori's face lit up at the sound. The *shoji* slid open and Rosamund knelt there, looking at her friends joyfully. Midori looked at her and wondered if she would ever get used to Rosamund's looks. Waves of yellow hair the color of spun gold. Pale, pale complexion almost like that of cherry blossoms in bloom. Full red lips and fuller breasts that rose firmly under the loosely-tied sleeping robe. Formally she was Matsudaira Konnosuke's prisoner, actually she ruled his household and him with a will of iron and a touch of the whip.

"Goemon, make Midori comfortable," Rosamund said in her accented Japanese.

Goemon rose and poured sake for Midori with his own hands.

"The problem is," he said when he had resumed his seat, and had described Ito's request for an interview, "that I can't just pull him in and question him. He's a retired retainer of the Mito elector clan, and a man with many ties, right up to the Presence himself. For all we know he might have been the tutor of the future Presence. I've heard some peculiar things about the goings-on in his household, and I'd like more information. That's where you come in, Midori. May I ask you to do something extraordinary? Not risky, I believe."

"Of course!" she said sincerely. "I would be honored."

"Ito is supposed to have some . . . well . . . peculiar sexual tastes ["So do you," interjected his consort]. I want you to enter his household and spy on him for a few weeks."

"Of course I will do it," she said, and blushed. They all knew she, a simple country girl, was overwhelmed by the company she found herself in. Okiku laughed and made a coarse pun, and even Midori had to giggle.

"What am I to look for?" she asked.

"Anything out of the ordinary. I don't know what. All I know is that he wrote of a terrible problem he wants to talk to me about when he can. Until he makes up his mind, I want to know more about what goes on there."

"I'll have to find a way to get in there, . . ." Osei said thoughtfully.

"That shouldn't be too difficult," Goemon said. "I

gather he fancies women, and often selects passing women for his pleasure . . ."

"By force?" asked Okiku, raising a shapely eyebrow.

"No. Not like that at all. He pays well. Just fancies commoners. I'd think that all you'd have to do is present yourself and make yourself, ah . . . indispensable as it were."

"I didn't ask my question idly," Okiku interjected. She told them about the attempted kidnapping. Goemon's face grew grim.

"I will institute inquiries. It is intolerable that anyone should engage in such a violation of the social order. *That* is a heinous offense. It disturbs the commoners and they are likely to make disturbances."

"And the women don't care for it either," added Okiku acidly. Goeman was apt to turn pompous in matters relating to his office.

Goeman stared at her, trying to decide whether she was joking or not, then nodded his head in the affirmative. In truth, he had not thought of it in those terms.

"I will sniff around this Ito mansion. Just in case. And I'll also be able to covey any messages needed to the City Office."

"Thank you, Elder Sister Okiku." Osei was clearly relieved. She knelt and bowed formally, ready to take her leave.

CHAPTER 8

MOMOE WAS STARING RUEFULLY AT HER RED AND PAINFUL hands when a commotion in the small fishing hamlet caught her attention. The women were clustering around a stranger. He was dressed in the clothes of a merchant. Simple cotton kimono, hiked up for travel, and a plain sash. On his back he carried a large basket which, as Momoe watched, he swung from his back. He squatted in place, a plump man whose muscular short legs showed in the sunlight. He chaffered with the fisherfolk, dispensing small knickknacks as he talked. He laughed uproariously at crude jokes and the shy fisherfolk followed suit.

He was obviously a townsman and Momoe, curious, felt compelled to put on the ragged robe 'Cho had given her. The fat man looked at her as she approached. He whispered something to one of the old crones, and she cackled and whispered back.

"Ah, young lady. Never seen you here before, have I? Not a fisher are you?"

Momoe smiled shyly at the familiar accents of Miyako. "No," she said in a low voice.

"Here's something for you then," he grinned and handed her a cheap comb.

"Kind of you," she murmured.

He laughed at the common Miyako politeness. "Miyako girl are you then? Intending to stay here?"

Momoe indicated her indecision by bowing her head.

"Why not come with me then? I could use some help in my business."

"Yes, go with the man," the crone urged her. The other villagers whispered and smiled at her good fortune. "Yes, go with him. Take ye t'the city he will . . ."

Uncertainly, she nodded, and when he smiled broadly, nodded agreement more emphatically.

He sounded kindly but there was something insincere about his offer that made Momoe want to refuse. On the other hand, her hands were blistered and she was exhausted from the days with the fishermen. And 'Cho's nightly demands were taking their toll too. She nodded silently, not really caring. The portly man laid a proprietary hand on her back and stroked the roughening skin.

"She's coming with me," he called out cheerfully to the group of fisherfolk. Only the fisherwife seemed to pay any attention. She ran over to Momoe and hugged her, then shyly handed her a small worn bag. "Some needles. It's all I got t'gi' you."

Momoe bowed her thanks, choking back her tears as the portly man led her off, back in the direction of the capital.

"My name is Yukio," the portly man said. "I make *kamaboko*, and you will help me."

Momoe nodded dumbly. She could see from the glint in his eyes that that was not the only thing he had in mind for her. Oddly enough, the thought was not displeasing. Suddenly she discovered that the pleasures of her body were the only things she had left. She was no longer a respectable daughter of respectable parents in a respectable occupation, but rather was as free as the winds. And the portly man, though not comely, was not displeasing. There was a certain animal delight about him, and a sly mystery that made her want to see what he had in mind.

"I am fortunate," he said to her later, as they reached his establishment on the outskirts of the city, "that my work is also my pleasure. I love *kamaboko* you see, and as I make it as well, I make it to suit my own taste." Indeed, most of the fish he had ordered from the fishermen were suited for the making of the bland-tasting fish paste which was featured in many dishes.

The morning work started early. There were fish to boil, bones and all, and their flesh to filter with other ingredients to create the right consistency. It was hot in the shed in which they worked. Yukio's operation was a small one, but Momoe saw that it would grow. The plump man was indefatigable, hopping from place to place, supervising and managing the cooking and filtering. The hired help left towards evening and Momoe, exhausted, slumped in a corner. Yukio still bustled about, tasting the finished product, seeing that the packages were ready for distribution.

"You are tired," he said, bending over her and helping her to her feet. His words and actions were both solicitous, but Momoe sensed there was more to it than the words. "Let me help you restore your energy," he whispered. "Here, come here." There was an undercurrent of excitement in his voice, and as she brushed against him Momoe could feel the erection that bulged his loincloth.

They were both naked from the waist up, and suddenly he was holding her, clutching at her rounded breasts. Momoe tried to resist but she was too tired, and in any case, ready herself for the feel of a male. His tongue sought hers and as his hands stripped off her underskirt, he rubbed blunt thick fingers through the soft hair between her legs. She swayed as she stood there, half from lust, half from sheer exhaustion.

"Ah, you are tired," he murmured in the steamy heat of the shed. He led her to a cutting table on which the rolls of finished product were packaged, now scrubbed clean of work and smelling faintly of fish and cedarwood. "Come, lie here and I will help you. I and *kamaboko*." Beside the table were several vats with *kamaboko* paste that had not hardened yet to the desired consistency.

He took a handful of the paste and rubbed his bare chest, then approached her and squeezed a generous handful between her legs. She moaned encouragingly, and he took another handful and rubbed it carefully through her hairy mound. It was hard for her to elevate herself much in her spread position on the low table but she pushed up as well as she could. He grinned and fisted another gob of the white paste. With great sweeping motions of his hands he began coating her entire body, until nothing but her head showed above the paste. His eyes glowed with lust and she wiggled and anticipation, making the paste shimmer whitely. His hands, coated with the white substance, roamed her body. His fingers explored her insides, slipping easily between the portals of her lower lips. Her nipples responded, peeking perkily out of mounds of the paste, like reverse mountains: the flanks snowy, the peaks brown. She floated off into a reverie as the *kamaboko*-maker's hands massaged her tired muscles. Gradually the tension left her limbs and entered into one hot spot, concentrating at the pit of her stomach, causing her to sound with lust. Shudders overcame her as his fingers, still coated with the paste, dug deeply into her salty interior.

"I'm hungry," Yukio complained, and he lowered his head to the pasture of her cunt, sucking and licking the paste up in great gulps.

Momoe cried out and almost sat erect. She had never felt the like before. The demanding touch of the man's lips and tongue on her sensitized cunt was almost too wonderful to bear. She cried out and clutched at his head, driving the searching tongue deeper into the sweet folds of her own flesh. Yukio obliged and drove his tongue like a vibrant miniature cock deep into her quim, carefully licking out every trace of the bland *kamaboko* paste and the salt of the girl's juices. She shivered and tossed her kerchief-wrapped head in the throes of an orgasm. Her heavily lidded eyes closed and her hips and bottom moved silkily, slithering on the slick table. At last the tremors subsided. Yukio looked down at her, then climbed onto the table between her legs. Her golden skin, tanned by her days with the fishermen, glowed against the snowy white of the paste.

Momoe noted that his erection was stiff as an iron bar. He found it difficult to bend it to her entrance. She aimed it for him and he slid into her, shuddering uncontrollably at the pleasure of it. He could find no purchase to jog into her and she soon discovered that the only way was to rotate her hips under his weight and clench internal muscles she did not know she had to increase the friction in her cunt. He gobbled greedily at her breasts, her chin, her belly, arching his body comically.

He burst into a powerful orgasm inside her and she tried to clutch his slippery form to hers. White sticky liquid oozed out from the pressure of their two bodies. His semen and her juices blended into the fish paste. Idly she ran a finger down their clinched bodies and examined the white paste that collected there. She gulped the gob, and it was the best *kamaboko* she had ever tasted.

The morning was like any morning in her new life. The *kamaboko*-maker made no sign that they had enjoyed the pleasures of the night before. The delivery men came and went, taking orders. She cleaned the vats and utensils, ran minor errands.

"Yukio-san," a breezy voice called from outside the shop. The *kamaboko*-maker left the vat he was examining and opened the door.

"Ah, the person from Sakamotoya. Welcome, welcome."

"We are having some guests. Special customers from the country. Could we have a special order?"

The two men chaffered for awhile, and Yukio made up the order. "Shall I have it delivered? It is rather a lot."

"If you can send it on right now . . ."

"All I have is one female assistant . . ."

"Send her then, by all means . . ."

Two hours later, a laden basket on her back, Momoe was on her way to the Sakamotoya: a store famous throughout the city for the quality of its service and the worth of its goods. It was one of the new stores in which the customers had a wide variety of goods to choose from in the greatest of comfort and elegance.

"Yes?" a clerk inquired as Momoe hovered uncertainly at the entrance.

She explained her mission and he directed her through the wide opening into the interior of the store. Momoe tarried a second by a bolt of silk stuff. She examined it with a critical eye.

"Well? What do you want girl?" a sharp voice interrupted her. "Get on with you. Miyako Tamba silk is not for the likes of you."

"Oh?" Momoe said cooly, angry at the hatchet-faced chief clerk's rudeness. "I would have thought it is country-made Tamba, not Miyako-made."

He looked at her in disdain. "Ha. As if Sakamotoya would sell such low-class goods . . ."

"Then Sakamotoya has been badly misguided." She bowed perfunctorily and hoisted her basket.

The kitchen was warm and busy. Maidservants and cooks were scurrying about, preparing food for the expected customers. She was relieved of her burden, offered a bowl of *udon* wheat noodles with a pounded rice cake by way of thanks, and hurried off on her way back to work. She crossed the large courtyard and passed through the main store again. The hatchet-faced clerk was off in a corner talking to an elderly man in rich-looking clothes. Other assistants attended patiently to customers. They would send messenger lads off to the storerooms with the customers' requests. The boys would stagger back loaded with bamboo baskets full of the desired merchandise. The chief clerk looked up and saw Momoe's passing figure. He muttered something in an undertone to the man beside him. At a word from the elder he hurried after Momoe.

"Miss. Excuse me, miss."

She turned with asperity, and the old man rose and joined them.

The clerk bowed slightly and said, "The master would like a word with you . . ."

"Could you look at the bolt you saw earlier?" the old man asked her politely. He indicated a pile of silk bolts on one of the mats.

Momoe unhesitatingly identified the poor-quality material. "There is another one there of the same make," she added offhandedly.

The old man sucked air in through his teeth. "And how did you know that?" he asked.

"I have worked as a weaver for many years," Momoe explained, conscious of his careful scrutiny.

"And now you are of Yukio, the *kamaboko*-makers household."

She shook her head, bowing in negation. "No. Merely temporary help I'm afraid."

"Would you like a job here?"

Her eyes lit up and she fell to her knees in gratitude.

† † †

Across the neighborhoods of Miyako, in a grander setting, another woman was being interviewed for a position as maid.

Ito looked at the young girl in front of him and stroked his chin thoughtfully. He was intrigued by her appearance. She claimed to be, and wore the clothes of, a seamstress. She had come to Haruko asking for work, and Haruko had immediately noted her unusual qualities. The girl had lustrous brown hair which she wore in a rough bun on top of her head. There was something elegant about the turn of her neck and her poise that made Ito suspect she might be the by-blow of some *kuge* aristocrat from the imperial enclosure.

She sat passively, eyes lowered, work-roughened hands in her lap. Ito licked his lips. He wondered if she would put up any resistance?

"Have you worked in any mansion before?" he asked severely. A bit of respect was instilled in the lower classes by assuming hardness from the start.

She lowered her head. "No sir," she whispered.

"You realize this is not like working outside?" he asked sharply. She bowed wordlessly. "In a samurai household, discipline and self-sacrifice are the rule, not the exception."

"I will do all that is necessary, master," she answered with bowed head. Ito longed to seize the nape of her neck and drag her to his crotch to assuage the sudden bulge in his *hakama* trousers.

"Not all that is necessary only." He said. "All that is required or asked of you . . ."

"Yes," she agreed.

"There is no going back!" he warned her.

"I understand," she said. "I will serve you and your lady loyally."

Ito turned and stared at Haruko, who was kneeling in a corner of the room. His face was flushed and tiny beads of sweat had popped out at the base of his nose. She knew the symptoms, and nodded.

Breathing rapidly and swallowing convulsively, Ito laid one hand on Midori's head, forcing her to bow closer to the floor. The touch of the unusually soft hair sent tremors through his frame.

"You will be part of the Ito House," he said formally. "You will be obedient and hardworking."

She nodded, her forehead knocking against the floor.

Ito raised her, holding her chin with a trembling hand. "Do you accept?" he asked hoarsely.

"Yes Master," she said.

"You will be Mistress Haruko's maid, but just now I have greater need of you. I will borrow you from time to time." He lunged forward, overcome by his own lust, and pulled her to him. She started to resist then, remembering her oath, sank softly and nestled into his arms. Her passivity excited him to a frenzy. He tore off his clothes, making a mental note while he still could that she be supplied with better. He spread her on the *tatami* and knelt, his knees by her ears. "Undo me!" he commanded with a trembling lust-filled voice. She hastened awkwardly to obey. He stood up and his brocade silver-threaded *hakama* fell to the floor and covered her head. He moved swiftly to one side and placed a victorious foot on her breasts, kneading them strongly with his almost prehensile toes, clutching at the soft, defeated flesh. She cried properly and moved the fabric of his garment aside, then peered up fearfully at his full bollocks and hugely erect pole. He was staring off into the distance, left hand on the dagger in his sash, right fist on his hip. Slowly his face bent down to glare at his captive. He gripped his dagger tightly, almost withdrawing it.

"Surrender!" he whispered hoarsely.

Cowering away from him, the captive spread her legs unwillingly.

He moved deliberately, with a heavy tread that shook the matting, and stood between her splayed legs. He raised a foot and a toe dug deeply into the wound between the captive's legs. Ito laughed in delight at the pleasure of victory and the evidence of his powerful blows. He dropped to his knees and rolled the body over. The captive flopped helplessly, ready for him to consummate his lust. His sword pointed at the target and he lunged forward, burying himself to the hilt.

Midori felt the brief tearing sensation of his invasion of her rear end. She had been expecting it and consoled herself that no harm was done, though, in her professional capacity, she regretted not being able to prepare herself better for his pleasure. She smiled inwardly. Ito's little charade seemed perfectly harmless to her. Since she had joined Osatsuki as junior partner she had participated in several such playlets. And the conclusion was always the same. Modelling herself after her Elder Sister, she displayed outward passivity and surrender while urging the man on with subtle motions of her hips and movements of her hidden muscles. His thumb joined his cock, exploring and tugging urgently at her cunt hole and she responded to the stimulation eagerly.

Ito Haruko watched her husband fall on the helpless new girl with amusement. His quirk was so familiar and so repetitive by now that she knew all the permutations by heart. She watched her husband's fingers dig into Midori's ass with approval. The girl barely moved, tolerating the moderate and controlled violence with fortitude. Haruko smiled to herself. The new girl would keep him busy while she would be able to attend to her own affairs without bother. In the meantime, she might as well enjoy her own pleasures. She rose and approached the couple, opening her robe as she did so. She lay down before Midori and beckoned. Midori lowered her head, smiled in acknowledgement, and started licking at the proffered cunt with a dexterous and knowledgeable tongue. As she did so she began squeezing Ito's cock with her anal muscles, encouraging and timing her customers' reactions so that they would both climax in her willing body at the same time, but so subtly that they would not realize she was guiding them.

Ito, lost in fantasy, saw the fields around him filled with corpses. The captive was dying beneath him as he stabbed and stabbed again at the soft flesh. Another body, legs sprawled, also fallen to his sword, lay before the first. His sperm rose in a rush of violent spurts that flooded Midori's anal canal just as her tongue extracted the flood of dew that Haruko let down. They collapsed together in a heap, Midori smiling in happiness at having performed the difficult feat without her mentor, Osatsuki.

CHAPTER 9

THE WOMAN WATCHED CALMLY AS ISEI APPROACHED ACROSS the clearing. She looked around casually, then smiled at him in open invitation. Dressed in blue-dyed and patterned jacket and baggy pants, he took her to be the farmer's wife. He had taken a shortcut, over the towering mountains that bordered Lake Biwa to the east. This modest farmhouse was the first he had seen on his way. It looked prosperous with a smug sort of satisfaction that came from hidden wealth.

"Would you like some hot water?" the woman asked as Isei came up to her. He bowed his thanks and after a casual look around, she went into the thatched house. Huge twisted black beams framed the roof. There was a sense of stillness and mystery.

"The master is away?" Isei asked, sitting down, his feet on the pounded earth floor of the *genkan* entrance.

"Yes," she said meaningfully. "For the rest of the day. Surely you would like to come up and sit comfortably?"

He followed her into the house, over polished wooden floors, through two large rooms to a smaller one on which was thrown a loose woven mat. Real *zabuton* sitting pillows, an innovation Isei had never seen before, beckoned to him. He sat down cross-legged and she brought the hot water, a grass infusion steaming in it. She sat down at his side and looked at his face.

Her hand casually brushed his thigh. He sipped his drink, ignoring it. There were weapons hung on the darkness below the thatch, and a strange looseness to some of the rear wall panels. She stroked the length of his thigh and he finally turned and smiled shyly at her. She touched his stubbled face with light fingers.

"They will not be home for a long time," she said,

61

pulling him down to her. He slipped his hand through the opening of her striped jacket and opened her baggy *mompei* pants. Her bush was full and her nether lips plump and covered with her liquid. He nuzzled her neck and pulled her robe open. She had wide tits with large oval aureoles. He squeezed the mounds and rose to his knees. She helped him slip off his nether garments. She was twisting now with passion, silently, with nothing but her heavy breathing to accompany the sounds of their bodies. Isei nibbled at her neck and her jaw and explored her mouth with his. She raised her knees somewhat and he cupped her full hairy mound in his hand.

She started pulling at his head, trying to force him lower. He obliged her, remembering that his own woman had liked having her breasts bit a bit. She squeaked when he bit down on her prominent nipples, but kept on pushing him down.

"Go *on*," she mumbled. "Down. Do me lower. With your mouth. Now. I need it so . . ."

Puzzled, he fought his way up and tried to introduce his prick into her. She grabbed his long hair and pulled him down towards her hips. Isei rolled onto her, his prick rampant, ready to thrust and bury itself in the joyous channel between her thighs.

She fought him. "No. I'm not ready. Lick me. Please. I'll do whatever you want afterwards. Lick me. Suck. Tongue my bud. Oh . . . oh . . ."

Her mutterings made no sense to him, and he felt he was playing in some strange game whose rules he did not know.

He pushed against her, and now she started resisting him in earnest.

"If you won't do what I want, you can get out of here," she blazed at him. By now though Isei's lust was aroused to a fever pitch. He slammed his full weight at her. She resisted and twisted in his grasp, tried to leap away from him. He caught her slick hip and forced her down with his weight. She struggled against him furiously, though still silently. Isei's superior strength began to tell and her struggles, which were motivated by lust at the start, became an attempt to escape his embrace as they progressed, rolling about the ground. By the time she had remembered and tried to employ the devices her menfolk had taught her, she was immobile, spread on the ground, and the mountain man's full weight was resting on her buttocks. She scratched at him futilely with her hands and he responded by whipping a length of her sash around her hands. He pulled down her baggy *mompei* trousers and exposed her full brown moons to view.

"These are lovely," he said thickly, stroking each half-moon affectionately, then pulling them apart. She cursed as she felt the length of his thick cock probe between her buttocks and nose at her anus. Unwillingly she raised her buttocks to facilitate the man's aim. The swollen knob of his tumescent organ probed between the full lips of her cunt. Isei thrust forward, burying himself between the soft moons. They supported the full weight of his belly and he pushed forward again. She began to feel the start of her own pleasure and raised her buttocks, burying her face in her arms.

Isei rocked back and forth on her, finding the pleasure of her buns mashing into him almost more than he could bear.

"So deep, so deeeep," she muttered finally.

She was lost now to the world, he saw, enjoying the pleasure of his masculine movement. He squatted over her buttocks, humping into her and she began muttering brokenly, urging him on to greater efforts. Her muscles clenched around the base of his cock, nipping at the long shaft. He saw her bare her teeth in a rictus of pleasure. He was ready to turn her over and pulled back just as she slammed herself forcefully into him. Globs of his seed showered her interior and flooded down her legs. Isei ground himself, almost unconscious with pleasure, into the waiting hole.

At last he recovered and pulled out of her. Dribblets of his come followed, trickling between her thighs and pooling on the polished wooden floor. She rolled over and watched him dress. The expression on her face was unfathomable. The only thing she said as he left had no meaning for Isei.

"You should have eaten me," she glowered into his eyes. "You would have had nothing to worry about then. *They* never do it to me . . . She turned her face to the wall, not wishing to see him go, then pulled on her clothes and went in search of a rag to clean the floor of the evidence of her visitor.

The meaning of her words soon became clear to Isei. He became conscious of the stalkers soon after they had gotten him in sight. Isei grinned to himself. To a villager or townsman their stalk would have seemed ghostlike. Completely silent. But a mountain-man had to learn to be able to get close enough to a rabbit to stroke its fur. He wondered why they were stalking him. Perhaps they were friends of the dead samurai and the woman had been a trap? Or had she some reason to dislike him? Unlikely, he decided. She had enjoyed herself after all. Nonetheless, they did not appear to be stalking him for fun and he quickened his pace. The slope rose above him and he slipped through gnarled roots and bushy passages with the ease of long practice. Listening carefully he noted that one of the pursuers was lagging behind the others. He reached a stream and started wading up its rough, moss-covered course. The stream widened somewhat and Isei found a place he wanted.

Three of the pursuers paused above his hiding hole. They conferred in whispers.

"He could not be far off."

"Scatter quietly. Find and kill."

A latecomer joined the others. "*Kacho*," one of the men called quietly. "He is hiding around here."

"Good," a breathy voice answered. "We'll find him. Someone has gone to fetch the rest of the house. I want his balls. No one can have one of our women without being punished. Damned *sanka*."

Isei would have shook his head in amazement. He could not understand what the men wanted from him. Or the woman. She had enjoyed it as much as he, and she was the initiator. He sank soundlessly into the narrow hole waiting patiently for his stalkers to leave.

Rising slowly from the fox's earth, a boulder before him resolved itself into the wet back of a brown-clad man lying silently and watchfully in the water. Part of the trap. The others were no doubt trying to cut him off. Isei thought for a moment. These brown-clad, masked men were something new in his experience: They moved almost like born mountain men, but spoke like townsmen. Curious. And dangerous. He carefully unpacked his blowgun from the pack at his side. The shiny steel needles were unlike anything any other mountain man owned. But then many of the *sanka* retained items that were at odds with their present humble existence: evidence perhaps that the dim ancestral memories of former glory were true. Isei's needles, like his *nata* hatchet, were made of finest steel. The flights were floss of mountain flax. He put it carefully to his lips and waited, patient as the hunter until the *shinobi* raised his head cautiously out of the water to peer around him. He never heard the slight puff that drove the steal splinter from six feet away into the soft spot at the base of his skull. Nor did he make a sound as he sank back into the water and drowned, unable to move.

By the time he was dead, Isei was heading away from the net. In the late afternoon he was climbing a high pass leading in a westerly direction. Cover would be sparse until he descended the other side. He cast a look back. Brown figures were racing after him, heedless of being seen. Isei climbed further, crossing a meadow almost recklessly, rising higher until bare rock was under his feet. He paused and looked back again. Only three men were after him. If they caught him here, in the open, he would not survive the encounter. He turned and rested his butt comfortably on a sun-warmed rock. His slow match was soon lit, and he eyed the three assassins' approach with equanimity.

The three *shinobi* stopped at the edge of the meadow. They conferred for a moment, then split up and stationed themselves at the edge of the wood. Hidden, or so they perhaps thought, from his eyes. It was clear they were aware, cautious but contemptuous, of his weapon.

Suddenly they sped together from the shelter of the trees. They zigzagged across the meadow, tumbling and weaving to spoil his aim. Isei smiled and raised the matchlock. The lead slug took the slowest *shinobi* by surprise. It smashed its way down the length of his back. The others heard the shot and saw the plume of grey smoke. Internally they relaxed. Matchlocks, however accurate, took almost a full minute to load. The second slug tore into the lead *shinobi*'s chest. He coughed, amazed, and fell. The last man suddenly realized that he was not dealing with a common musketeer. The knowledge took him by surprise. He changed his mind, trying to melt into the bare meadow, changed it again and tried to race for the shelter of the trees. Panting, he turned and peeked back at the talus slope where the *sanka* hid. He was a master of camouflage and the venerable oak provided almost perfect cover. For a moment he could not see the quarry, grey as the rocks among which he hid. Then the *shinobi* could not see a thing as his eye and brain filled with the pressure of Isei's slug that tore through his skull.

Isei turned to go. The *shinobi*'s self-confidence amazed him somewhat. Didn't the man expect a hunter to be able to shoot a man's eye at two hundred paces? And did they really think an experienced hunter would wait any more than three seconds before having his matchlock ready to fire again?

CHAPTER 10

SUGIYAMA PATTED HIS MIDDLE AS HE WALKED. HIS SMALL medicine box was missing. It had been attached to his belt by a silk cord ending in a toggle. The ends of the cord were cut. The courtesan must have removed it, perhaps as payment. Well, all the common people thought of was money. He was mildly disappointed. He had thought she was above such considerations.

The outskirts of Miyako were rising above him. Houses clustered together thickly and he passed shops and inns. Walls enclosed the villas of the wealthy. The jostling travellers kept a decent space from him, but nonetheless their presence was irksome. Also, the previous night's exertions, pleasant as they had been, had made him sleepy. Sugiyama wandered into a lane in a small village. Spying a half-ruined wall and expecting to find an abandoned villa behind it, he leaped the barrier. A large formal garden in the Chinese style, poorly kept but still very elegant, met his gaze. Through the trees and bushes he could make out the roof of a small thatched hut or outhouse and he made his way in that direction.

He broke into a clearing and saw that he had made a mistake. Though unkempt, the garden was not abandoned. Beyond a pond, on the far side of the hut he could see the outline of a large dilapidated villa. A middle-aged woman was standing at the hut. She heard Sugiyama's step on the gravel that ringed it, and turned expectantly.

When she saw Sugiyama her face changed to an expression of alarm. "Who are you? What are you doing here?"

Trying to put a good face on things, and not wanting to be mistaken for a mean robber, Sugiyama strode confidently forward.

"Sugiyama Tamasaburo. I heard the water and came for

a drink," he said gruffly and walked past her. He was halfway to the pond when he discovered he had made a second mistake. A young woman was drawing water from a stone cistern served by a tiny stream of clear water by the pond's edge. And from the interior of the hut he could hear the sound of movement. He walked on, ignoring the baffled stares of both women. He reached for the bamboo dipper the young woman had dropped and helped himself to a drink.

"What are you doing here, eh?" a male voice addressed him from the hut. An exquisitely dressed middle-aged samurai strode over to Sugiyama while the young girl ran for the shelter of the hut.

"Drinking," said Sugiyama succinctly, and put the dipper carefully down on the parallel golden bamboos that rested on the stone basin. The bamboo thumper, filling and emptying its load of water, accompanied his words with a timeless tock, then another.

The samurai strode over to Sugiyama and stared at him insolently. "I am Ueda Masahige, of the Satake clan, and I am not used to being addressed that way."

"Sugiyama Tamasaburo. And I don't care how you like being addressed."

The two women huddled together by the hut.

The samurai clenched his jaws, slid back a step and drew his sword in the elegant motions of the *Tamashii-ryu* school of sword fighting. He balanced on the balls of his feet. His blade was held pointing slightly forward in *chudan kamae* ready position. His left hand gripped the blade at the pommel, right near the guard. His eyes focused lightly on Sugiyama. He breathed lightly, alertly.

Sugiyama grinned coldly, then lazily drew his plain sword from its plain lacquered scabbard. He held the sword loosely at his side, one handed, in no recognizable position. His weight was distributed fairly on both feet, completely relaxed. The Satake swordsman smiled slightly. The *ronin* was a fool. That overconfident pose was good for impressing the yokels with one's insouciance, but he was an experienced, high-grade swordsman. He inched forward slightly, improving his position to the optimal distance.

As Ueda's weight shifted, Sugiyama slipped forward in

a deep *zenkutsu-dachi* stance, his right foot extended well forward. His sword flashed out at knee level and he snapped back to full height stance. Ueda stared down horrified as his shin fell to one side, his uncontrollable weight to the other. He had time to see Sugiyama's eyes move from his own falling body to the horrified eyes of his wife and her maid.

Sugiyama strode forward, reversing his sword. The back of the blade deflected Ueda's feeble blow and he plunged his own tip, backhanded, into Ueda's solar plexus as he passed. Ueda's body tried to arc off the ground as Sugiyama pulled his blade free. He stopped before the two women, smiling hungrily. He flipped the blood off the blade automatically, wiped it with a tissue from the store in the bosom of his robe, and started to resheath. The moment's inattention almost cost him his life as the samurai's new widow drove her *tanto* dagger straight at his belly.

Sugiyama twisted aside and seized her forearm, twisting her to the ground with his hip. She fell heavily, but tried to rise and attack him gamely.

"Run Ocho," she screamed. "Run!" but the younger girl was trapped between the interior of the small hut and Sugiyama. Panic had paralyzed her and she huddled in the corner watching the older woman fight the samurai with wide eyes.

Breathing heavily Sugiyama strove to control the woman's struggles. Her elaborate hairdo became undone and her long hair turned dusty with her efforts. The struggle had also disarranged her expensive silk kimono. She had stocky legs tipped by white *tabi* socks. Her lacquered black *geta* clogs had fallen off. Sugiyama finally got her in the grip he wanted, her arm twisted painfully behind her back. He grinned down at her and she turned her face away, as if aware of her immediate future. Sugiyama crushed her to him then forced her thighs apart with his knees. She cried out, still trying to struggle as he exposed his long flesh sword. It threatened her with a blind eye. The paralyzed girl within the hut looked on and the single eye at the end of the man's organ seemed to wink at her hypnotically.

Sugiyama's blood was pounding in his ears as it always did after violence. Forcing the woman down with his weight and locking her in place with his hand, he fumbled with his other for her opening. She tried desperately to twist away but was unable to avoid him. The soft crown came into contact with the lips of her cunt and Sugiyama forced his way into her brutally. She cried out in pain as his ravishing member tore up her canal. One final cry and then silence as their hairs met, mashed between their pubic bones.

She stared blankly at the trees as he moved inside her. Her body began betraying her and responding to his thrusts. She struggled to maintain her control, not to betray to her ravisher the touch of pleasure she felt.

Sugiyama turned his head from the sweaty face of the woman he was in and peered into the tea hut. The young girl, her breasts barely budded, was squatting against a wall. Her eyes were bright, focused intently on the juncture of the couple's thighs. Her hand crept to her crotch. She saw Sugiyama's eyes on her and snatched it back. But then, like an independent-minded organism, it crept slowly into her lap. Sugiyama's senses were aroused. The hand moved to open the pink kimono she was wearing and expose smooth thighs and a juncture of faint black down between them. She opened the lips of her pussy and displayed her treasures to Sugiyama's enraptured gaze. He pumped furiously into the woman beneath him, who grunted with the effort of his body. The girl was staring at Sugiyama directly now, her little finger diddling a tiny clitoris not six feet from his head. His hips were moving without pause into the body of the elder woman, her arm still twisted painfully beneath her.

The young girl started rubbing her cunt furiously with her hand. She was smiling dreamily now. Sugiyama clutched the plump body of the dead samurai's wife and gritted his teeth. He did not want to climax before his ghostly paramour did. She rubbed harder, and her other hand moved to her chest and exposed her young breasts to the *ronin's* gaze. The young woman started jerking suddenly, her eyes rolled back into her head and her eyelids closed. Sugiyama's sperm boiled out of his balls at the same moment and he jerked and twisted above the soft body of the woman. She cried in pain at the pressure it put on her arm.

Sugiyama collapsed, panting heavily. The young girl rose from her seat next the wall. Sugiyama rose to his feet. His cock, shiny and trailing a faint string of milky fluid, stood out horizontally from his black *hakama* trousers. The young girl smiled once, whirled, and slid quick as an eel through the tiny rear opening of the tea house.

The woman on the ground groaned and opened her eyes. Sugiyama looked down at her, then at the back of the hut. It would be useless to search for the girl now. The woman followed his gaze with concern. When she saw the hut was empty, she smiled with triumph and braced herself for his reaction.

"I only wanted a drink," Sugiyama insisted calmly. He turned to go and the woman watched his back, pulling her kimono over herself.

CHAPTER 11

THE WORK AT "SAKAMOTOYA" SHOP WAS HARD AND EX-
acting. As a beginner, Momoe had to do all the work
disliked by the senior maids, and in addition, occasionally
had to assist Mr. Sakamoto in his examination of the
various stuffs he had purchased for his establishment.

She was scrubbing the woodwork in one of the smaller
display rooms while next door a well-padded matron examined material brought her by scurrying shop boys. Passing by her bent figure, the chief clerk beckoned to her in
his usual curt way. "Mr. Asano, one of our valuable
customers, is waiting for his wife, who will be some time.
He is taking tea in the Pheasant room, across the main
courtyard and up the stairs. Go and attend to him. And no
unseemly noise or behavior, mind."

She walked up the steep wooden steps. The bottom and
top steps squeaked musically to warn the occupants of
visitors. Otherwise her feet were soundless on the polished
wood. Asano was a thin man, dressed expensively in a
brown silk-lined kimono. There was grey on the sides of
his head, though his topknot, lying diagonally across his
pate, was black as ink. He looked at her as she poured the
tea and offered him cakes.

"You are new here?" he asked.

"Yes sir," Momoe said and bowed.

"That's very thoughtful of Sakamotoya. I must compli-
ment them. Move the tea things aside please."

She did so, and was surprised to see him beckon to her.
Momoe knelt before him, asking what she could do for
him. The merchant examined her thoughtfully. He stroked
her neck lightly, then opened the lapels of her robe. She
started to pull back then remembered the chief clerk's
words. It seemed she was expected to do as Asano wished.

She shrugged her shoulders mentally. He looked pleasant enough, and there was not much he could do with his wife downstairs.

Asano exposed her breasts and admired the full mounds. He flipped back the skirt of his brown robe, then opened his snowy loincloth. A monstrous prick, only half erect, emerged from a nest of iron-grey hairs.

"I think I'd like your mouth," he said conversationally.

Momoe gaped at him.

"Come girl. Come here." He pulled her gently down to his crotch.

The memory of yesterday's time with the fish-paste maker came back to Momoe. It made sense that if she enjoyed having a mouth on her pussy, men would enjoy the same thing on their cocks. She bent forward without any further urging. The cock had a strange bitter smell. Peculiarly attractive. She touched the tip experimentally with her lips. It was soft and dry, slightly spongy. Asano let her have her way. Her tongue peeped out, a tiny pink mouse. It licked at the cock head and scurried quickly home, back to its nest. The second time she tried she was much bolder. She laved the tip of the monstrous prick with the wet tip of her tongue. Asano moved appreciatively. She became bolder still, running the oral digit around the broad crown, under the two lobes that formed a base of the plum, then across the hole. The tiny blind eye exuded a transparent substance and she sipped at it like a bee. It was faintly bitter, smelling of male and lusty promise. She tried an experiment, running her tongue down the length of the shaft. The skin was soft and loose, covering a stiffness she had never had the opportunity to explore before. Asano gave her her head, allowing her to explore him and provide his pleasure at her own time.

Momoe cupped the large wrinkled hairy bag below the shaft. Inside she could feel two soft eggs moving around as if encased in oil. She raised her head and looked at the tip one more time. The single hole regarded her with a blind stare, dripping a single tear. Opening her mouth she engulfed the entire head, taking care to cover her teeth with her lips. Asano quivered slightly. The taste was nice, Momoe decided. Salty and bitter and entirely male. She hollowed her cheeks and sucked more of the shaft into her mouth. Her tongue pressed moistly against the shaft, pressing the cock to her palate.

She withdrew to examine her handiwork. The entire plum head was glistening with her saliva. The prick quivered, straining at its leash. She became conscious of Asano's quickened breathing above her head. The sound made her realize that she too might join in. Her left hand stole between her legs as she bent again to her task. She sucked at the flesh pole and released her cheeks, then sucked again. The desire to see how much of the hand-long shaft she could take in occurred to her. At first she found it very difficult. The end of the penis hit the back of her throat, causing her to gag. She withdrew somewhat, teasing only the tip with her tongue and lips. Trying again she found she could ease it in further, then further again. She set to work in earnest, pulling in more of the warm quivering length each time, pulling back and assuaging the cock's hunger by licking the tip each time the deep penetration became too much to bear.

Finally she learned the trick and found herself with her nose buried deeply in the black iron-gray hairs at the base of Asano's muscular belly. She was in a haze of lustful accomplishment. She doubted many women could do what she had just done. Sucking mightily and stroking her own clitoris with a thrumming violence, she set about trying to make both of them come. Asano's hands were about her. He stroked her head and nape, the backs of her ears, then loosened her kimono and squeezed her round breasts unmercifully. All that was almost unnoticed by Momoe as she found her pleasure rising with her accomplishment and with the feel of her own hand, slipping in and out of her wet cunt channel.

Asano's hips started jerking furiously into her. His balls started contracting. He grunted rhythmically. She pulled back against his hands. She wanted the pleasure of his sperm streaming into her mouth, not just vanishing down her throat. Reflexively he tried to force her deeper but she held onto his cock with her mouth, squeezing and milking it with lip-covered teeth. A wash of warm thick liquid filled her mouth. She gulped at it and swallowed, wishing to take it all. Another spurt followed on immediately and Asano's grunting increased in volume and frequency. His hips jerked uncontrollably now. A driblet of sperm she was unable to control ran down Momoe's chin. She felt it go regretfully but her mouth was filled again with a final major spurt of his male essence. She swallowed gratefully, noting how the liquid assuaged a soreness in her throat. Finally she licked his softening cock clean, tasting and swallowing all his juices. She gave her own clitoris a final stroke. A tiny shiver of orgasm shook her frame for a brief moment, and then she was kneeling before Asano again, peering modestly downwards, helping him rearrange his clothing.

Asano's eyes were closed. His breathing slowly returned to normal. He slumped slightly. Opening his eyes he smiled slightly at Momoe. "That was very well done. You have had much experience in the toothed vagina?"

"No," she said, suddenly shy. "This is the first time . . ."

"Indeed? Remarkable. You are a true asset to Sakamotoya. I'm afraid we must end this delightful session. My wife will be here soon. However, should the opportunity arise, I will call for you again. Please accept this as a token of appreciation." He laid a small paper-wrapped package on the floorboards and slid it over to Momoe. She bowed appreciatively and poured him some tea, then put the parcel in her sleeve. It was an oblong silver *momme:* A craftsman would have to work for an entire month to make as much.

After Asano left to join his wife, Momoe made her way to the quarters she shared with the other maids. The flavor of his sperm still seemed to linger round her mouth, though she tried rinsing it out from the waterbucket. One of the older maids, plump and fortyish, looked at her with sympathy.

"Been with that old pig Asano, have you?"

"Yes," Momoe shrugged indifferently. She was becoming used to the varied responses of her body, and besides, in the sophisticated atmosphere of the Sakamotoya she did not want to appear an innocent waif.

The other woman laughed coarsely. "He always does the same, doesn't he? Here, come with me. The pressure's slacking off and I don't think they'll miss us. I've got something to get the taste out of your mouth."

She scrabbled in the small chest that held her personal

belongings and produced a gourd-shaped bottle. Uncapping it she took a healthy swallow, rolled the liquid around in her mouth and said "Ahhhh. Try some."

Momoe followed suit. The liquid smelled like the wine she occasionally smelled on her father when he came home after an evening out. It seemed innocuous enough. She gave a cautionary sniff, then seeing the look of superiority of the older woman's face, tilted her head back and took two healthy swallows. The liquid streamed like hot silk down her gullet, then burst into a warm coal at the pit of her stomach. Momoe blinked in surprise then took another swallow. Her head began swimming pleasantly and she giggled.

"You're already red!" the other maid exclaimed and snatched the flask away. They took alternating sips of the bottle as night descended around them.

"Gone, all gone," the maid tilted the bottle down and sighed regretfully. Momoe rose unsteadily to her feet and made her way, weaving, to the stairs leading down from the long gallery in which all the maids slept.

"Where you going, Momoe dear?"

"Tge' . . . Tgetch . . . To get some more." Momoe hiccuped then giggled.

"No, not there. See you drunk, they'll shrow you out."

"Careful," Momoe waggled a solemn finger. "I'll be careful. Find a sake seller. Careful." She eased herself slowly down the stairs. With a drunk's cunning she made her way out a side door of the "Sakamotoya" and wandered off into the night.

The lights and laughter drew her to the small isolated shed by a large unpainted shrine building. She peered blearily through the cracks. A group of young men sat around a couple of lanterns weaving straw rope. The short *happi* coats they wore proclaimed their membership in the neighborhood's youth association. They laughed as they talked, and the large ceramic bottles beside them rose frequently to their mouths. Momoe saw the bottles through the cracks then hiccupped loudly.

"What was that?" one of the men turned his head.

Momoe giggled, tried to stifle the sound, and hiccupped again.

The men rose to their feet and advanced on the wall.

Two of them slipped suddenly through the door and had her by her arms before Momoe could react.

"A woman," they said, laughing, as they dragged her into the light. "Looking for a drink, no doubt," one of the men said smiling. They all laughed. "And some fun besides." One of them pushed a bottle at her, and Momoe took a large swig, trying to bluster her way out of the situation.

"Hmph. Now you wouldn't harm a lady would you?" she asked coquettishly.

"A lady? Of course not. But you, you will be nice to us, won't you?"

She looked at them, bronze chests shimmering in the lantern-light, and liked what she saw. "But I'm so terribly thirsty," she complained. They laughed again and encouraged her to drink again. She took a large swallow. The sake did not taste so bad now that she was used to it. And the men were nice and attractive. "What are you celebrating?" she asked, more to have something to say than out of any real curiosity.

"Why, we've just finished preparations for the festival. We're going to dance . . ." Someone chimed in, ". . . and wrestle . . . ," and another added, ". . . and vie for the ladies' favor."

One of them, his topknot awry, leaned confidentially to her and asked, "Are you a good judge?"

Momoe hiccupped and looked at him, then blinked the bleariness out of her eyes. "Of what?"

"Of things, you know, various things. I'm sure you're very good . . ."

"Of course I am," she said with drunken gravity. "I told them at Sakamotoya didn't I?" She hiccupped again.

"You sure did!" the men encouraged her. The leader smiled again. "Then you can do us a favor, since you're so discriminating . . ."

"Of course I can . . . can . . ."

"We've been arguing, and we want you to be the judge."

She swayed slightly and took another ladylike sip from the large bottle. "Anythin' I cn . . . cn . . . can do t'help."

"Here," he said, whipping off his loincloth, "Judge

our cocks. Which is the best, d'you think?'' He was grinning broadly and winking at his companions.

Momoe looked at the semi-erect penis gravely and blinked. She shook her head. "I can't tell. S'only one. Gotta see the rest.''

There was a flurry of movement and she was faced with a row of expectant cocks. Some were erect, others slowly rising to erection, still others limp, barely showing between their owners' thighs.

"Gotta have them all in the same state," she mumbled and moved towards the nearest one. Several of them reached promptly for their cocks and started stroking their shafts with their fists energetically.

"You're trying to cheat!" Momoe said furiously. "Stop it!" She reached for the group leader's prick and stroked the shaft hard with her soft hand. It rose proudly. The shaft was a pale brown, the head a fiery brownish-pink. When the member was erect to her satisfaction, she reached for the next one. The young men crowded around her, shoving their cocks in her direction.

"Sit in *seiza*!" she commanded and slapped the nearest half-erect shaft. They obeyed and Momoe was faced by a row of young men in blue-happi, sitting on their knees, cocks exposed. She stroked the first one in line, a stubby cock with an enlarged head like a mushroom. The young man smiled at her, his breathing frantic. She looked at her handiwork critically while sipping at a cup of sake someone handed her. Then she turned to the next one. Many of the shaven pates sprouted beads of sweat as they watched her progress.

Momoe paused at the end of the row. The men sat, some smiling dreamily or lustfully, others watching her curiously. Before her stretched a long row of erect pricks. Thick and thin ones, some longer, some shorter. She smiled. "There, that's better."

"Well?" The one who had suggested her office prompted. "Which is the best?"

"I don't know," she said. "They all look gorgeous. But how can I tell which is the *best*?"

"There's only one way to tell," said one of the men slyly.

"Yes, I imagine you're right." Some of her drunkenness had left her at the thought. She took another long swallow. The liquor did not burn at all as it went down this time. She looked at them thoughtfully for some time. They peered back anxiously, as if she were a real judge deciding their fate. With slow erratic motions she opened the bosom of her robe, then hiked up her skirts and tucked them into her sash. One of the men rose, his prick bobbing before him as he rushed to fetch an old quilt from a corner of the shed. He spread it rapidly. She waited until he had returned to his place. Before them the men saw a young woman. Her thick eyelids were half closed. Her lips were full and generous, her face the rounded beauty of Miyako. Some peered in anticipation at the small black patch of fur between her full white thighs. She opened them slightly as she stood there, then one of her hands descended past her obi. A finger inserted itself gradually into the bottom apex of the fur and stroked lightly, once, then again. The men held their collective breaths. She knelt gracefully, wriggled herself into a comfortable position, then spread her legs wide and motioned to one of the men. They could see, at the juncture of her thighs, the faintly darker slit where they all longed to bury themselves.

The lucky young man knelt quickly between her legs. The others clustered around as he fumbled with his erect prick, trying to lodge the head of the iron-stiff bar into the waiting entrance. Momoe put her hands behind her head and looked at him with amusement. How silly these young inexperienced men were, she thought gaily. The excited youth fumbled with her cunt, knocking against her thighs with the tip of his prick. His friends urged him on silently. In his lustful excitement he could not manage to make any headway. At last Momoe raised her knees slightly and with a twist of her loins helped him lodge the tip of his prick between her soft full nether lips. He reached for her breasts, throwing himself forward as hard as he could. The long shaft tore its way up her damp waiting channel. The expectation was too much for the man. His balls suddenly pumped and a flow of liquid bathed Momoe's insides, soothing and lubricating her interior. The young man buried his face in her breasts, his hips stuck lustfully to hers. Reluctantly, trying to put a good face on his quickness, he rose from her.

His place was taken by one of the nicer cocks Momoe had seen in what she now regarded as her private collection. Fatter and heavier than the rest, the man mounted her enthusiastically. His cock, curved like a bow, widened her eager cunt lips and reached deep into her belly. She raised her hips to meet his thrust. This time there would be no quick end. He gripped her hips and rammed himself again and again against her clitoris. His curved cock sought out all her best parts and she panted with delighted lust. He sucked at her erect nipples, mauling them with teeth and tongue. Clutching him to her she felt the first of many orgasms overcome her as glazed and lustful male eyes peered at the couple before them, waiting their own turn.

Momoe lost track of time. The straw was warm and comfortable under the robe, and the face of her lover kept on changing. She found in herself an endless capacity to love. Her body was racked with orgasmic flashes as the prick in her body replaced itself ever anew in a different form. The men discharged lustfully into her, without regard now for her pleasure, having seen that she took from each as well as they received. Her cunt overflowed with the men's discharges, and the rocking of their slick bodies on hers conspired with the alcohol in her blood to lull her to sleep.

CHAPTER 12

ISEI COULD HAVE WALKED ALONG THE MAIN ROAD LEADING from the north, but the mountains, as usual, called to him more than the shores of broad Lake Biwa. Between the pine and larch he could see the shining blue waters of the lake. He knew that soon he would reach some path leading up and over the mountains in the direction he wanted to go. In the meantime he was fascinated and somewhat fearful of the broad expanse of flat water.

Before him he could see a figure dressed in black and white, wearing a wide-brimmed hat. A priest then. One of the lowland shavers, not a hairy *kebozu* priest, the only ones he had had any contact with in his mountain fastness when they came to serve the population. He kept his distance. One never knew when a priest would curse one.

They maintained the distance throughout the day. At noontime the priest stopped to rest way ahead of the forester. There had been something peculiar about the way the priest moved, and Isei stooped to examine the tracks of the prelate's straw sandals. Puzzled, he stood up. The steps in the leafy mould were the in-turned ones of a woman! A woman priest? Isei shook his head in bewilderment. He left the narrow path and climbed up the mountain, circling down further to catch a glimpse and satisfy his curiosity. He caught sight of the black-and-white robes—without the priest. A small rill ran over the path. Below the path the water formed a shallow pool. Isei's sharp ears caught the sound of splashing. He grinned. The priest was having a bath then. He slipped closer, wondering if priests were built like other men. This one at least wasn't, and Isei stopped his advance, petrified. Slowly the truth dawned on him. Not a priest. A woman disguised as a priest, even to the shaving of her hair. She was probably a felon escaping justice. He watched her bathe herself, panting almost audibly, running his tongue around his lips. This was the longest he had ever been without a woman.

The argument he had with himself was short. She would hardly dare complain, and . . . and. . . . In the meantime, as he secured his matchlock in a hiding place and eased closer, he saw that she was bathing herself with slow, tantalizing, almost ritualized motions. She had a full smooth body, its curves accentuated oddly by her shaven head. She was sliding her palms slowly over her flanks, then stroking her breasts, pinching the nipples. One hand dipped between her thighs, splashing cool water into the dark shadow.

The sound of her splashing hid his approach. He stayed for a moment, slipping easily out of his own clothing while she splashed water onto her face, then raised her closed eyes to the sun. Then Isei charged through the shallow pool. The shaven-headed woman turned to face him. Her alarm returned to calm instead of fright when she saw the cause of the noise. His stiff erect prong leading, Isei splashed towards her. He reached for her slick pale body crying victory when her face crinkled in disgust and ducked under his reaching arms, tripping him into the water in the process. He pulled her slick body into the water with him, and she did not resist, only rolling him about with her.

They rose together and he groped for her, panicked that she might run. She smiled at him through the water drops that beaded his sight.

"Phew. You stink," she said firmly, not resisting when he reached for her again.

Taken aback by her simple statement he asked, "Stink?"

"Stink! Smell bad! I won't have you that way."

"Have me?" he asked again.

"Do you have to repeat every word?" she asked pettishly. She caught sight of his semi-erect pole and reached for it. "Wash. I won't have a man that smells as bad as you do."

Isei soon found himself being laved by her skillful hands. The rub of sand, then moss, on his skin offered a soothing luxurious sensation he had never felt before. And gradually her movements brought about an exciting fire in

82

his loins that seemed to burn brighter than it ever had before. She bent forward and sucked lightly at the tip. Bemused and rather embarrassed by her action, Isei said his first words for some time.

"You are not really a priest. What are you hiding from, eh?"

Much to his regret she raised her head from his erect pole and regarded him with surprise. "I am a nun, of course." She noted his puzzled look and added, "A sort of female priest. Haven't you seen one before?"

"Ah! A shaman! But where's your divining bow then?" he asked suspiciously.

"No, not a seer. A nun. We devoted ourselves to religion. I am from a nunnery—sort of a monastery but only for women—called Dosojinin. I'm on my way to the monasteries of Mount Hiei. Who are you?"

"Isei," he answered shortly, reaching for her and leading her unresisting to the bank. "From the mountains." He pulled her to the ground and spread her legs, then knelt between them. She looked at him expectantly. He applied the tip of his prick to her lower lips and pushed into her without further ado. Her face registered disappointment. Her cunt was damp and soon gave off the oils that made it a delight to its owner and possessor. Isei bucked into her, his rump rising and falling with the speed of his movement. He found her bald-shaven head an added attraction, though, since he was interested in her lower parts and not her top, it would not have mattered anyway.

He glared at her face lost in his pleasure as his climax approached. Slick as an eel, she pulled out from under him and squeezed the base of his prick with a strong hand. He groaned, then yelped in frustration, then turned to her furiously.

"Wait!" she commanded.

She rolled him onto his back, stroking his limp cock softly until the pain passed. Then she did something Isei had never imagined before. She took his cock in her mouth. For just a brief second Isei thought he was about to die. The pleasure was so unexpectedly intense he almost spurted his seed then and there. The nun removed her head, then mounted him. Her legs well spread, he could see the length of her cunt, its prominent hood and full red slit, as she lowered herself onto his rampant prick.

She moved slowly over him, guiding his hands about her body. First her flattened, slightly sagging breasts, then her firm rounded belly, then finally to the curve of her lips where his cock disappeared into her. Her mode of making love was entertaining, Isei decided. His enthusiasm was soon lit and he began exploring her on his own. He lifted and weighed her breasts when he discovered that gave her pleasure, tickled the nubbin of flesh hidden beneath the hood and was rewarded with contractions of her vagina around his erect tool. With her hand she directed him to insert a finger into her cunt along with his cock. Her powerful hole relaxed and accommodated both his digits, the bony one and the one of pure muscle. She stroked her sides and flanks, and encouraged him to do the same. She writhed deeper on his cock in reward, driving him deeper into her depths. His hand came around to her buttocks and she leaned forward to allow him easier reach. They were pleasant to squeeze, and becoming adventurous and curious, he inserted a finger between the half-moon. She encouraged him by widening her thighs and licking his chest with tiny touches of her tongue. His questing finger penetrated the tight rings of her ass and he was surprised to feel his shaft of gristle beyond a thin membrane.

Without removing him from herself she rolled them both over. Isei started pumping slowly, and she urged him on. Faster and faster he thrust into her welcoming body. She responded with movements of her hips that seemed to grip the length of his cock as it had never been gripped before. Her legs went over his back and locked behind him and her fingers scratched at his back, his nape, his ass, inside his anus, awakening feelings he had never known before.

"Now! Now!" the nun commanded, leeching to his neck with her mouth, her entire body glued frantically to his. Isei contracted his balls in a mighty explosion. A wash of boiling liquid rushed up his cock causing him to loose all sense and thought. He was a tiny mote flickering and shattering blindly into pleasure. The nun met him with a force of her own, her body and his melding into a single organism. They lay as one for a long moment, and then Isei, his pleasure spent, moved to extract himself from her embrace. She opened her eyes and looked at him accusingly, then allowed him to go. Streams of white liquid splashed from her opened channel to the ground.

Isei rolled onto his back and the nun rose on one elbow. She examined him minutely, then stroked the length of his body. He tolerated her touch, though what he really wanted was to go to sleep. She smiled knowingly, then suddenly pinched the skin of his belly. He jerked and turned to her furiously.

"There is much you do not know about love," she said conversationally.

"Why, weren't you satisfied?" he almost snarled. This was the first time any woman had doubted his prowess.

"No." she said simply.

"You certainly dropped your moisture," he pointed out truthfully enough.

"Yes. But that does not mean I was satisfied. For instance, why did you not stay with me after you had finished?"

"Huh?" he rose on his elbow as well and peered at her. "But we'd just finished!"

"Not at all," she smiled. "There is before, there is the middle, and there is after, like in all things. *Zanshin*, perfect finish, is as important as all the other elements of lovemaking."

He considered her words thoughtfully, then snorted his disbelief. "Fucking is just fucking," he asserted.

The nun looked at him severely, then began dressing. "I will teach you," she said serenely.

Isei grunted his disbelief and began dressing too.

"I will go with you," the nun said determinedly. "You have the potential of salvation and I, as the rules of my order dictate, must help you on your way."

He scowled at her. "I don't need any help."

"Yes you do," she said, following him back to the path. "You are searching and cannot find, and my way is the only one for you. I will instruct you in the way of *tantara* and you will be saved. For an untutored savage you have a remarkable capacity for the joining of female and male. But it is untutored and needs improving."

"No one's complained yet," he snorted.

"Possibly because they were untutored like yourself,

possibly because they were too polite. But we of the Dosojinin know that the true Way is above politeness. You have the quality. Many men think quantity is what counts, poor things. We women are well ahead on that score, and know the way better than men. I shall be your tutor on that way.''

He grunted and walked away, hoping to lose her along the path. Between the trees he saw a phenomenon he had heard of but never seen: a large seemingly endless sheet of water.

Never having seen such a large body of water, Isei angled towards the shore of the lake. The waters stretched off into the horizon, dotted here and there with the white sails and brown hulls of fishing craft. Rather than forest, Isei found himself soon enough walking through cultivated areas. He reached a path leading from one village to another and followed it, hoping to find a farmer who might be prevailed upon to trade for some vegetables. He eyed the full fields hungrily. There would be good eating here, if only he could get some.

Looking at the field and eagerly expecting a farmer, Isei suddenly found himself facing a young samurai intent on his own business. The man was dressed in scruffy *hakama* and worn straw sandals. His swords were plain and his entire look was shabby. Nonetheless he strode along arrogantly, a grass hat tilted over his shaven forehead. Seeing him, Isei knew trouble was on its way. He looked around for some place to step off the path and kneel or fade into the forest. To his right was a tall embankment, to his left a drop into a low-lying field of taro. He stepped tentatively and nervously forward, hoping to find a broadening in the path.

From the look on the samurai's face Isei knew he was in for a hard time. The man smelled ready to vent some deep-seated rage on anyone crossing his path.

The samurai saw Isei on the path before him. He recognized him immediately as a forest nomad, a low-class fellow. One barely within the confines of the law.

The samurai's left eyelid twitched. ''Get out of my way, filth.''

Isei stared at the warrior without moving for a second, then bowed and moved to the side. The samurai grimaced and strode forward, gathering the skirts of his wide hakama trousers. His attention was on Isei and not on his footing. He tripped, and the straw rope of his sandal tore. His foot twisted and he came down heavily towards Isei, kneeling at the side of the path.

The samurai executed a perfect roll as Isei twitched aside reflexively. The warrior rose snarling.

"You bastard *sanka*," he said, drawing his sword. "You tripped me!"

Under normal circumstances, Isei would have turned and run. But he was tired, and moreover, he had suddenly had his fill of overbearing plains people. The stone flew from his hand as he came to his feet, grazing the smooth brow and disarranging the topknot still further. The samurai charged with a shout of anger. Sparks leaped forth as the *katana's* blade clashed against the heavy metal of Isei's woodsman's hatchet. Isei twisted the tool and the notch at the base of the square-cut blade near the handle almost forced the sword from the samurai's grasp. Isei brought his knee up sharply into the samurai's unprotected crotch, but the warrior twisted away, trying to get some distance from his opponent.

For a long moment the two men stood facing one another. The samurai suddenly realized that the fur-clad mountain man would not be easy prey. The law might be on his side—after all, he was entitled to cut down any attacking commoner, not to mention outcasts like the *sanka*—but his opponent seemed ready to give battle. And to turn and run was unthinkable.

The samurai slid foward, stabbing two-handed at Isei's exposed midriff. Isei twisted aside and sucked in his belly. The curved blade scraped along his tough vine belt and was deflected. The samurai recovered and raised the blade to eye level preparatory to delivering a cut to Isei's shoulder when the heavy *nata* leaped forward. For a moment the reality failed to register with the warrior. He stared stupidly at the stumps of his wrists as hands and sword fell to the mossy ground. Two bright spouts of blood shot from his cut wrists. He stared at them in fascination as his blood pressure dropped precipitously, then fell to the ground. Isei watched him impassively for a long moment, then set about disposing of the body. He knew and feared the penalty for what he had done, justified as it seemed to him.

"That was well done. And evil too," a feminine voice broke into Isei's black thoughts. He spun around in surprise. It was the nun.

"Who *are* you?" he snarled fearfully. If she told what she had seen. . . . And she had been following him . . .

"One who wishes you no harm." She smiled enticingly. "Did you know that you have many good qualities?"

He grunted.

"Yes," she continued. "I will need to help you develop them . . ."

"I don't need any developing," he snarled.

"We all do," she said pacifically. "I meant, however, that you are blessed with a remarkable sexual constitution, one that needs more polish . . ."

He drew back from her in alarm, instinctively fumbling for his crotch. He looked at her out of the corner of his eyes, fearful she was some female succubus: a hollow woman, or a ghost.

"My fucking is my own concern," he almost whined. "Let me go!"

"But you don't do it to yourself, do you?"

"Nnno," he said, "Except sometimes." His mouth snapped shut. Why was he talking about himself to a fake-priest?

"Then it involves someone else too?"

"They like it well enough, those cunts."

"Yes, but they should like it better."

He laughed. "Why should *I* care? I have my fun."

"Ah," she said. "The buddhas and the kami have commanded us to ease our burden in this lifetime, and the teaching of our sect demands full release. Only then can one be truly free from desire. Desiring someone or something and not being released inhibits buddha-nature. . . . Remember the woman in the mountain!!"

He turned surlily, upset by her glib tongue, and walked off. He was loth to admit to himself that there was something in what she said. She hurried after him, still spouting the nonsense that drew attention to his own ignorant state.

CHAPTER 13

THE WOMAN WAS LIMPING BADLY. HER WHITE PILGRIM clothes were stained, and her hat was frayed. Sugiyama was resting in the shade of a small grove when she passed him on the way to Miyako. He watched her through the bushes, unnoticed by the group of rough-looking commoners who were eyeing the same woman from further along the path.

The men talked among themselves in low voices, casting looks at the young woman all the while. There was much subdued laughter, which became more furtive as she came opposite them. One of them, dressed in worn blue-dyed pants and a ragged gown that was tucked into his belt rose and sauntered casually into the path before her. He stretched hugely and looked to either side of the path, then nodded. The pilgrim woman slowed down to pass the lounger.

"Well sister," he said, grinning at her and peering beneath thick brows. "Why the hurry? Wouldn't you like to stop awhile? Hungry and tired, aren't you?"

She looked at him with a worried expression and made to pass. Another of the ruffians stepped into the path behind her. Suddenly he was gripping her elbows and the other two rushed from the shade, laughing.

"Stay with us awhile sweetie," they said.

She tried to scream but the first loiterer had his hard palm across her mouth. She was borne rapidly into the woods, beating at the strong bodies impotently. They laid her down by the stream and started pulling off her clothes. Finally she was cowering at their feet, scratched and slightly bruised, dressed only in stained white gaiters that covered her shins from ankles to knees. She tried to cover herself with her hands while one of the men held her shoulders down and licked greedily at her small breasts. The other three stripped rapidly, and the fourth stood before her and waggled his cock playfully.

"Only for a while, dear."

The leader, his head stubbled, crouched over her loins. She held her thighs determinedly together. He grinned and ran a hand into her dark fluffy bush. She shrieked and one of the men whipped a bandana around her head, gagging her. The man over her clutched at the dark hairs. His forefinger poked at the top of her slit. She struggled as the other two knelt on either side of her, watching their companions and waiting their turn.

Stubble-head thrust the blade of his hand forcefully between her legs. He added another hand, keeping her hips flat with his elbows. At last he managed to pry her legs open. He gazed lustfully at the open slit, then grasped her ankles suddenly and raised them to her head. Doubled over, her cunt was suddenly exposed to his gaze. He laughed and the others laughed with him. She grunted with the effort, the sound muffled angrily behind the gag. His thick finger was suddenly inserted into her dry cunt, bringing a cry of pain from her. He spat on his hand and rubbed the insufficient moisture against her purse, made prominent by her position on the ground.

He crouched over her for a moment, glorying in her shame, wishing her to see and appreciate the humiliation to which he was subjecting her. Then, guiding his cock with his free hand, he descended into her. The broad crown of his cockhead parted the lips easily. She tried to move but was held down by three pairs of hands. Slowly, looking at her eyes cruelly all the time, the ruffian lowered his lips. His thick nobbly shaft disappeared slowly into her cunt lips, which seemed to shrink back with fear at the pressure. At last his scrotum rested on her upraised buttocks. He paused and pinched the soles of her feet through the straw sandal straps.

Holding her legs by the ankles he widened her to a V then set to work, raising and lowering himself into her. A shiny froth appeared as he progressed and her passage became looser, oiled by her own involuntary discharges. She grunted unwillingly as his body weight pushed her down. His movements speeded up and he began to grunt and mumble, extolling the virtues of her slick cunt and smooth legs, delighting in the feel of her body. The other three pawed at her breasts and thighs, squeezing her flesh painfully and exchanging remarks that left nothing to the imagination. She turned her face away, knowing that her fate was sealed.

The wash of hot liquid into her aching cunt was a relief for the pilgrim. The man above her humped violently into her, enjoying the last dregs of his triumph and pleasure. She could see the white stream, residue of his discharge, trickling down her upside-down cunt and pooling on the creases of her belly. The man withdrew and lowered her legs to the ground. Helplessly, her muscles tired from the uncomfortable posture, she let them fall apart.

Another of the ruffians was quickly upon her. His cock was inserted into her overflowing cunt. The penetration was not as painful this time. She turned her face away and contemplated the tops of the trees while the man grunted above her. He slobbered on her breasts, then spewed his load, shaking her supine, unresisting form with the heady rush of his passion.

When the last of the rapists rose from her, she breathed gratefully and tried to sit up. Between her legs spread a pool of male cum, matting the large patch of black hairs at the juncture of her thighs and muddying the leaf-strewn ground. She tried to rise to her feet but was dragged down wordlessly by the ruffians. They leered at her.

"Not so fast dearie. We haven't finished yet."

She tried to run, was dragged back just as Sugiyama walked across the small clearing on his way to the stream on the other side.

"Hey, what the hell you doin' here?" one of the ruffians said. "Get out."

"You do not speak to a samurai that way," said Sugiyama icily, going down on one knee to drink and ignoring the commoners. They were no concern of his, the woman least of all.

Without a word one of the men drew a dagger from a plain wooden sheath in his clothing and struck at the exposed back. Sugiyama spun around under the blow and his *katana* blade whispered from its sheath and without pause cut the man in two at waist level. For a brief second the tableau froze. The commoners could not believe what they just seen. Sugiyama relaxed in perfect *zanshin:* final movement. The would-be murderer could not feel anything below his chest, did not know for the second before his blood pressure dropped that he was dead.

Sugiyama rose sideways to avoid the rush of blood from the twitching, falling corpse, and shook the blood off his blade. The three other men jerked to life like suddenly animated puppets. Two rushed for their clothes, looking for weapons. The third, more practical, groped for a stone. The *kozuka* flashed from Sugiyama's dagger sheath into his eye before his fingers reached the rock. Sugiyama stepped forward and his great blade, wielded with one hand, severed the bent neck of one of the men. A two-handed blow met the charge of the last, and cut his belly open.

Sugiyama looked impassively at the four bloody rag dolls, one of them cut neatly in two. His pulse quickened, now that the action was over, as it always did after he had killed. His attention shifted to the shocked gaze of the woman pilgrim. He stared at the juncture between her legs and she tried to cover herself up in vain. He stepped towards her and she rolled over onto her hands and knees, trying to crawl away. Sugiyama stopped her with one hand on her smooth back. She paused resignedly, her head hanging.

Incuriously he examined her sopping cunt. His heart was pounding as usual after killing. He loosened the tapes of his *hakama* trousers. His cock sprang erect. He lowered his sword to his side while his other hand explored her sopping interior. The feel of his fingers was infinitely more gentle than what she had just experienced. She responded by arching her back.

"Please, ..." she whispered, and it was not clear, not even to her, what she was begging for.

Sugiyama adjusted his height and pushed forward. His cock slid easily into her moist interior. He pulled it out slightly, then pushed in once again, deeper this time. She moaned, with pain or disgust, resignation or lust, he was unable to tell. The samurai felt a faint twinge of remorse at taking her this way, but after all, the lower classes were there for the ease of the gentleman class, and he needed her services.

He stroked her hanging, quite full breasts, then started jogging his rump easily into her. She responded to his movements as her body shook with sobs by grinding her hips against his loins. Sugiyama explored the front of her body with his hands and she forced the pace, raising and lowering her head and humping her full ass against him. Her cunt contracted suddenly and squeezed his cock. He was not ready for the paroxysm of sobbing and of twisting, grasping hips against him. His own climax boiled up and he sank into her brutally. On all fours they shook like a pair of mating dogs, his white juice seeping from the joint of his shaft and her channel.

Sugiyama released the woman when the last of their tremors was over. He straightened his clothes and stuck his sheathed sword back into his sash, then strode off in the direction of the road without casting a glance back.

She looked at the samurai's departing back, then at the corpses at her feet. Dressing, her reddened swollen eyes dry now, she spat at them in fury, then bent to rob the corpses. She had had her revenge on four of them, and would probably never revenge herself on the samurai. So be it. She still had many miles to go on her arduous pilgrimage.

CHAPTER 14

THE WESTERN SLOPES OF THE MOUNTAINS THAT BORDER Miyako on the east are cut by many steep gullies. These flow with water, and are covered by lush vegetation. They are dotted by small villages making a living off the produce and crafts they sell in the city. They are isolated and generally peaceful. Isei strode boldly through one such small hamlet. The nun followed patiently behind, engrossed in her meditations but keeping Isei in sight. He ignored her, trying only to control the urgency in his loins at the thought of her figure following him. The path twisted downwards, between the houses and small yards. A bamboo-basket-maker raised his head, saw the rough-looking, armed mountain man. He stared, then decided it was none of his business and returned to his basket. Peasants in the tiny fields among tree-clad cliffs did the same. Further down the path, the valley opened up somewhat.

In the midst of a clearing stood a house rather larger than the rest. It had a low wall surrounding it, and even a thatched gatehouse. A gaggle of excited people were congregating before the house, blocking the path.

Isei shouldered through, ignoring the commotion. A hand fell on his shoulder. He turned furiously.

"Wait!" the nun said. "Listen!"

They peered through the gate. The owner, on his knees before his own house, was a strange sight. Beside him cowered his wife, much younger, still attractive. From inside the house came the mingled screams of a child and the oaths of some rough male voice.

"What is happening?" asked the nun.

"Ah, your grace, your grace! A robber. . . ."

"No, *two* robbers!"

"Yes, two. Perhaps. I saw only one . . ."

94

The villagers, concerned but also excited by the event, took to arguing.

"Two," said Isei with finality, cocking his ears. "One heavy, the other much lighter. And a child."

"Yes, yes. They were apprehended breaking into a storehouse. They took the landowner's child hostage. Someone has run to fetch the officials, but by the time they arrive . . . They have threatened to kill the child unless they get some money. . . ."

Isei shrugged and turned to go.

"This man will help you," said the nun loudly.

Isei turned and glared at her. He had no such intention. Villagers abused and feared his kind. He owed them nothing. The nun stared back steadily, and he lowered his eyes.

"Call the owner. Say he will be saved, if only he believes."

Isei snorted amusement, then ruefully smiled. He would have to think of a plan . . . He looked at the house again. He could see one or the other of the two robbers through an open sliding door. But never both of them at once. Presumably the nun wanted him to save the child, not just dispose of the robbers, though why this should be so, he could not imagine: It was not her child after all. He considered the possibilities as the elderly, pot-bellied landowner came puffing up, wringing his hands.

"It's my daughter. My only daughter," he said, weeping. "They will not let her go."

"Give them what they want," said Isei.

"No, no!" said the villagers. "If we do, and let them go, the authorities will blame us for assisting criminals. The entire village will be punished!! We will not allow it."

The landowner turned on them, but fearful as they were of him and his threats to their livelihood, they feared the official executioner more. Isei had to admit that his sympathies were with them. He knew that in any event, the poor people would be made to bear the blame. But still and all . . . The nun stared at him and said again, "This man will help you . . ."

Isei scratched his nape, and then his beard thoughtfully. "We'll need some trays, the kind used for gifts and such. And a rice bale. And a large basket. I saw a basket-maker above. And someone to talk to the bandits . . ."

"I will do that," the nun said firmly. "They will not attack me."

The villagers rushed off to do Isei's bidding. The nun listened to his instructions, then walked easily into the house compound. The house owner joined his wife, kneeling halfway to the house platform, their backs to the gate.

The nun knelt on the house platform before the entrance to the house proper and spoke in a low voice with the robbers. They responded with inarticulate screams that gradually turned to a threatening murmur. She returned and reported to Isei.

"One of them will come out and examine the ransom. The other will stand at the window with a knife at the child's neck. If there are any problems, he will kill the child on the spot."

Isei nodded. "That's what I would have done in their stead. Good. We are ready. Take the trays in."

Three villagers quickly bore the footed trays into the compound and laid them on the ground midway between the house and its cowering owners. The woman had not ceased her sobbing, which intensified every time the child within whimpered.

"We are preparing the rice bale," the nun called, as instructed by Isei. "Please do nothing hasty, it will be here right away!"

Isei knew this was the one chancy part of his plan. If the robbers insisted on having everything ready at once . . . But no. The robbers were impatient at the sight of the covered trays. The sliding door slid further open and one of the rough looking men, dressed in loincloth and ragged sark and carrying a short sword, stepped cautiously out onto the platform. Another, no less ragged, appeared behind him, clutching a girl of five or so to his chest. A sharp knife rested against her neck. The robbers peered fiercely in all directions, then the forward one descended the steps. The nun hurriedly moved back. Isei shouldered the rice bale and, bent almost double, stumbled clumsily into the courtyard.

The robber paused, started to retreat, then thought the better of it.

"Lay it down right there, you bastard," he yelled. The other, the one in the window, jerked the child to him which brought a wail from mother and child alike.

"Aya, boss," Isei mumbled, laying down his burden and kneeling beside it. The rice bale was a large one, obviously hastily assembled. It bulged unseemingly, its straw mat covering straggling into a lengthy, lumpy sausage-shape rather than the compact barrel-shape most bales were pressed into. The robber grinned and approached the covered tray. He bent over the covers in anticipation and snatched them back.

Isei flipped open the rice-straw matting that made up the bale and whipped out his matchlock. He raised it, smoothly and casually and squeezed the trigger lever with the butt at his hip. The robber at the window grew a third eye, set neatly between the other two, and dropped both knife and child. Isei rolled forward to get away from the thick grey smoke of his shot. The basket spun from his hand. He had laden the rim with carefully balanced river pebbles, and it flew true. The live robber, charging back to the house, found that he could not see as the large tub-shaped basket settled neatly on his head. While he struggled to comprehend the cause of his sudden blindness, and eventually tried to remove it, Isei was leaping forward. The robber managed to remove the basket and turned. He was just in time to see a bearded, wild figure in a sleeveless fur waistcoat charging at him. The robber screamed, raised his short sword. He felt a blow and Isei's heavy *nata* hatchet swung though flesh and bone and caved in the front of his chest. The return swing took him in the neck. The robber fell, spouting blood.

"You did not have to kill that poor misguided man," the nun said severely.

"What?" said Isei, horrified. "Leave him to the public executioner? To have his head sawn off with a bamboo saw? I would never do such a thing. That is how they serve us, the wild outcasts."

She bowed her head. "I am mortified. You are correct. Better to die as he did."

The house was a small one, even if larger than that of its neighbors. As farmers go, those in the neighborhood of the imperial capital did well. Isei would have much preferred to sleep outside, but the nun had spoken for both of them, accepting the landowner's profuse thanks and hospitality, no less effusive because they had refused any reward but supper and a night's rest. The landowner's wife, younger and pleasanter aspected than he, had pre-pared delights for them with her own hands, and served them herself. She cast silent glances of admiration at Isei, dressed in a conventional kimono for the first time in his life.

Pallets were prepared for them in the main room of the house, a screen separating their sleeping places. Isei felt uncomfortable. The pallet was too soft, the house too well sealed, and the creaks and thumps of the house settling in the night made him uneasy.

"You are uncomfortable, Isei-san," a pale form said beside him.

"I am not used to this," he responded in a whisper to the nun's question. "It is too soft, too. . . ."

She chuckled. "It also has some advantages. Let me show you."

She stripped off her white sleeping robe and laid down on the too-soft bedding. He looked at her, conscious of her nudity as a desirable thing. His cock responded almost instantly. He was ready to leap upon her figure. The dark patch at the juncture of her legs, barely visible in the light of the single lampion, beckoned enticingly.

She smiled approval at his self-restraint. "The first lesson," she said didactically, "is to please the other." Without any visible effort she flipped her legs high and stuck her shoulder through the back of her knees. Her cunt was exposed prominently to view, her head seemingly detached from her body. Isei gaped at the sight and the longitudinal opening of her full purse gaped pinkly at him in return. She motioned him forward.

Hypnotized by the sight, Isei followed her beckoning finger. He peered fearfully at the hairy mound gaping in the middle. She pointed out its parts, enumerating them by their secret tantric names. She parted the outer lips, displaying the treasures inside. A sweet musky scent arose from her and Isei sniffed appreciatively. She smiled over his head. Then her hands started stroking his face, caressing his cheeks, bringing his hypnotized eyes closer and closer to her waiting femaleness until the individual hairs and parts disappeared into a haze. She rubbed his nose deeply into her and he followed the scent, burrowing with his nose as deeply into the moist woman-smelling cavern as he could. She jogged herself against his broad nose, wetting it thoroughly with her juices, then withdrew him. His face was inches from her own and she tilted it up to see into his eyes.

"You have two cocks," she said. "In addition to fingers of course. Both are pleasurable in their own way, and you must now learn to employ the Small Opener before knowing the proper use of the Great Triumph. That is what the woman in the mountains wanted, and rightly too. And when you refused to supply it, she rightfully set her kinsmen on you."

He nodded dumbly, not really knowing what she meant. Slowly and deliberately she extruded her tongue, thickening it by rounding her lips. Suddenly he realized what she meant. For an instant he was overcome by revulsion at what she expected. Then the sweet warm smell of her cunt came to his nostrils again. Attracted and repulsed he lowered his head once again. He licked tentatively at the outer lips. The taste was salty-sour with a fragrance that reminded him of some wildflower. He tried again, and she rubbed her cunt the length of his partly-willing tongue.

Suddenly a strange lust overcame his reluctance. He lapped at the hairy lips with great gulps, extracting as much of her moisture as he could. But as soon as he had gathered her honey, her infinite depths produced more. She stopped him with a gesture and a whisper.

"Point your Vermillion Rock at my Lotus Gate first." Not knowing what he was doing, he allowed her to position his head as she wished. She rubbed his tongue against her clitoris then described long characters against the length of her inner lips. Finally she poised his oral cock against the entrance to her tunnel.

"Thrust!" she said urgently. He pushed forward with his head, tongue stiffly extended. The flesh of his nose pushed and rubbed down against the nubbin of her clitoris. His tongue stabbed deeply, again and again, into her wet channel. She regarded his laboring head with approval and then allowed herself to relax.

Isei felt shudders, tiny at first but growing rapidly, go through her body and focus on her cunt into which his tongue was digging so blindly. The tremors grew to massive shivers and spasms. Her cunt grabbed at his slippery tongue. He felt her orgasm the way he had never felt a woman's pleasure before. His mouth was inundated with her salty-sweet juices. He clutched at her buttocks with his hands, but she batted his fingers away. On all fours, head buried between her legs, he felt his own cock responding to her pleasure. It jerked tightly against the muscles of his belly. The release of tension without any touch, his own or another's, was so intense he cried out into her welcoming lower mouth. Her cunt responded by a further series of shudders and a final jerk that buried him deeply into the tight chasm to heaven.

He pulled away from her and regarded the small pool of his jetted milk with confusion and chagrin. She followed his gaze and her eyes lit up.

"Wonderful, Isei. You have leapt ahead on the path. Not many men can do that—pleasure themselves solely by pleasing their companions—it is a valuable gift."

He looked at her in confusion as she sought her own bedding behind the screen.

He closed his eyes and fell quickly into a deep sleep. There was a soft sound as the *fusuma* sliding door moved aside. A pale figure stood there. Isei, wakened by the tread outside, could smell the body fragrance of the landowner's wife. She knelt inside the door and slid herself forward.

"Isei-sama," she whispered.

He raised his head slightly.

"Could you come here a moment?"

He slipped quietly out of his uncomfortably soft pallet and followed her noiselessly. She entered a room crammed with bales and boxes of household goods and knelt there in the light of a tiny candle.

"Isei-sama, I wanted to thank you myself. My husband is so gruff you see . . ." She pushed a folded bundle towards him. Isei touched it doubtfully. It was a handsome though worn suit of clothes: pantaloons, and a robe. He bowed in thanks. She stayed still, on her knees. Her dark eyes were fathomless in the candlelight, as if she was waiting for something. He noted that her light summer *yukata* was loosely tied. Her breasts were full and showed clearly at the opening of her robe. A quiet motion from the corridor behind him attracted his notice.

He cast a look backwards and was surprised to see the face of the nun smiling at him from behind the door.

The landowner's wife knelt and bowed a second time. One of her full breasts popped out of the robe. She made no attempt to replace it, raising her torso instead to allow him a full view of its size. He raised both breasts with his hands, thumbs on their prominent nipples. She closed her eyes to mere slits and breathed rapidly through her nose. Isei pulled her to him and nibbled at her neck. It occurred to him that the nun's lesson might also apply to her mouth, and he sucked at her lips, inserting a questing tongue into her. Not only did the woman not object, but she responded fervently, running her own lips across his, licking back at him with her tongue. Isei explored her full body joyfully. She twisted and moved with his exploring hands, obviously enjoying the prolonged sensation of his palms on her, his lips on her own. They stripped one another in the dimness and she allowed him to enjoy the sight of her plump body in the dark. She had a small scar on her belly, perhaps from childbirth. Otherwise he found her perfect, plump and thick in the thigh and shoulder. She rolled over against him, her full buttocks digging into his loins.

He turned his head and saw the nun smiling encouragingly at him. She made pursing movements with her mouth, then indicated the woman's buttocks with her hand. When Isei failed to respond, she crept over to the couple and pulled at his hands. Instructed by her he slid lower, parting the woman's full buttocks. She writhed against the pressure, allowing him liberty to explore her. The nun pushed his head lower and he understood. His tongue licked out, striking between the mounds of her bottom, searching for the sweet hole of her pussy. The woman bent almost double, holding still in expectation. He found the hole and pushed in with his tongue. It was tight and resisted his efforts. She had been to her bath and her hole was still dry. He moistened it with his tongue and began working slowly at the hole, enlarging it while he explored. The nun, her head bent close to his, whispered into his ear.

"Very good. Explore her with your fingers. Encourage the flow of her essences to supplement your own."

The woman was trembling now, her ass butting against Isei. She raised her upper thigh and stuck out her ass. Her hands came around to feel his head and she led his hands forward along the almost hairless meeting of her thighs. Isei was lost in his pleasure, though he was now conscious that of the woman's two holes, his tongue was slipping into the lower one. His lover guided his head and without missing a beat he began probing her higher up. The sensation was different, looser and more flexible and she jerked as wildly as before, then forced his head back against her anal ring. Isei obeyed her desire and the shaking of her body increased.

"Very good," the nun whispered. "Do it again. Move from one to the other. Use your fingers on her. Sooth her belly."

Isei obeyed and the nun moved back, then twisted his hips so that his painfully erect cock was directed straight up. He felt her warm breath on him and redoubled his efforts with his tongue as the nun's mouth sucked strongly at his erect penis. She engulfed the entire staff, sucking and milking it with the entire length of her mouth and throat. Just as Isei felt he could take no more, she withdrew. At his mouth the woman was convulsing with a series of explosions that spattered his mouth with the juice of her cunt.

The nun slid into the shadows as the woman turned and held out her hands to the mountain man. He rose on all fours and positioned himself above her. The woman's eyes were closed and she urged him on with clawed fingers on his neck. The nun's hand came out of the dark and grasped the base of his root forcefully.

"Not yet," she said in a whisper audible only to his trained ears. "Walk about the grove awhile first." He did not recognize the simile until she started running the tip of his rampant cock through the woman's sparse cunt hairs. Beneath him the landowner's wife moaned and begged incoherently for his maleness. The tip of the cock stimulated her fantasies and she could feel her desire fanned into a second orgasm. Her hips twitched and moved uncontrollably. She thought she heard a female voice call commandingly, "Now!" but it must have been her own, distorted by the lust of her orgasm.

Isei plunged forward at the nun's command. He feared the landowner's wife would hear the nun, but the naked woman was so deep into her own pleasure that she might have been dreaming. The crown of his cock found her entrance unerringly and he drove himself to the depths of her clutching hole with all his might, her knees clamped at his side as her mouth clung to his. They moved together violently, the frequency of their body movements increasing to a blur. As his own pleasure rose Isei felt the nun directing his fingers to the woman's sweating ass. He dipped a finger between her buns and scratched at the muscles of her asshole just as she let down a final spray of moisture, erupting violently against him. He exploded as well, flooding her thirsty interior with his juices and grinding mindlessly against her like the minks he had seen coupling in the snow.

"Excellent, wonderful," the nun's low voice congratulated him.

"Yes, excellent indeed," the other woman echoed.

Isei rolled away from the plump, naked woman below him. The nun's voice arrested his motion. "Not so fast," she whispered. "Make her remember you. Play with her some more."

Obediently for once, Isei stroked the woman's heaving sides, squeezing her breasts lightly, and slipped a finger into her gluey crack. He was rewarded by a diminishing series of spasms and a grateful sigh.

The nun was nowhere in sight when the housewife rose to her feet. Isei started getting up too but she motioned him to wait. She returned after scrabbling in a series of chests. She bore a small parcel and knelt before him, still gloriously naked.

"You are the best man I have ever had," she whispered. "My husband is older than I, and of course quite adequate, as a girl . . . Well, no matter. We are a good family, my people are former *ashigaru* of Honganji temple at the capital. Please accept this as a token of my appreciation." She pushed the stiff cloth bundle at him. "If, as you say, you are on pilgrimage to a temple at the capital, this will allow you to move freely in the town. They are suspicious of mountain men there, such as yourself. Please accept it . . ."

He unfolded the bundle. A sleeveless *jimbaori* doublet unrolled before him. In it was a long brocade sleeve with tasseled ties. He puzzled over it for a moment, then understanding struck. It was a covering for his matchlock.

"The *mon* device on the back of the coat will allow you to move freely," she said shyly in a whisper.

He bowed to her. "We are then both of gunner families. I am grateful to you, Elder Sister."

She simpered as he gathered his gifts and padded back to his room.

"That was very well done," the nun said from behind the partition. Isei fell asleep, warmed by her appreciation.

CHAPTER 15

THE RHYTHM OF HOURS AT THE ITO MANSION WAS RELATIVELY unchanging. Midori adapted to it quickly. Cleaning and other duties kept her busy. The other women sniped at her, not the least because she was, for the time at least, the master's favorite. Less enviable was the fact that Haruko too had taken a fancy to her. She was a demanding mistress, making use of Midori's skills or her presence or her body as her whims and moods dictated. Midori bore the beatings and the rough sex cheerfully, knowing they were temporary and secure in the hidden knowledge that she was not what she seemed.

If sex with Haruko was straightforward and demanding, sex with Ito was theatrical and bordered on the ludicrous. He dressed her in fantastic costumes, threatened her with a variety of weapons, most of which were genuine antiques, few of which were serviceable because of their extreme elaboration. He seemed also obviously worried about something, but she never managed to identify the reason. With him there was none of that lazily pleasurable time after sex when questions could be asked and confidences exchanged. He rose from her supine body, sometimes painted a garish red to simulate hideous wounds, with a shamefaced look which barred any intimacies. He would hurry away to his duties, his writing, his endless conferences with Hori his secretary or Uemura, the young man who Midori knew to be Haruko Ito's lover. But he never looked back at her. She tried to snoop, but she was not very good at it, and never came up with any information worth reporting to Matsudaira's agent, who came by in one disguise or another once a day.

Resting on her knees, her exposed ass rising to greet the sun, Midori considered all these things. This afternoon Ito had dressed her in a massive-looking gilt armor patterned after some hauberk of five hundred years before. She feared its weight and was pleased it seemed lighter than it suggested. He armed himself with a great curved sword and declaimed a mumbled set of lines in classical Chinese she could not understand. He thrust deeply into her wet cunt, his balls banging against her clitoris. She wriggled imperceptibly to encourage him, mindful as always of her Elder Sister's exhortations to be in control at all times. Ito's movements approached their climax. She wondered what he saw with his mind's eye. She watched his shadow before her. He rose, massive and threatening, and his curved sword rose higher until it poised before him, ready to slash down just as his flesh sword spewed the contents of his balls into her.

Midori heard a muffled bang. Ito gave a cry and fell over her. She waited passively for his next move, but instead he rolled off her. The body moved with the leadedness that characterized a man after he had spewed his seed. She looked over her shoulder and sniffed. There was a peculiar burning smell. Ito's eyes gazed back at hers, uncaring. She sprang erect, careless of her appearance. Flames rose from his dead body. The giant sword he held was still clutched in his fist, hidden beneath the body from which pungent smoke was emerging. Midori covered her mouth with her hand to suppress a scream. Death was no stranger to her, but this reinvoked the supernatural fears of her earlier training.

She rose convulsively and backed away from the cadaver. Ito seemed to stare at her accusingly. She turned and ran towards the villa, screaming hysterically. Ito's guards were slow to arrive. All the residents of the opulent mansion were used to the sound, and even the sight, of hysterically screaming, naked young women. They knew better than to interrupt their master's pleasures. Midori herself was practically incoherent. She burst finally into Haruko's rooms and collapsed panting onto the *tatami*. Haruko, still involved in arranging her hairdo, looked at her severely.

"What are you bawling about, girl? Go back to the master right away!"

"B . . . but . . . but he . . . he is dead!" the brown-haired girl wailed. She was trembling and the sound of Haruko's laughter rang strangely in her ears.

"Nonsense," Ito's wife said callously, "He is only playing a game with you. Go on. Go back or he'll have me administer a beating. I'll like that," her eyes gleamed. "Maybe I'll do it anyway. Go on, now."

"But mistress," Midori cried, "he is dead. I heard the shot. I saw the hole in his face . . ."

"What?" Haruko was suddenly on her feet. "What shot?"

"He was killed!" Midori practically screamed.

Haruko looked at Midori for a second then rose and dragged the hysterical girl, still dressed in her gilt armor, to the garden.

Haruko looked at Ito's supine body from the porch. "Stay here!" she ordered Midori, then ran to the side of her husband. "He is dead?" she cried after a moment's examination. "Call the guards!"

Heedless of her strange habiliments, Midori rushed to obey.

Ito's retainers stood indecisively at the edges of the garden, peering this way and that for the killers.

"Don't come close!" Haruko screamed at them. "Let the magistrate's men do that. Someone run and call them."

† † †

Matsudaira Konnosuke, though high in the estimation of those near to him (and perhaps, who knows, of the Presence Himself) was nonetheless slave to certain requirements. At set times he needs be at certain places, dressed in certain ways, and with very little leeway. He enjoyed some of the ceremonial—that part that related to his substantive activities—and hated other parts.

Social demands were part of the ceremonial he liked least. None of that showed on his face as his secretary read a report of a disturbance in one of the commoner quarters. Visits by retired Senior Clansmen were an unpleasant but necessary part of the job. He checked the detail of the room with one eye. His hands lay flat on his thighs, his elbow barely brushing the silk tied hilt of his dagger.

"Lord Ito is late, Lord," the secretary murmured quietly.

"Hm. Yes. Try to find out what's happening. Discreetly. Let's try not to insult the old bird."

The secretary bowed. One of the attending samurai bowed as well and slipped out of the room. The secretary continued the reading. Half an hour later the samurai came in. He bowed perfunctorily, approached Matsudaira quickly and whispered in his ear. Matsudaira's eyebrows rose and he signed for the secretary to stop.

"Lord Ito was murdered before he left his villa." There was an outburst of excited babbling. "Quiet please. Muto, take some of your senior men and seal the villa. I shall be arriving as soon as possible. His villa is in Daimonji ward it is not? Have some of the *chonin* detectives see if they can find any rumors. I will be there presently." Four samurai, led by Muto, a square-faced elder, rushed out of the room. Matsudaira rose, turned. The sliding doors opened and he strode out. The doors closed silently behind him.

Matsudaira stood at the scene of the crime and examined everything with minute attention to detail. Behind him were the villa and his men, crouching motionless on the small secluded veranda. Before him was a stretch of gravel, and then a mossy rise. Beyond it was a small pond with gold and silver leopard carp swimming in its limpid depths. Beyond the pool was the villa's high wall. To one side he could see the exposed rafters of a large building. He vaguely recalled that the temple—its name escaped him—had requested permission to rebuild after a period of neglect. The distance to the temple roof on one side, or to the mountain straight ahead, was considerable: several hundred feet.

"Was anyone with him?" Matsudaira asked Muto.

"There was a woman . . ." Muto answered and there was some hesitation in his tone. Matsudaira walked out onto the garden, taking care to step only on the half-sunken paving rocks. The body was still there, covered by a woman's kimono. He motioned Muto closer. The other retainers held back.

"Well? What did you not say?"

Old Muto scratched his jaw. "It's kind of delicate, Lord. Ito had, . . . well he had some peculiar sexual tastes. I think Saga-san may know more about that. Anyway, he dressed his women in armor and . . . ah . . . had them that way. He was actually on top of the woman when he was shot.''

"The woman was one of his own household? Did she say she saw the shot?''

"Newly employed, I gather. One of the commoner constables interviewed her. She is still in armor. She was bowing before him and saw nothing.''

"I'll go and see her. You've gone over the ground?''

"Of course, Lord. No identifiable footsteps beyond Ito, the concubine, and the wife. One set each. We're holding the concubine, but the wife stated that the concubine was on all fours when Ito was shot.''

"I'll see them both,'' Matsudaira ordered.

Midori was ushered into the room where Matsudaira stood, his brows creased thunderously. Some of her ancient fear of him rose to the surface. He took no notice, merely asking, "Are you the woman Midori?''

She bowed on the floor and answered in the affirmative. The constable, dressed in striped short robe and blue pants, looked at her severely as if wishing he could tie her up and lead her to execution. Matsudaira turned to him.

"Where is Mr. Muto? Find him and bring him to me. I'll oversee the woman.''

The constable bowed and departed at a run.

"Don't worry Midori,'' Matsudaira said kindly, kneeling by her side. "I'll have to be severe with you, and I'll order you sequestered at the mansion. Don't worry. Is there anything you need to tell me?''

She nodded her head wordlessly, reassured, as they heard hurrying footsteps. He rose just as Muto and the constable burst into the room.

"Lord?'' Muto inquired.

"Muto-san, there are some peculiar aspects to this case. And of course we must treat it . . . with delicacy.'' Muto nodded. "We can't even seal the villa. Have the constables go over every inch of the ground. I want a full report and a plan of the villa. Confiscate the armor and everything else that was at the scene of the crime. Have some men close off and search the area immediately behind the villa and the mountainside.''

Wordlessly Muto indicated the servant girl.

"Have her taken to the magistracy. I will interrogate her

there. There is no need to tie her," Lord Matsudaira said as he left the Ito mansion. Muto bowed and turned back.

Midori, under escort, arrived at the official mansion and was brought to a familiar door. Matsudaira, Miura Jiro, and Rosamund were waiting for her inside. She found she was more comfortable in the august company than she had felt before. Matsudaira/Goemon was smiling, a smile which wiped out the severe impression he had given in his persona as examining magistrate. He poured her a cup of tea with his own hands and she thanked him with a shy smile.

"Now tell us about it. Don't be reserved. I know what the general setting was."

Midori bobbed her head and described the scene.

"He was holding a *sword*?" Jiro asked incredulously.

"He liked to pretend he was a great warrior. It was pretty uncomfortable in that old armor."

"I saw it," Goemon confirmed. "I've had it confiscated. All the rest too."

"What does it have to do with his death?" Jiro asked.

"I don't know. Not much I imagine. He was shot," said Goemon thoughtfully. "The shot must have come from the hill. Hit his chest bone, then through the heart and entrails. Very high angle of entry. There's nothing before him but the garden wall, which would have been too low, the temple, which is off to his left, and the mountain."

"I only heard a very muffled sound," Midori said tremulously.

"It must have been from a great distance. You are sure you did not hear the gun closely?" Jiro asked.

"I am sure, Miura-sama." Some of her composure had returned. "It was muffled, from a distance. Perhaps beyond the garden wall. His clothes were scorched, smouldering."

"The hillside?" said Goeman thoughtfully. "That would be five hundred feet away, at least. Some shot. And the burning clothes. That sounds like a shot at close range. It doesn't fit together."

"Or else, from below the wall. At an angle." Jiro mimicked a high trajectory shot with his hands.

"In either case, he'd have to be some shot!" Goemon's lips were pursed. "But what about the flames?"

"My father . . ." Jiro was groping for words. "He used

to tell me, something, what was it . . . Yes. They would heat cannonballs red hot, then ram them into the guns to fire at enemy ships and set them alight.''

"It would blow up the powder!" Goemon objected.

Jiro shook his head. "No. They used a wadding of wet clay . . ."

"Possible, barely possible. Or else his sins were catching up with him and it was divine wrath." His eyes grew thoughtful, and Midori shrank from them, her awe of the divine surfacing again.

"Oh, stop scaring the poor little girl," Rosamund broke in. She turned to comfort Midori.

A page spoke from the other side of the *shoji*. "Mr. Muto wishes to speak with you, Lord."

"Wait here!" Goemon said and reassumed the severe expression of Matsudaira Konnosuke. He slipped out of the room and Midori closed the sliding panel behind him.

Muto and Saga, his senior advisors, were seated in a small informal audience room Matsudaira used for private audiences. They bowed as he entered and seated himself.

"Any information?" Matsudaira asked shortly.

"Not much more about the Ito case I'm afraid, Lord," Saga, the younger of the two said.

"We've got to solve it quickly," Matsudaira said with a frown. "Ito was quite high in his clan's councils. We will have to inform them. And report to the Pavilion. I can't understand what he was doing here in Miyako at all."

Muto's pug face cracked a grin. "We don't have to hurry and inform his clan, Lord. They sent him here, and it wasn't a promotion either."

Matsudaira glanced at Muto. The mastiff-faced counsellor had served his father, and his special expertise was politics, of which he was a mine of information. "Do tell," he said thoughtfully, then turned back and ordered his page to bring tea.

"Ito has always been rather sickly," Muto explained, his face creased in effort. "He's served the Mito domain very well, but always in administrative capacities. I think that rankled. Anyway, he fancied himself a warrior, and it got mixed up with his sex life somehow. He just couldn't get it on unless he was playing the warrior. He played too hard one day and killed his wife. It was an accident, but the elders decided he'd better remove himself elsewhere. His present chief wife used to be his Second. Apparently she didn't object to his tastes and got sort of promoted to chief wife. She's from a lower-class samurai family of Mito. I don't think he was vicious or anything, just eccentric."

"We have to check into motive. What about Uemura, the young ward or disciple or whatever he is?"

Saga cleared his throat. "Hm . . . There's something about him. He lives way too high. I think we should look at him carefully. *Maybe* he has a motive."

"Yes, but what about the method?" Muto objected. "We're looking for a *superlative* gunner. The constables haven't found any trace of a man: wadding, footsteps, anything. We'll just keep looking. But Lord, there is something else. There's been another murder."

"Another mu. . . ." He held Matsudaira and Saga's attention fully. "Same method?" Matsudaira asked quickly.

"No. Quite a different affair. A *ronin* fought with a samurai of the Satake clan in the latter's mansion. He gave his name."

"The Satake man challenged him?" Matsudaira asked. "That's no affair of ours then, surely."

"It was a challenge. But he apparently took advantage of the man's wife as well."

Matsudaira rose, his face flushed with blood. "Find him and arrest him! This is intolerable. Some samurai seem to forget their duty and remember only the privileges! I will not have this in my city. Muto, you are responsible for bringing the man in!" Matsudaira thought for a moment then reseated himself. "I'll try another method too, just in case. From my own resources. Get me a description of the man!"

The two counsellors bowed and Matsudaira rose and strode out. They walked out. "He's shaping up quite nicely," Muto said in a low voice.

Saga chuckled. "A chip off the old block. The Old Lord would have been proud. It's a shame they quarreled before the old man's death."

The two old retainers smiled at one another knowingly. They had served Konnosuke's branch of the Matsudaira family all their lives, and gone through the civil wars that brought the Tokugawa family to the Shogunal seat in the

Old Lord's train. The family's position was dear to them, and young Konnosuke was beginning to show he was made of the same stuff as his father.

Behind them, Matsudaira and his half-Barbarian friend discussed Sugiyama's future.

"You know," Jiro said. "The description sounds familiar. I got a message from Satsuki."

"Is she back from her pilgrimage?"

"No. But she sent me this and a tale." He showed Goemon a small lacquered box. It was the kind carried by men of fashion, which divided into five compartments, each one for a different medicine. "She took this off a samurai who was about to attack Matsuo, her bodyservant. The events sound similar." He handed a sheet of paper to Goemon.

The slim young man read the letter quickly. He grinned. "Too much Chinese scholarship as usual," he observed. His tone turned serious. "At least she is all right. Yes, it sounds like the same man. Well, we've got a description at least. Think you can try and look yon gentleman up? You know, it might be best to dispose of him quietly. Arresting a samurai always leads to trouble, and I've got too much to handle just right now. Did you know there's a report of false coinage turning up? Saga told me this morning. A merchant complained of receiving counterfeit *momme* silver coins. And two, now three murders. At least finding this *ronin* and disposing of him should be no problem. Wish I had that job."

Jiro grinned and rose to his feet. "Tough," he said succinctly. "I've told you before: You should have stayed an itinerant doctor."

His arms folded, Matsudaira stared down at the mat, lost in thought. His giant friend silently took his leave, grinning slightly in anticipation.

CHAPTER 16

"WHAT ARE YOU DOING HERE?" A ROUGH HAND WAS SHAKING
Momoe and adding to the discomfort in her mouth and the
pounding in her head. Momoe slowly raised her bleary
eyes. A fierce face topped by a kerchief and characterized
by dark piercing eyes under bushy brows was peering at
her. The dawn light was turning the alleyway pink.

She moaned. "Ow, my head. Ah. . . ."

He shook her again. "Nothing but the aftereffects of
drink. I repeat, what are you doing here? Are you a
whore? Where's your *goza* mat?"

"No, no." Momoe protested weakly. "I'm not a whore.
Only drunk." Then the enormity of what had happened
struck her. She could not now return to Sakamotoya.
Having once abandoned the premises without leave, they
would not take her in again. Tears started to run down her
cheeks and she bowed to the dirt in shame.

"Stop that caterwauling." The fierce man shook her
angrily. "What's the matter? Explain calmly and with
balance!"

Not knowing what else to do, she told him her story. He
peered at her, his brows knitted in thought, then rose from
his crouch. "Follow me," he said over his shoulder. "I'll
give you work."

Not knowing what else to do, Momoe followed his tall,
thin figure.

He led her to a modest house in one of the city's
northern quarters. Workmen and petty traders hurried by
her and Momoe prayed that none would recognize her as
Momoe from Gion quarter, the weaver's daughter.

They entered the house and he motioned Momoe to a
seat before him. She looked around at the gloomy room.
The plain floorboards were worn. He did not open the

shutters and the guttering candle barely lit the cobwebby interior. Dried bunches of herbs and roots hung close to the rafters. Through a half-open sliding door she could see what appeared to be a laboratory. There were jars and pots, several mortars and pestles of various sizes, and more bunches of herbs and other unfamiliar materials.

"I am Terauchi Hideo. I am a doctor and herbalist. You will help me domestically as well as with my business."

"What business, may I ask?" she said timidly.

He stared at her thoughtfully down his nose. "You should know that I am the master of many arts. I know how to preserve the body and to protect the bodily essences. The four corners of the earth yield to me their secrets." His bushy eyebrows seemed to quiver. "All their secrets. Except one. The ancient sages knew it, and I shall too!" He voice rose almost to a screech.

She nodded fearfully at his outburst, then hastened to obey when he ordered her to clean the house. With the exception of his laboratory she was to have complete responsibility for the domestic arrangements.

"And your work?" she asked timidly. "How can I help you with that?"

"You will find out in due time," he said, and returned to his secret compounding and mixing.

Much later he intercepted her as she hauled in a large bucket from the communal well in the neighborhood.

"I sell a compound that increases the virility of men," he said abruptly. "You will assist me in doing so."

She nodded humbly.

"With the initial dosage you will approach the customer so that he might try for himself the quality of the elixir."

"I do not understand master," said Momoe uncomfortably. She had a strange feeling that . . .

"Stupid girl," he said in a monotone. "You will fuck them of course."

"Me?" she said surprised. "But I am not, . . . that is I don't. . . ."

"Stop your silly protestations," he broke in. "You will do what I say so that I can get the coppers from those foolish men and apply them to my real work: the elixir of the sages."

"I am not a whore," Momoe said tearfully. "You must not demand this of me . . ."

"Shut up," he roared. "Do you really think I have need of your petty domestic tasks?"

"I cannot do that . . . that . . ." she answered with some spirit.

The doctor peered at her forcefully from under his bushy iron-grey brows.

"You will do what I say, you drunken slut, or else I will ram my walking stick up your stupid cunt and throw you out into the street!" he snarled.

Momoe cowered away from him in fear. The memory of the way he had found her returned to her eyes. She fell on her knees, her heart pounding, then peered up at him from under her straggling hair.

He was looking at the curve of her ass against her kimono thoughtfully. "That's better," he said approvingly. "Stay as you are!" he commanded. He slipped off his traveling pantaloons and displayed a semi-erect, thin but long cock with a peculiarly dark cast to the plum tip. He knelt before her and raised her head. Momoe drew back instinctively from the prick presented to her mouth. The doctor gripped her by her nape and brought her face to his crotch again. She sniffed cautiously. The heavy bitter smell was reminiscent of Mr. Asano at the Sakamotoya shop. Unwilling, yet fascinated, she felt her insides begin to tingle with the familiar, and by now desired, sensation. She closed her eyes and opened her lips, moving them foward. He rubbed the tip against her lips. The spongy tip left a sticky residue. Her tiny tongue licked out and met the bitter flavor hungrily. The doctor raised the tip and began stroking her face with it. He poked her eyes lightly, then painted her cheeks and nose with the sticky trail.

Momoe sighed deeply as the fire in her loins grew. She fumbled with her clothing and her plain cotton *obi* came loose. She reached beneath her and began stroking her juicy lips in the same rhythm the doctor was using on her face. The cock tip circled her mouth like a predator waiting to pounce. She made an O of her lips, and finally managed to capture the head, almost biting at it in her eagerness.

He pushed forward steadily and she sucked him in,

116

supporting his balls with her delicate hands. He indicated his approval with a glance, and then pulled back, only to thrust it in again against her soft tongue and palate. The speed of his thrusts grew and Momoe sucked with all her might, reluctant to lose the mighty flesh pole. She caught sight of herself in the polished sides of a piece of the doctor's equipment. She was crouching, one knee raised and her hand disappearing between her legs. Her breasts were filling out and her skin was smooth and golden. Her striped robe, soiled now, fell loosely and enticingly from her shoulders. Her chin was small, and her lips, from which grew a monstrous shaft, were full and red, extruding and everting as the man moved into her. Over all she could see her heavy lidded eyes, peering back at herself seductively. The vision was so enticing she felt as if she were watching another creature, a creature towards whom she yearned with all her might, a creature who was making love to her at the very same time. A warm pink flush suffused her skin. Her nipples rose to hard points. The thrumming of her hand against her cunt moved to a fever pitch and she felt the first tremors of her climax just as the doctor's prick started swelling and jerking in her mouth. She sucked lustily, longing to taste the male juices again, no longer ashamed of her own appetites.

By now she was familiar with male reactions and she knew what the swelling and pulsing meant. Her tongue laved the shaft and she urged the flow on by stroking the doctor's hairy ball bag. Terauchi pulled out of her mouth and she raised her head in reproach.

"Wait!" the doctor said softly. "I must not waste the vital essences." He knelt behind her and she guided his rampant prick into her hungry hole. Moving backwards lustfully, she impaled herself until she could feel his ball bag slapping against her buttocks. He pulled her back and folded his legs under her. She supported her weight on her forearms and forced herself down on him until her ass could touch his belly. He helped support her body, allowing her to move freely. She rubbed back and forth, creating the friction she needed by rubbing her body in circles like a woman pounding seeds in a mortar. Her breathing grew faster and she felt moisture drip down the buns of his ass and wet the patch of rough hairs at the base of his cock. He looked on approvingly, passively allowing her to reach her own pleasure, merely tweaking her pink nipples.

"I am glad you take to this so well. A major part of your job," said the doctor, "will be to demonstrate the worth of my secret elixir. Your nature is a bit too lustful for what I need, but you will learn control. It is important to demonstrate to the customers that the elixir is working and of good quality."

"Is it not?" she asked, not really caring, sunk in the pleasure of his erection as she churned it from one side to the other.

"Of course, of course," he said. "Nonetheless, it is of no importance beyond what it brings in from the credulity of the commoners."

"Yes, yes, oh yes." She suddenly came again, clutching at the floor and rocking violently in his lap. He clutched at her smooth buns, pulling her to him until the spasms were over, then used the same handholds to remove her from his prick. She crawled off reluctantly, feeling every bit of the pole as it slid out of her hungry hole. She was surprised and delighted when he turned her on her back and mounted her again, crouching between her knees and allowing only his long cock to rummage the length of her cunt. His breath smelled faintly of some unknown spice, and Momoe breathed in deeply. She determined to let him have his pleasure this time, and set forth energetically to do so. Her inner muscles closed on his member, milking it as far as she could. He withdrew, then plunged in again, and she repeated the movement. His thrusts became deeper, his returns slower and more reluctant. To her delight she found him pounding into her, grinding his loins strongly against her while his mouth, rather than spouting instructions, was fastening onto her breasts alternately.

"Yes, yes," she cried, crushing his stringy body to hers and hooking her ankles together behind his bobbing back.

She was twisting her hips eagerly, approaching her climax, when he pulled suddenly out of her and hit her a stinging blow on her vulnerable, partly open cunt. Momoe shrieked and folded on herself. "You must *not* try to make me spurt in you too quickly!" the doctor said in a calm, terrifying voice. "Do you understand? Control your own lust and control mine as well. Let us do it again!"

Momoe nodded dumbly and he mounted her, laying his full weight upon her belly. His long prick was soon rooting in her again. They lay for hours, changing position time and again, the doctor forbidding her to rest or to gain any relief. Gradually she learned to control her reactions, and she found that the longer she lasted, the more powerful was her initial orgasm. The doctor looked at her growing self-control with approval.

"Now we will see if you can control yourself positively as well as negatively." He returned with a flat lacquered box out of which he extracted a long thick prick made of smooth shiny horn. Momoe looked at it with some apprehension. It was larger than any real prick she had ever seen, almost the length and thickness of her arm.

"Must I really do this?" she asked nervously.

The doctor frowned at her under his bushy brows but forebore to answer. Instead he tipped her over on her back and brought the tip of the monstrous *harigata* to her well-irrigated opening. "You must be able to control the largest prick," he said, and thrust it in.

At first Momoe felt she could not take all of it, but then the flexibility and youth of her channel prevailed and she watched, her head raised, as the shaft slid deeper and deeper into her. She could feel the head nudging the tip of her cervix. The doctor knelt between her legs, his cock erect. The *harigata* was obviously hollow, for his own cock disappeared into the artificial one. It was then tied by two tapes behind his back.

"I will not be gentle," he said, still frowning. "Let us see if you are able to absorb this." He pumped suddenly and violently into her tender inflamed cunt. Momoe shrieked with the pain of the sudden insertion of such a large object. Mindful of his previous instructions, she clutched his stringy body to hers. The doctor was staring off into the distance. His long hair was disarrayed, his features were contorted. Sweat had sprung up on his face and ran into his eyes. But his butt kept up a triphammer movement, and gradually Momoe began to feel comfortable with the monstrous thing in her. Her body responded then,

119

uncontrollably, as his motions grew wilder and he bit hard at her nipples.

"More, more you old dog. Give me mmmooore," she squealed in a voice that was only barely hers. She pummelled his back with her fists, scratched and bit back at his neck, her head thrown back until a final massive orgasm built inevitably in her loins. The fire ran through, raising goose bumps on her skin, forcing her to clench her jaws so as not to scream aloud. And her elastic insides closed around the enormous cock that pummelled her, seeking its juices as she let down her own.

She came to lying on a pallet in the room. The door to the doctor's study was closed and strange smells drifted from it. Momoe roused herself painfully. Her cunt was tender, but surprisingly, as she touched it, she felt a shock of pleasure. Experimentally she inserted a finger into her own vagina but found no difference in her cunt. Whatever stretching it had undergone, it had soon returned to its original tiny size.

She cleaned what she could of the house, trying to wipe away years of grime and neglect.

The doctor emerged from his study trailing indefinable vegetable smells, not all of them appetizing. He bore a small vial in his hand, eying it thoughtfully.

"Momoe!" he called. She paused in her scrubbing and wiped her hands on the dirty and torn apron she had managed to find in one of the kitchen's unkempt cupboards.

"Yes master?" She scurried to him.

"I may just have it. Observe my face. See if my physiognomy changes as I ingest this elixir. It is compounded of . . . well, no matter to you. But it is likely to cause my face to change as the internal humors rise. The face, as you know, is the expression of the internal person. A well-trained man such as myself can easily read character from a face. I read yours right away," he added as an aside, and she barely forebore to ask what he had seen there. "No matter," he continued. "Observe my face closely, notably the inner folds of the eyes, the corners of the mouth, and the lines between nose and lips." He drained the little ceramic vial and remained sitting on his woven mat while she observed his face closely.

At first there was no sign of change. Then gradually a

deep rich blush began to suffuse his skin. He began breathing heavily and a pulse jumped into prominence in his neck. He closed his eyes as if to savor the feeling. The heavy breathing passed after a minute or two but the flush remained. The doctor's hands rose as claws into the air and his eyes snapped open, but he obviously was not seeing anything. Foam came to his lips. The strong tremors and the rigidity of his neck passed gradually and his claw-hands fell to his lap where they groped at his crotch as if possessed. Suddenly his features relaxed. His eyes glittered darkly and he eyed Momoe with parted lips. She wanted to move, to escape, but was mesmerized by his expression. His hands leaped forward like those of an eagle and he dragged her to him, pulling apart the lapels of her kimono and exposing her breasts. She had the merest fraction of time to notice the enormous erection that bulged his loose trousers, and then she was held to him with a grip of steel. One of his hands was between her legs, the other prying at the ties of his own pantaloons which he tore impatiently. His cock sprang out. It was fiery red, engorged with blood and nobbled now with thick blueish veins that had not existed there before. He threw her on the hard floor and mounted between her thighs. His hands crooked brutally into her hips and he was muttering incoherently. She tried to match the speed of his movements, tried to extract some pleasure out of his mouthings and powerful thrusts, but long before her own pleasure arrived she felt her insides flooded with his sperm.

Still lying in her, his bony hips oscillating, he muttered into her ear, "I have failed, I have failed again, miserably. This is not the elixir of life. I cannot even avoid discharging such of my own internal juices as I control. Feel us, you are completely flooded with my male essence and my own life-force is diminished accordingly." He pushed away from her with his hands but his demanding cock thrust back at her, rubbing against Momoe's slick and delicious insides.

"But master, you are wonderful. You have created the proper elixir of love which you can sell now truly."

"Bah!" he cried, sunk in his mental anguish as his gonads took over. "I wanted life eternal, not this damnation. Look, it is doing it again!" His hips began jerking at her thighs again and he watched with horror, as his engorged cock, seemingly with a life of its own, thrust deeper and deeper into Momoe's hidden recesses. She fell back gratefully, urging him on and the doctor fell on her again, roughly squeezing her skin, breathing the perfume of her cunt that washed around him, and thrusting, thrusting, thrusting deep into the willing depths of the girl beneath him.

At dawn he managed to stagger away from her. Momoe was grateful. She enjoyed the hammering of his prick at her cunt, but by now it was becoming painful and raw. He dithered in the half-light of dawn and she could see that his cock, which was suffused with purple and red, was still as hard as an iron bar. He staggered in the direction of the water bucket, croaking hoarsely. His hands trembled as he helped himself to some water. Suddenly his face contorted and he reached again for his member, then turned to her. Momoe braced herself, knowing he was about to leap on her again. He staggered and crashed to the floor, breathing convulsively. His eyes opened briefly and he saw her spread legs. His fingers hooked into the boards like claws and he struggled to pull himself forward, staring at the semen-flooded cunt. His face suffused with purple. He gurgled suddenly, then fell forward. His forehead knocked against the floor and he moved no more. Without pause Momoe leaped to her feet. She knew he was dead. She dressed hurriedly and ran out of the house into the pale sunshine beyond. Not looking back, afraid of seeing his emaciated face crawling after her, she set off to leave the city. She paused towards midday at a teahouse on the western outskirts of Miyako.

The area bordered one of the highways that led from the Inland Sea provinces to Miyako. Several tea houses faced a canal. Outside each establishment stood maids trying to entice travellers in. Some made extravagant promises to potential guests, extolling the quality of the lodgings, the food, or the compliant disposition of the establishment's maids. Some simply attached themselves bodily to customers that caught their eye, leading them almost willy-nilly into the inn or tea house.

Momoe sat for a while observing the waters of the canal and pondering her future. She was no better than any prostitute now, she decided. She had slept with many men, and was far from the virginal maid of several days ago. This was where she belonged, where anonymous men could enjoy her body and she could expiate her own sin. She turned into the tea house to apply for work as one of the maids.

CHAPTER 17

THE SOUTHERN ENTRANCES TO THE GRAND CITY OF MIYAKO were always busy. People seeing others off, caravans of porters getting organized or arriving. Merchants on their way to Osaka and Sakai. All of these steered well clear of the ragged samurai with the wicked look in his eyes. Sugiyama spotted a tea house. Red felt covered the benches outside, and a young tea-girl called out enticingly to potential customers. But the felt was ragged and the tea-girl, though pretty, was awkward and badly trained.

Sugiyama sat himself down on one of the benches, his long *katana* between his knees, and gruffly ordered tea and pounded rice cakes. She scurried off to obey and Sugiyama casually observed the traffic passing before him between the tea house and the narrow canal that ran from the river.

He sipped his tea, and Momoe, after ensuring that his cup was full, contemplated him for awhile. He was handsome, not as handsome as others she had had, but definitely pleasing except for the cruel sneering expression he wore so haughtily. While she mechanically tried to entice customers into the tea house, her mind wrestled glumly with her perennial problem: Now what? She knew she could not return home, the shame was too deep. And life as a tea-maid was no better than any other of the positions she had tried. Truly, a woman's lot was hard. She stared sadly at the ground before her until, suddenly remembering her duties, she raised her head guiltily to see if any other potential customers were approaching. The samurai was still sipping at his tea and there was a momentary lull in the traffic on the road. From the south a train of merchants was approaching: from the direction of Miyako a few travellers, one of whom was a tall, broad shouldered samurai. She watched the large samurai's advance with some puzzlement. He seemed unable to make up his mind, stopping now and then at one of the inns and tea houses lining the highway. When he got closer, the reason for his hesitation became obvious. He was questioning people along the route. Momoe's heart sank: Perhaps he was after her? To question her about the doctor's death? For some unknown sin? But then she noted his unshaven pate: A *ronin* then. Masterless, and obviously not an official.

Forty feet from the tea house he noted Sugiyama still impassively sipping his tea. A strange light came into his eyes. Momoe cowered back into the shade of the entrance. Sugiyama stared back at the giant *ronin* with no discernible expression. Jiro slid forward, coiled tension in every step. Sugiyama rose slowly to his feet as the giant stopped ten feet from his seat and bowed slightly.

"You are perhaps Sugiyama Tamasaburo?" Jiro asked politely.

"So?" responded Sugiyama.

"This is yours then?" Jiro extracted the small lacquered medicine box from the bosom of his robe and showed it on his palm.

"It is. I lost it."

"No. It was taken from you. By a friend. She asked me to deal with you."

Sugiyama did not answer. His hands slid to the hilt and sheath of his sword and the blade was extracted smoothly. Jiro followed suit.

They faced one another cautiously, eyes wide-focused. Both held their sword loosely in front of them, jutting out at an angle like two great curved steel cocks. Jiro shifted his balance a bit and the other carefully adjusted his stance.

Jiro stepped forward and to his right, bringing a bright arc of steel down at Sugiyama's left hip. Sugiyama twisted back and then forward, avoiding Jiro's blow and striking for his neck. Jiro's blade came up to vertical guard and both blades shrieked against one another, sparking. The two samurai separated again. Onlookers kept their distance, but continued watching with great curiosity.

The two contestants eyed one another more carefully now. Sugiyama noted his opponent's massive build and huge workman's hands. Jiro overtopped him by more than a head, and was broad to match.

Jiro examined the slimmer man cautiously. He had fine regular features but his thin lips betrayed a vicious sensuality. For perhaps the second time in his life, Jiro felt he was equalled. He did not dare think he was outmatched. He thrust his hips, both hands on hilt towards the other's stomach, then twisted to one side for a reverse *kesa giri* cut: from hip to opposite shoulder. Sugiyama avoided the attack and attacked in turn with a flurry of forward and side cuts that forced Jiro, step after step, to retreat. His feet stood suddenly at the paved edge of the canal. Sugiyama cut at his stomach with an unavoidable blow that would have cut him in half. The training Okiku had put him through came to his aid. He squatted for a roll. Instinct made him roll backwards where training and reflex would have him roll forward into his opponent's knees. Where he would have arrived a thin *kozuka* throwing knife, drawn from the notch in Sugiyama's scabbard, sprouted from the ground. Jiro himself was not there. He had disappeared from the face of the earth, and for one panicked moment Sugiyama almost spun around expecting Jiro to drop in magically from heaven. Then his mind processed his eye's images and he laughed, peering down into the canal where a splash marked the giant's whereabouts.

Sugiyama watched the giant being swept downstream, and he laughed loudly and unpleasantly. The onlookers hurriedly scuttled away. Sugiyama turned back to his tea, amazed that one of his victims had actually made it away alive. Unless he drowned of course. His heart was pounding in his chest with pleasure again, as usual. His eye fell on Momoe cowering in the corner. As was always the case with him, violence fanned his lustful nature. He took two quick steps and was up on the platform standing over her. He grasped her lapel and pulled her to her feet. Shaking her slightly he said, "A room?"

She motioned helplessly, and in her confusion, indicated her own sleeping corner in a small hut behind the building rather than one of the public rooms. Sugiyama hastily dragged her in the indicated direction. She tried to scream, to call on the help of the inn owner or the servants, but there was no answer. None of them were foolish enough to interfere in the murderous samurai's activities.

Sugiyama slammed shut the torn *shoji* of the outhouse

and dropped Momoe unceremoniously onto the floor. He loosened his clothes in two rapid movements. She trembled, tried to resist, and was slapped soundly for her efforts. Soon his long erect prick was threatening her face. Automatically she opened her lips and sucked the staff in. Sugiyama's fingers tangled in her hair and he pulled her face to him. Notwithstanding her willingness, Momoe began to choke. The samurai pulled out of her and stripped slowly. There was a glazed look on his face that she did not care for. He pulled open her robe and examined her breasts, tweaking the pink nipples roughly. Then he sank to a seat on her bedding which she had hurriedly pulled out of the small chest on the floor.

"Strip for me girl," he said.

She swallowed convulsively and hurried to obey. Her striped robe slipped to the floor. He held up a hand and she removed her fingers from the ties of her red underskirt. His hands suddenly slashed out in a blur of motion and he slapped both her breasts. She squealed in terror and tried to escape but the look in his eyes rooted her to the spot.

He enjoyed the sight of her. Two red blotches appeared on the outer sides of her breasts. She was quaking with fear, her hands trembling. Her body was slim, hips broad. The eyes were screwed shut, then opened wide in panic.

"Your skirt," Sugiyama said conversationally.

She untied the garment with trembling fingers and the length of cloth fell to the floor. He looked at her mound, topped by fluffy black hair, then ordered her to turn around. She did so with alacrity, fear in every line of her body. His hands parted her buttocks leisurely and he enjoyed the sight of the tiny beard visible between her thighs. She flinched at his touch and immediately felt the slap on her buttocks. She knew better than to run.

He turned her to face him. She was still trembling. He lay back on the futon. "You like using your mouth, is that it? You will use it on me," he commanded. "Lick me."

She fell to her knees and did as he told her. Her generous mouth encompassed his member and sucked it in to the root. He pulled her ass towards him and examined it leisurely. The delicate pink inner lips were shadowed by soft hair. He parted them and examined the tiny hole and the little clitoral nubbin at its bottom. An urge to taste it possessed him and he forced her to straddle his mouth, applying his lips and fingers to her hole. Momoe started to move on the samurai's face and he immediately slapped her to immobility.

"Attend to your business," he said.

She continued lapping his thin long cock with her broad mobile tongue. Soon her moisture was dripping down and he shoved her away. Fearfully she waited for his next move. Sugiyama examined his cock. It was in a fine state of erection, shiny and wet. His eyes lit on the crooked old beam that held up the center of the shack.

"Stand up," he commanded.

She obeyed with alacrity. Sugiyama posed her under the beam and made her raise her hands above her head, then tied them there with his sword cord. The silk bit into her wrists. He stepped back to admire his handiwork.

"Pull yourself up," he commanded. He grasped her hips and forced her high, then let her drop. The head of his cock disappeared into her waiting hole and she rested immobile against his form, her feet not touching the floor, her weight supported only by her bound hands and his cock. Sugiyama grinned at the sight and started flexing the muscles of his thighs. Momoe bobbed up and down on him. The pleasure of his cock, deeper in her than anything except the doctor's *harigata*, soon overcame the pain at her wrists. She twisted and moaned, tied to the beam, trying to maintain a precarious hold on his cock with her cunt muscles. He started jerking into her, puffing strongly, his hands at her soft breasts, his mouth biting at her neck. She squealed slightly as she felt the gush of sperm shoot into her canal. He pulled Momoe to his chest, squeezing her bum roughly and muttering obscenities.

When his cock wilted and then plopped from her cunt, she felt a stream of his liquids run down her legs. He untied her with a jerk on the cord and she fell, muscles turning to water, onto the old futon the innkeeper had supplied her with. Sugiyama turned indifferently to dress, then noted that dark was covering the sky. He shrugged and looked at her again.

"What's your name?"

"Momoe, sir," she said.

"I'll stay here the night," he said. She bowed, shivering with fear. "Bring some food," he ordered.

Momoe scurried to obey, and the innkeeper laded a tray with a pot of rice, some pickles, a piece of grilled salted fish and a bowl of soup. Sugiyama ate it all unquestioningly, then stripped Momoe once again. She knelt, quivering, on the futon.

"Clean me," he ordered.

She hurriedly leaned forward to comply, licking the drying remains of their mixed juices from his cock and balls. The male cudgel soon came to life, rearing its head, which menaced her like a snake from the stories her grandmother had told her. Sugiyama seized her breasts and squeezed them painfully. She knew better than to protest and he grunted with satisfaction. He brought them together. Momoe's breasts were erect round mounds, and she liked squeezing the pink nipples. But they were by no means large. By forcing them together he managed to make a soft cushion for his erect cock. He started rubbing his cock at them furiously. Momoe rocked back and forth with the power of his movements. His thrust became violent, spasmodic, and suddenly she felt the fluids spurt against her chin and trickle their way down her chest. He released her and she sank gratefully onto the futon. Sugiyama lay himself down beside her. He grinned at her in the dark as she wiped his sticky sperm from between her breasts, then squeezed her breasts again. She wondered for the thousandth time what would become of her. Seeing her abstracted expression Sugiyama grew thoughtful in his turn. He rose suddenly and found the long scarf that she tied underneath her *obi*. Turning on her, he bore her to the ground. She protested meekly, trying not to arouse his ire, hoping that whatever he did with her body would be over soon. True, when he entered her, she felt her own lust rising, but he was inconsiderate and seemed to take pleasure in her pain rather than in her body.

Sugiyama roped her hands together behind her back, then tied her wrists to her heels. She was now bent backwards like a bow, and he dipped his head at her cunt. It was prominently displayed because of the posture she had been tied in. His tongue whipped in and out of her cunt, driving her to a frenzy of lust she could not fully satisfy. Her desire grew stronger, fanned by the unremitting tongue. She moaned deep in her throat. This violent lingual rape was not something she had experienced before. She longed to grasp his head, to pull at his body, guiding him to the spots he missed in his labors.

An uncontrollable howl burst out of her as her body searched for release. She writhed in her bonds, thrusting her pubis as hard as she could against the stiff tongue. Sweat and female juices poured down her legs in equal proportions and she collapsed unhappily against the futon. He bore her back, her torso arched and his long thin cock plunged into her worn and tired pussy. She closed her eyes as he hammered unmercifully at her cunt, slipping in and out of her helpless body. At last she felt him stiffen, his hands clawing at her ass, and he collapsed by her side.

"Untie me please, Mr. Samurai. This is terribly uncomfortable . . ." she whispered timidly.

"You'll stay that way. I do not want to be awoken during the night to attend to you, and in any case," he grinned suddenly in the dark, "I enjoy it this way. I'll have you during the night as you are."

They slept. Momoe, exhausted by the day, was barely conscious as Sugiyama, true to his word, woke her several times during the night by stabbing his prick into her unprotected cunt. In the morning he was gone, with only the marks of the scarves on her wrists and ankles to remind her of the ordeal.

CHAPTER 18

ROSAMUND LAY BACK ON THE BARE TATAMI AND PARTED her legs. She piled some flat *zabuton* seating pads under her head to raise her face. Matsudaira ignored her, engrossed in his reports. She pulled open her robes, but even the slithering sound of her stiff silk *obi* sash failed to rouse him. She sent her hands down the length of her belly and stroked her golden bush.

"Goemon," she called softly.

The subliminal signal caused him to raise his eyes unwillingly. He caught sight of a pink slit being opened by long delicate fingers. A bright red tattooed rose glowed on the perfect white skin. Its stem was rooted deeply into the pink cunt hole that was now being opened for his gaze by her questing fingers. One of the tapering long digits insinuated itself into the slit, stroking the long inner lips, then twiddling the extraordinarily long clitoris that arched out to meet the finger. Rosamund smiled at him over the pink-tipped mounds of her breasts.

He tried to return to his reports, but the sight held him mesmerized. Rosamund wet her middle finger slowly, turning it about in her mouth. She examined it for a moment, then, left-hand fingers holding open the rose pot, inserted her finger delicately into the depths. She moved the finger about while her hips began to squirm on the silk futon. A pearly sheen emerged on the inner recesses of the pink cunt. She jerked her hips violently, and when Goemon looked away, moaned loudly to accompany the motions. To Goemon it sounded like the purring of a large cat. Her left fingers parted and Rosamund's exceptionally long clitoris, curved like a claw, emerged and was stroked carefully by her wet fingers.

She turned on her side and raised her thigh. Her hand

went around her buttocks and exposed the entire juncture of her thighs to Goemon's gaze. He gritted his teeth and returned to reading his report. Rosamund stroked the entire length of her slash, from the top of the golden bush to her tiny pink anal entrance. Her fingers, first one, then two, then a third, dipped deeply into the waiting hole. Goemon's breathing quickened and his perusal of his papers became more perfunctory.

Rosamund rolled onto her stomach. She reached back with both hands, parting the full, pale half moons and exposing herself fully to his gaze from another angle. "Goemon," she called in a low voice, "come and fuck me. Beat me lover, come on. Here it is."

The sight and the sound acted on Goemon like the smell of a bitch on a male dog. His breathing quickened and he rose from his seat, unconscious of his duty or anything else. Rosamund smiled into her pillow. She was tired of being ignored just because her man had to work, and her power over him proved to be greater than the power of duty.

Not watching where he went, his shin smashed against the low table he was working on. The pain, and particularly the sight of the documents falling to the mat brought him back to his responsibilities.

"I am busy," he said angrily. "There was a robbery of a sake merchant," he tried to explain. "Three men forced their way in and stole his cashbox. They were armed. Now we have to look for them as well. I have two murders, one of which has no motive and the other too many and no murder weapon. What is the world coming to? . . ." He turned back to his desk and its reports.

"You're always too busy for me," she hissed, her face contorted in anger. "You cockless bastard, I should take on one of the serving lads." She picked up a hard rice-bran filled pillow and threw it at his face. He leaped to his feet, the pillow passing unharmed by his face. Taking one angry step towards her, he collided again with the corner of the desk, sending the papers flying. The pain spread a red sheet before his eyes.

"Stop that you . . . you . . ." Loosing control, his hand lashed out and he struck her face. She yelled and clawed out at him. At first Goemon fell back, so unexpected was her attack. Then enraged by her curses and flashing hands he struck at her once, then again. She fought back and he hit her violently, his hands connecting again and again with her shoulders then with her large soft breasts. He rolled onto her, forcing her body down while he pummelled at the soft flesh that struggled under him. She tried to bite at his restraining arm and the sudden sharp pain of her teeth made him lose his reason completely. He forced her down on her back, his hands punching mercilessly into her soft parts again and again. She started to cry in pain and he ground his body violently against her, discovering as he did so that his cock was in violent erection. He threw off his loincloth and parted her legs urgently. She fought him, drawing blood from rips in his skin. His cock found her opening and he forced himself inside her. She responded with a triumphant cry, pushing her hips up against him. He rode her while slapping intermittently at her full breasts. They turned a flushed pink and the nipples came erect as if thirsting for more or clawing at his skin.

Rosamund started climaxing long before Goemon. Her heels locked against the small of his back and she scratched violently at his chest. Her lips fastened there as well and drew bloody marks as she alternatively kissed and bit him. The sharp pain of her resistance drove Goemon to a raging frenzy. His cock hammered into her and he tried to fend off her attacks and force himself on her. He knew that at that point nothing would stop him except his death or orgasm. He changed his tactics, pulling violently at her ass, he pulled the buns apart, causing her to shriek loudly as he buried two fingers in the resisting warm ring of her ass. At the same time he lowered his head to hers. Partly to defend himself, partly because he was impelled to do so, he forced her mouth open, then drove his tongue forward, raping her mouth. She fought the lingual member with her own, while at the same time sucking it in greedily. Bucking against him she felt her insides explode time after time. Gobs of her own juices inundated their joined pubic mounds and ran down between her buttocks to wet the torn entrance to her anus.

Goemon exploded violently too. His cock was searching out her inner recesses and he felt the spurts of semen whipping into her like gunshots. Feeling him climaxing Rosamund clenched her powerful well-trained cunt muscles. The sudden constriction hurt Goemon's cock as he was coming, and he forced another fraction of his fleshy man-root into her, mouthing her tongue and tearing at her ass as he did so.

The two figures lay as if dead. Finally the darker one rolled off and collapsed on the mat, staring dully into space. She laid her golden head on his muscled chest and softly kissed the marks of her teeth and nails. Some were slowly oozing blood. She smiled happily. He looked fondly at the golden mass of hair on his chest, stroking it lightly. There was work to be done, but not just now.

† † †

Okiku thought long and hard about the best way to go about finding the kidnappers. Obviously, what she needed was some bait. Then again, she had to find out where the kidnappers were working. Knowing her temperament, Jiro had made her swear she would not attack the men alone. She was pleased with his concern, yet annoyed at the implication of protectiveness. The big lump was more in need of protection than she had ever been.

She dressed with care. Light mesh armour went on under dark pantaloons and sark. Over these she wore a kimono slightly thicker than necessary for the warm weather. She checked her bag of tricks and regretfully left her sword-staff behind. It would not fit the role she had to play.

At dusk a slightly inebriated young widow was complaining loudly that she was lonely and alone in drinking places around the Kitano shrine: the site of several earlier reported disappearances of young women. Several men took the hint, but she brushed them off, and on one occasion had to run off into the dark to avoid a too-persistent suitor.

At last, after innumerable cups of bad sake, most of which ended covertly on the floor, she struck lucky. A heavy-set man in simple workman's clothing had been watching her in one of the drinking stalls as she loudly related her imaginary troubles. He was present at the next bar she came to. This time he was not alone.

She left into the dark, weaving slightly. The two followed. Fewer people were moving about and Okiku dipped into an alley. It was a matter of a second to drop her bright colored kimono. She stuffed it regretfully under a house, then leaped lightly, dressed all in black, onto the house's low roof. Two figures came around the corner.

"Where is she?" the slim one whispered.

"Stupid, she got away from us." The other voice came from a burlier man who moved with the lightness of a professional thief. They sped to the far end of the alley. Okiku dropped to the alleyway behind them and followed. The three of them skulked about the neighborhood for some minutes. At length the two potential kidnappers gave up.

"Lets get out of here. We'll try again tomorrow. The boss will be angry though."

The men split up and Okiku followed the bulkier leader. They ended up in a small well-kept house among a welter of similar ones in an artisan neighborhood. Okiku climbed lightly to the roof of a neighboring house. The grey tiles felt familiar beneath her feet. She inched along until she could see inside the compound. There did not appear to be any place to securely hold a prisoner: The house was built as simply as all the rest. She leaped the wall and began prowling around.

A maidservant tripped out of the *genkan*, then turned to say good night to her mistress. It appeared that the slaver lived an exemplary home life. Okiku grinned. Not unlike herself and Jiro.

She waited for the house to settle down then dropped to the ground, silent as a butterfly alighting on a flower. With a quick twist of a small tool extracted from her pouch, she lifted one of the external door-shutters that ran around the house and slipped inside. She felt carefully for nightingale floors, ankle-breaker holes and other traps. Listening quietly she could hear the owner and his wife, both snoring in different keys.

Okiku prowled through the tiny house, not finding anything that could in any way be termed suspicious. She wondered if perhaps she was mistaken. She paused before the room in which the owner and his wife were sleeping and slipped inside. Just then the man's snoring stopped. She crouched quickly so as not to be outlined against the white paper of the *shoji*. The man's breathing indicated he was awake. He stretched and one of his hands touched Okiku's sleeve in the dark. He was still sleepy and his reflexes slow, but he would soon become conscious of the fact that there was an object where none should be. For a brief second Okiku wondered whether she should kill him. Then a better solution occurred to her. She crawled rapidly to his side, flipped up the light quilt and burrowed her head inside. She found his crotch without any difficulty. The man's hands found her head and he guided her to his unfurling cock.

Okiku laved it with her tongue and the member began to swell.

He started pulling her towards him, intending a sixty-nine position. She resisted, knowing he would find her armour. Then the idea began titillating her. She shrugged rapidly out of her pantaloons and rolled the light flexible armour high up her waist.

The kidnapper nuzzled at her wet sweaty cunt. Apparently he was so sleepy, or so unused to his wife's smell that he could detect no difference. Okiku, crouched fearfully on his face, began enjoying the situation. He was inexperienced but lustful and his tongue stroked the entire length of her pussy. He caught her hairs in his teeth and pulled on them, then sought out the tiny button of her clitoris. His thick mobile lips sucked at the fleshy pearl and Okiku had to struggle to control the sounds of her delight. Instead she applied herself vigorously to the head of his cock. He had a pleasant member, she decided. Not too thick or large, yet substantial enough to give her mouth pleasure. She lavished her best caresses on it, licking delicately below the head, then sucking in the shaft as far as it went. With her left hand she stroked the length of the knobby shaft and delicately lifted the hair sack that contained his soft jewels. He slobbered at her cunt, grasping her slim ass and pulling it to his mouth. She sucked in the entire length of the shaft and worked her throat expertly. He jerked quickly and moaned into her cunt, sending her into a paroxysm of lust. She ground her hips into his face as his come spurted luxuriously down her throat in ever diminishing loads.

The man settled back onto his hard cushion and Okiku rolled rapidly off him, hoping he was not the kind to talk in bed. He rolled over contentedly and Okiku crept soundlessly around the sleeping figure of the wife in the neighboring futon. The burly kidnapper rolled over again and fondly patted his wife, thanking her for the pleasure she had given him all unknowing. Okiku thankfully resheathed her dagger. Had he raised an alarm, he would have had to change his tone in the middle of it. The knife at the root of his manhood had added spice to her enjoyment of him. She chuckled to herself as she moved silently out of the room and into the night.

CHAPTER 19

MATSUDAIRA KONNOSUKE HAD BEEN RESTLESS THE ENTIRE night. He had just decided that sleep was no answer, was about to reach for his senior concubine whose blonde figure slept beside him, when he heard his guard call at the entrance to his private chambers.

"Lord, excuse me."

Matsudaira slipped out of the bedding. Rosamund protested feebly as he walked quietly out, holding his short sword. He crouched several feet away from the entry. He could hear no indication of trouble.

"What is it?"

"Permit me?" the guard replied. "There is a message from Mr. Muto."

Matsudaira opened the door. The messenger, a young samurai from the police office, bowed to the floor then rose to a one-knee crouch. Matsudaira recognized him as one of the samurai constables . . .

"What is it Yanagisawa?"

"Lord, Muto-sama has instructed me to tell you that there has been another robbery. This time at a silk merchant's. He says there are some serious aspects. His men are chasing the culprits who were seen."

Matsudaira nodded. "Get me a horse. It will be quicker than a palanquin." He turned and rushed back into his private quarters.

Rosamund, blonde hair dishevelled and one full pink-tipped breast exposed, sat up in the bed.

"What is it?" she asked.

"Another robbery," he said, throwing on a day kimono. Over it he tied a pair of loose flowing trousers— hakama—that were the privilege of samurai alone. A black *haori* coat with his crest of three pine needles went on top.

She pouted. "Again? You don't have any time for me now!"

He was in no mood to quarrel, and lacked the time to soothe her properly. "I'm sorry. There are too many things to handle. I will see you in the morning." He hurried out of the room, peering regretfully over his shoulder. He knew the look she wore on her face: It meant a great deal of painful pleasure for him in the future.

The silk merchant's warehouse was lit by the lampions of the magistrates office. Muto detached himself from a small group of assistants and rushed over as Matsudaira dismounted. His runners and guards puffed around him as the ride had been a long one.

"Well?" Matsudaira demanded.

"Same gang," Muto said. There was something in his voice that made Matsudaira signal him aside.

"Lord, it was young Uemura." Muto's bulky face was blank.

"And?"

"I thought, since we know who it is that is heading these robberies, that we should perhaps wait with the arrest . . . You may have some other use for him."

Matsudaira grinned boyishly. "We might, you know. We just might. A second pipeline into the Ito household might prove to be useful . . ."

Muto started at the "second." The young master certainly was shaping up. He had had no idea the young magistrate had been able to move so swiftly.

"What shall I do then?" he asked, a shade more deferentially.

"Nothing for the meantime. I'm after much bigger fish."

"It would be embarrassing to have him arrested," Muto prompted. "His father is a senior member of the fief council in Kanazawa."

"What about his associates? Any knowledge of them?"

"He has been going about with a group that is writing some new form of poetry to replace the traditional *waka* verse. But they are all commoners, or men of no antecedents. Some of them *may* be involved. In any case, we could arrest them without any problem."

"Don't do it yet. Have them observed and be ready to

arrest them if I decide to arrest . . . or rather if he has an accident of any sort.''

Muto's respect for his superior grew another notch. He had an idea what form the accident would take. The large samurai who lived in the direction of Gion visited the magistrate frequently. He taught fencing, among other things, and he seemed very close mouthed about his affairs. Well well well. The youngster was of the same mettle as his father. Muto remembered a couple of incidents from their shared youth. . . . "It will be done, Lord," he said formally.

Matsudaira nodded an acknowledgement. "Let me see the scene of the crime. We cannot afford to be captives of our own preconceptions. Who saw Uemura?" They moved away, deep in discussion. Across the town an angry Rosamund was pounding her fists against her pillow. Suddenly an idea occurred to her. She smiled brilliantly and stroked her cheek thoughtfully, then went in search of a certain chest.

In the early hours of morning a nun, her head wrapped in a purple hood and covered by a broad hat, scuttled out of a small side door in the magistrate's mansion. She kept her face down and her hands hidden. But on her black-clad shoulder a single strand of golden hair lay forgotten, fallen from a head that should have been shaven bald.

† † †

In the city's northern quarter Haruko reached out a slim hand. "Come here," she said. "You're late. Where have you been, eh? Running around with your prissy friends writing new-fangled poetry?"

Uemura bent and bit her palm, then slid a hand over her naked body. "Do you really think I should be here? Much more enjoyable, of course, but won't people be a little bit suspicious?"

She laughed. "Why should you not be here? We have explained your presence. You are a bona fide student of my husband's. What could be more proper than that you console the widow?"

He grinned. "This way?"

She pushed his head between her spread legs. "Of course."

"I want more money," he said, his voice muffled by her hairy mound.

"Sometimes I think you like me only because I help support you."

"No. I now have . . . sources of my own. What I get from you is only a token of your appreciation."

She drove four nails into his ass. Beads of blood appeared.

"Would you like to have my new maid?" Haruko asked.

"One of the most delightful things about you is that you are entirely unjealous." He grinned. "Of course I'd like to have her again. That soft hair of hers . . ."

"Don't get too fond of her!" Haruko warned.

"Or else?"

"Yes, or else, you could end up like . . ."

He rolled onto her and shut her mouth savagely with his own. She resisted fiercely. "I am not one of your maidservants. You may not take me like that! You do as I say."

He retreated from her fury, but not so far as to relinquish control of her conical breast. "You *owe* me!" he said, bringing his face to hers.

"How is that?" she asked, still angered, but puzzled.

"Ha! As if you don't know. If I hadn't come by . . ."

"What do you mean?" she asked, suddenly alarmed. "What did you see?"

He grinned evilly. "I saw enough. And acted too. And if I act any more . . . well, the *eta* untouchables have a hard hand with women prisoners. And I have a hard hand for you." He squeezed her breast suddenly, and though she winced, she did not pull away. He pushed her onto her back and straddled her chest. He pulled her breasts together and rubbed his erect cock between them, then shoved his meat forward to her lips.

"Suck me!" he commanded. As if still surprised at his sudden tone of command, she obeyed. Unlike other times he did not deign to reciprocate. Then her domination had been absolute, now she was doubtful, and with lack of certainty came a greater balance between them. As she sucked and nibbled expertly at his erect cock she wondered what he knew.

The cock quivered in her grasp. She wanted to withdraw. Haruko did not like having a man's come spurting into her mouth. She tolerated it when her husband had demanded it, but had managed to turn his interest elsewhere. So far she had never sucked Uemura to a climax. This time he seemed determined to force her to it. He held her elaborately coiffured head down to his crotch. His excitement became obvious. The tip produced a fluid that presaged what was to come. She tried to withdraw but Uemura held her down forcefully, and without creating a scene, there was no retreat. His cock jerked again, and she waited passively for it to erupt.

"Suck it, suck it you bitch, you darling, you woman, suck it!" he half-commanded, half-begged. She hollowed her lips reluctantly and a spurt of sperm filled her mouth, quick on its footsteps came another while he ground his hips against her face. She tried not to swallow, tried to spit the juices out but they flooded her mouth. Some dribbling back along the shaft, some penetrating her throat. At last it was over and Uemura relaxed. His prick lost its tenseness, becoming semi-soft though still engorged.

Haruko pulled away from her lover and spat the residue into a convenient sheet of tissue paper. She glared at him and he laughed.

"You were much less reluctant to have me come in your maid's mouth, weren't you?" he mocked her.

Her thin lips firmed and a glint came into her eye.

CHAPTER 20

H<small>IS EYES WIDE WITH WONDER</small>, I<small>SEI WANDERED THROUGH</small> the imperial capital of Miyako. He had never seen such splendid buildings in his life. The wall of the palace with its armed guards frightened him, and the crush of people in the streets and markets was oppressive. The nun walked behind him, volunteering nothing, keeping to her prayers. As the sun stood overhead at midday, he found himself standing before a long imposing temple. He eyed it suspiciously, then decided to examine the rear, just in case. He had been receiving odd looks throughout the day, but in the cosmopolitan atmosphere of the large city no one was actually ready to challenge his right to be where he was.

They circled the building to the back. A crowd had gathered at one end of the long open gallery that ran the length of the building in the rear. Isei peered at the other end, then heard a thrum and a "thwok" sound. An arrow sprouted just above the black-centered parallelogram that hung at the end. Using elbows and bulk, Isei shouldered his way to the front of the crowd. Men gave way to the wild, gun-carrying mountaineer.

Kneeling on the platform was a stocky man with tremendous shoulders and overgrown arms. His left shoulder was bare and held a seven-foot red lacquered bow. He let loose another arrow, then bent the bow again using an arrow held out by one of several assistants passing him the arrows. A man beside Isei looked at the sun and muttered, "Some time yet, until midday."

Isei looked at the target. The length of the gallery was about three hundred and fifty feet and was lined by pillars and roof beams receding in a straight row. An easy shot, he decided, at least for a gunner. For an archer though, . . . a very fair shot indeed. The low roof beams required a very flat trajectory which meant a bow with tremendous pull. He looked at the archer with greater respect. The pillars, roof beams, and the blackboard were well quilled with arrows. The target itself was obscured by arrows, looking somewhat like a strange flower.

Finally a gong sounded and the archer paused in his monotonous occupation of shooting one arrow after another. He rose smoothly to his feet, bowed to the target, then to the audience. Two official looking men began counting the arrows lodged in the woodwork. The archer looked on impassively.

"Five thousand and eleven! One thousand two hundred and eighty six!" the official declared.

"What is that?" Isei demanded of a man near him.

The man nodded and grinned at the ignorance of the country bumpkin. "Arrows shot. And arrows reaching the target. They changed it every once in a while. What an archer. What stamina! He has been at it since dawn!"

Isei could not resist the jibe and he sniffed audibly. "At this distance, anyone could hit a target."

The archer heard the comment through the commotion. His head turned slowly, his eyes panning the crowd deliberately until he focused on Isei's form. Their eyes locked. Isei examined the archer. He looked to be shorter than the mountain man, but his shoulders were easily half again as wide. His hair was shorn and he ran a hand through the rough greying stubble. He was about to remove his archer's glove, but paused.

"You can do better?" he asked softly, but in a voice that carried.

"More accurately. At a greater distance. Yes. With this." Isei raised the silk-covered bundle of his musket.

The archer's face tightened. "Show me!" he commanded.

"It would not be a fair contest," Isei retorted. "You are undoubtedly tired." He felt uneasy about the public display, but something prideful was rising in his bosom. He drew an odd comfort from the presence of the nun behind him.

"Show me nonetheless, that you are a worthy challenge?"

Isei grinned and nodded. He slipped the gun from its cover in one smooth motion and his flint rasped once.

"I would have pierced you with an arrow by now," the archer commented.

"In other circumstances, I carry the match lit," Isei retorted.

The archer hopped down from the platform, still carrying his bow while the officials removed the arrows. Isei turned, looking for a target. "The pine tree. Over there. See, it sways in the wind. But there is a topmost twig, sprouting above the mass of foliage." He raised his matchlock.

The archer stared unblinking at the top of the tree which swayed in the light wind. The crowd, which had been about to disperse, stopped in its collective tracks. The tree was easily five hundred feet away.

Isei squeezed the trigger lever gently and the match reached the touchhole. He swayed backwards with the recoil, then forwards again. The smoke obscured his vision as he moved to reload, but he heard the long, drawn-out "Ahhh" of the crowd and knew he had reached his mark. The archer's thin smile showed him more clearly the same thing. A young boy raced off to retrieve the pine branch.

"I am Wasa Senri," the archer said. "Come and visit me. Towards evening."

Isei bowed. Overwhelmed suddenly, he asked shyly, "Where does the master live?"

"Right here, on the grounds of Rengeoin temple. That pine tree was mine." He smiled again.

Towards evening Isei proceeded to the house. Lanterns were being lit and their warm glow lightened Isei's gloom. The houses, and no less their inhabitants, scared him. The nun had insisted he have a bath, but the bathing in an artificial bath with crowds of people had not been pleasurable.

They entered the small gateway together and were ushered into the guest room of the house by Wasa himself.

"I apologize," he said. "I live by myself."

The two men discussed the pursuit of their expertise. The nun served them patiently, otherwise sitting meekly by Isei's side, saying nothing. Wasa proved to be a jovial man with a broad knowledge, theoretical and practical, of all sorts of airborne missiles, from firearms through arrows, blowgun darts and throwing knives. Under his friendly professional interest the normally inarticulate Isei seemed to bloom. In his own ignorant way he had thought much about his abilities, and had even made improvements on his firearm.

Wasa examined the notched rear-sight block admiringly. Sighting through it he caught the nun's eye.

"You must be bored by the talk of experts," he said joking and held out his sake cup.

"I too am an expert," said the nun calmly.

"Indeed," said Wasa, somewhat maliciously. "In bead telling?"

"Nothing so simple as that," said the nun. "We of the Tantara school practice the *prana* of female and male."

Wasa looked at her speculatively. "I have heard of those practices. I have heard too, that they are esoteric. And banned."

"True," she nodded. "But that is neither here nor there. The government is always banning this or that, usually for the wrong reasons."

"And you are Mr. Isei's companion?"

"He is my disciple on the Middle Path." Isei stared at her in surprise. "Though he does not know it yet."

Wasa laughed. "A hidden master. In what art specifically?" "The cloud and rain art. The art of the body. The art of man and woman."

He laughed again, emptied his cup, filled it and passed it to her. "The art of short range fighting. Like a swordsman, you must come in close."

She smiled back. "We are striving to improve ourselves. In future ages, the art of rain and cloud will encompass all others as a way to *satori*. Come, let me show you."

She rose while the two men held incredulously silent and dropped her robes. Her body was smooth and slim and completely bare. She had taken the opportunity to shave her armpits and crotch. Her belly descended smoothly towards the full lips of her pussy, their outer surfaces slightly blueish from her shave. She stood with her feet together, and they could see a triangle of light between the lips and both sides. Her breasts were full, sagging slightly, the nipples still flaccid, brown nubbins set off center in lighter brown aureoles. She stood silently, unmoving.

"I will show you what is meant by the *tantara*," she said. "Observe my lotus." Raising one foot, she rested it on her thigh between crotch and knee. The two men could see the full outer lips, their inner surfaces slightly obscured by the thinner delicate inner labiae. She started to move the muscles of her lower torso. Her belly rippled and the ripples grew larger. Moisture appeared on the inner lips. She speeded up the movements of her hips and belly and was soon trembling on her one leg like a leaf in a breeze. Her hips jerked spasmodically.

In a perfectly controlled voice she said, "Examine me closely, please."

Both men crept closer in fascination and peered at her naked cunt. Tiny pearls of moisture shuddered between the pink lips.

"Examine closely now," she said. They could hear the faintest hint of strain in her voice. "Insert your fingers."

They both inserted a forefinger into her cunt. The hungry mouth clutched at the intruding digits and they felt the massive ripples of her self-induced orgasm squeezing their fingers wetly.

"You see," she said, lowering her leg. "The start of every art, as you gentlemen know, is control."

She turned to them and helped them strip. Wasa proved to have an enormous prick topped by a broad purplish plum-tip. They fondled her as she undressed them and she encouraged them with quick words. Finally they stood together, the two cocks pressed strongly against her thighs, a mouth on each breast, hands between her buttocks and on her belly, fingers exploring her crack.

The nun knelt gracefully and smoothly frigged both warm shafts. She sucked each of them alternately. Both men shivered convulsively as the warm silky mouth sucked them in. She alternated between the rampant shafts, frigging the one that was not enjoying her lingual caress with her hands.

"Control," she murmured, "Control yourself," as Isei felt the pulsing of an initial orgasm. He concentrated, thought of himself as addressing a target with his matchlock, and the peak he was reaching for receded into the distance. She screwed her eyes up at him and smiled in approval.

The nun observed both rampant glistening cocks with pleasure. Tugging slightly at his manroot, she had Isei lie on his back on the matting. The aristocratic-faced mountain man followed her actions passively, his face devoid of all emotion. She whispered an incantation, or perhaps exhortation, then straddled him. Touching him only with her nipples, she stroked his face and body. The tiny softly-hard tips scored his skin like brands of fire. They rolled over his face, digging electric traces into his nerve ends. The two reverse-mounds dipped lower, circled his chest, touched his arms and descended to his belly. His cock received its share of attention from the double cones, as did his pulsing jewel bag.

She rose to stand before Wasa, who had not moved. She raised one foot again and placed it delicately on Isei's roll of engorged meat. Frigging him gently with her foot she addressed her nipples to Wasa. His chest, then his belly and loins received the same attention as had Isei's. For all his fortitude and experience the archer could barely forebear to seize this enticing woman and hurl her to the ground. The fantasy grew in his mind but he knew that she was impossible to rape. She could accept anything he could do with equanimity, and return her contempt at ineptness that would be more wounding than any arrow. She kissed his lips appreciatively, an educated tongue licking out, touching his, and withdrawing, then she descended to the supine form of the mountain man.

She crouched, gloriously naked, over Isei. Wasa stood beside the two and he stroked his enormous curved penis to its root, then grasped the jewel bag there with delicate hands. Her mouth descended and Isei was amazed to see the full length disappear into her mouth. Her throat muscles moved and Wasa gave a groan of extreme pleasure. Her throat was as silky and as controlled as the rest of her. Her glottal muscles milked his member while incredibly, her tongue laved the base of his shaft and the top of his scrotum. He stood, his arms folded on his chest, barely moving as she demonstrated her skill and dedication.

Below them, Isei watched the archer's long shaft disappear into the nun's mouth. The large bag swung over his face. His own cock was buried to the hilt in her tight cunt. Though her body did not move, her interior muscles were milking his shaft with an energy and skill he had hardly known existed. He wanted to pinch, to stroke, to feel her lovely nakedness. Anticipating such a distraction, she had imprisoned his arms between her knees, and Isei subsided, watching the growing pulsations of the large male scrotum above him.

She ejected Wasa's cock from her mouth as his balls began to pulse, then led him behind her. Isei felt the pressure of the massive cock head against his own. His hands were released and he reached behind her body to find that she was stuffing her slit with both cocks simultaneously. Wasa's thick member entered easily and she looked back encouragingly. When he was fully in her, his balls rubbing against the mountain man's, she commanded him to be still. The two men luxuriated in the sensation of two cocks inserted in the same woman. Slowly the nun began to move, impaling herself deeply on the shafts, then withdrawing. Gradually she sped up her motions, and as she did so, ground her ass against both men. Wasa was unable to contain himself. He leaned his full weight on her and clutched at her breasts. Her face betrayed little of the regret she felt and she continued encouraging both men with grinding motions of her hips. The men cried out simultaneously as her motions raised them to a climax. They were deaf to the outside world as the nun bore down upon them, forcing every last morsel of flesh into her waiting cunt, her internal muscles squeezing both shafts together. Her enlarged interior channel was flooded with the discharge of two cocks pulsing together, draining both men to exhaustion. Wasa fell on her back as Isei bore the weights of both lovers above him.

The silence after sex was broken by the men's heavy breathing and a giggle. Wasa spun around as Isei slipped from beneath both bodies and streaked for his clothes and his belt. The nun rose from the matting, more composed than either man. At the entrance leading from the *genkan* hall to the room they were in stood a young girl. She was dressed in a striped kimono over which she wore a red apron stamped with the name of a well-known tea house. Her hairdo was simple, her face smooth, with the high brow, round structure, and heavy eyelids of the classical Miyako beauty. She smelled heavily of sake and bore a cloth-wrapped square package in her arms.

"Who are you, girl?" Wasa asked sharply.

"Momoe. Of . . . of Gion," she said defiantly. There was a faint hint of desperation in her voice that neither man heard. "I am delivering these bean-jam cakes for the tea-house. I only stopped, . . . I only stopped for a wee drinky. S'very far you know . . ."

"She is drunk," said the nun, peering with disapproval at the sodden girl.

"An you . . . an you . . . I know what you've been doing! And you a nun too!" Momoe wagged a finger playfully at the nun and grinned foolishly. "Anyway," she announced, straightening with drunk gravity, "I am a messenger from . . . to Master Wasa. The Master asked for some special . . . cakes from the teahouse, and I was the only one who could bring them. . . ."

She knelt somewhat unsteadily and proffered the cakes, then looked around the luxurious room with naive interest, showing no inclination to go.

Wasa looked at her and notwithstanding his drained state, wondered if perhaps. . . .

"Would you like to see two women?" asked the nun, almost divining Wasa's thoughts.

He looked at Isei. "Yes," both men said softly.

She approached the kneeling girl and stood beside her. "Come," she said gently, "you will acquire some merit tonight."

The intention behind the words was obscure to Momoe until the nun started undressing her with deft fingers. Momoe closed her eyes and enjoyed the feeling. The nun's musky body scent reminded her of Ocho, the girl at the fishing village, and Momoe surrendered gracefully to the knowing fingers that were busy at the juncture of her thighs.

The nun rose and clasped Momoe to her body. The two females contrasted delightfully. The nun slimmer and tauter, her body older but still full of knowledge and determination. Momoe's body fuller, broader at the hips, softer with a dark patch of hair at her legs. Trying to please, Momoe lifted one of the nun's breasts, slightly softer and lower set than her own, and kissed it lovingly, her tongue stroking the nipple which sprang erect at the touch.

"You are well set upon the path, my daughter," the nun

intoned, then led Momoe to the *zabuton* and laid her upon her back.

The nun mounted Momoe's prone body. Momoe raised her legs and threw them over the nun's firm buttocks. She searched between their bodies until she could find the nun's slit, then began rubbing the little clitoris that was hidden between the two sweet rolls of flesh. She masturbated herself at the same time while the nun's hands and mouth were busy at her own breasts. Momoe's nipples rose with the pleasure until they were painfully bursting points of desire.

Isei could no longer contain himself. He squatted at the girl's head and tilted her face back, then presented his aroused prick to her mouth. She tried to move away, then seemed to give a mental shrug. The knob slid into her mouth, then down to her throat.

"Breath loosely through your nose," the nun, her teeth nibbling at Momoe's neck, instructed. Isei pulled out to afford her some air and Momoe set out to suck his pole with a will.

Wasa squatted behind and examined the trio. The mountain man's face was contorted, but even so Wasa fancied he could see the lines of aristocratic heritage in the planes of the face. Many of the *sanka* were reputed to be descendants of the Taira clan who had pretended to the shogunate centuries before. Defeated, they had supposedly fled to the high mountains. The aristocratic lines of Isei's face seemed to lend credence to the story. Wasa ran his hands down the nun's smooth back. He parted her buttocks and she obligingly spread her legs. Her cunt was occupied by Momoe's busy juice-coated fingers. Wasa assisted the girls with his own strong fingers and the nun's behind twisted and churned with the added pleasure. Wasa examined his own erect prick for a moment. The arrow was ready, and he needed only to choose the mark. He did not want to spoil the nun's pleasure in Momoe's handiwork. Instead he knelt between the women's legs and aimed his shaft at the tiny buttonhole of the nun's anus. She raised herself slightly to oblige him and the knob, then the shaft, slid smoothly into her waiting cavern. She was tight and moistened by his finger laden with the moisture from her and Momoe's cunt. Wasa leaned back and spread her ass as far apart as he could. He could see the base of his cock disappearing into her enlarged hole, appearing and pulling the ring of flesh with it as she moved. He matched his movements to hers. Beneath them, Momoe gasped ecstatically at the added thrust of the nun's mound into her own soft lips. Meanwhile Isei's cock was shafting silkily into her mouth and she knew that she would soon be flooded with his salty juices . . .

CHAPTER 21

STILL SLIGHTLY DRUNK, MOMOE LEFT THE ARCHER'S HOUSE. They had laden her with gifts: a length of material, some sweet cakes, a hairpin, and a bottle of Osaka sake. She strolled happily through the dark streets of Miyako. Life as a vagabond was not so bad she decided. A man came out of an alley behind her. He seemed in a hurry and Momoe suddenly realized she was alone in the very early, and very dark, morning. She regretted her decision to return to the inn and had just decided to turn back and ask for shelter with the archer when she found herself surrounded. A sack was slipped hurriedly over her head and her legs were caught. She started to struggle and scream when she became conscious of a knife pressed to her face.

"Don't make a sound, or you'll be quite dead," a rough voice muttered at her through the sack.

Momoe quieted, but tears started to run down her face. Just as she got used to her life, something else came to stir things up. She had no illusions about her fate. At best she was about to be raped by a gang of louts. At worse, she would be sold as a prostitute to some horrible country house where the law was less careful about examining the prostitutes' licenses.

The three men carried her rapidly through alleys and abandoned lots, taking care to avoid lit places. Soon she was dumped on the hard wooden floor of an old and rotting storehouse. The whitewash was peeling and some of the wooden lathes were exposed by falling plaster.

"Here?" one of the kidnappers grunted. "Why not the usual place?"

"Because the boss says so. Usual place is crawling with nasty people with batons and ropes. Fancy a try then?"

The other fell silent. A third voice pitched in. "What about pay eh?"

x

153

"Boss bringing it with him. You wait. Don't leave yet. Lets see what we've got here."

They unrolled the victim from the sack, carefully keeping their faces covered. Momoe lay on the floor while they pawed among her belongings and shared them out among themselves. "Not bad looking," the burly man said. "Should fetch a nice price."

Momoe's heart sank. It was to be a brothel for her after all.

Above the group, peering through a crack in the crumbling roof, Okiku recognized the face of the weaver girl who usually delivered the cloth she ordered. She watched as the men debated something, the leader objecting, the other two insistent.

"We can't have her. The boss likes 'em fresh."

"She's no virgin," the thin man said. His examination of her cunt with a stiff finger had brought a cry of protest from Momoe and a slap from him.

"Turn her over," the thin man suggested. The other two licked their lips. They rolled Momoe quickly onto her stomach. One of them pressed her shoulders down while the other two spread her legs. Momoe knew it would be futile to resist. She was apprehensive about what was to happen, but there was a strange stirring in her groin and she herself could not tell whether the quivering of her skin was from fear or lustful anticipation. She twisted her neck to peer over her shoulder in order to see what they were doing. In any case, the feeling was growing on her that she enjoyed most of the things she did with men. And she was curious about their intentions.

"This won't hurt if you relax and let me do it properly," the leader said to her as he stripped. He knelt between her legs and Momoe felt his hands stroking the length of her taut back. She peered over her shoulder fearfully and the kidnapper holding her shoulders obligingly loosened his hold.

The leader cupped her firm slim buttocks in his hands and she automatically raised her hips. One hand slid down the crack of her ass, parting the full golden moons. She felt him stroke the length of her purse and her lips moistened in appreciation. He examined her behind intently, then parted the two half-moons widely with his left hand. A finger started working its way into her anus, and for a moment she contracted the muscles in surprise. He stopped, waiting patiently, and she relaxed again. The finger penetrated further and she relaxed her muscles, following each movement of the finger, wishing he would pay some attention to her hungry cunt as well. As if divining her thought, the man started tickling her clitoris with an available finger. She sighed quietly and relaxed completely. The finger was fully in her now, exploring her virginal passageway freely. A second joined it, widening the opening and loosening the muscles some more. The man bent forward and spat on his hand. He applied his fingers to the tiny ring of muscle.

"No, not there!" she said involuntarily. When he did not pause, she relaxed again, ashamed of her outburst, anxious that nothing should detract from the new sensation. His blunt finger soon worked its way past the guardian muscles, and she felt the sensation of the digit worming its way gradually into her muscular depths. The pleasure grew as he stroked her clitoris and the length of her rapidly moistening quim with another of his fingers.

She could feel the tip of the warm cock nosing at her rear entrance. The man rose, crouching over her. He aimed the shaft at her rear entrance manually, then lowered his loins. She felt her ass muscles part gratefully and the length of the shaft sank into her until his balls were banging at her buttock mounds. The girl from Gion spread her legs widely, lifting her pert bottom as she did so. The man waited patiently for her to adjust herself. Then he started moving into the sweet tight hole. He pulled apart the pale buns before him and watched as the muscles reluctantly released the shaft. He stabbed his muscular column into her again and she whispered her encouragement, twisting her neck back to enjoy the sight of him, lost completely in her own lasciviousness. His hands slipped under her. One worked its way into her flooded cunt, rubbing against the membrane, pressing against his own cock. His other clutched lightly at her pendant breasts. Momoe rubbed against him, moving her hips and her torso in rhythm with his shafting of her ass. She was conscious of the male thrust into her asshole, an entrance she had never considered for use the way it was now being used. She was conscious of his gentleness, attributing it correctly to his desire to avoid damaging the merchandise.

And finally, she was conscious of the keen delighted sight of the other two men. She would have called for them to insert themselves into her mouth but the man on her had just captured her tongue and his own was fucking between her lips as his cock fucked her other end.

Above them Okiku watched the man crouch over the supine woman. At first he crouched over his victim and all she could see was the movement of his thick hairy buttocks. The girl beneath resisted somewhat at first, twisting her neck in discomfort. Then Okiku saw that the motions were rousing her. Her head arched back and the other two men released her so she could enjoy the full pleasure of the man who crouched over her. The burly man leaned back in his pleasure and Okiku could see that his shaft was stuck deeply into the girl's ass, disappearing into her nether hole. He pulled out gently, then shoved back in again. The girl responded by raising her ass and digging her chin into her chest. The men's hands disappeared under the woman and Okiku knew that they were fondling her breasts and cunt. Irresistibly her own hand crept to the moist crevice between her legs. She fingered her juicy clitoris, rolling it between her fingers. Below her Momoe was rapidly approaching a climax, uttering soft cries and grunts as the demanding male pole searched her insides.

The kidnapper's movements quickened and she felt her own orgasm rise in concert with his, notwithstanding the unnatural penetration. His hands twisted at her body, gently gently, and she was conscious that he was exercising the utmost self-control. Finally he sank into her, his entire body trembling with suppressed violence. She managed to snake a hand back and stroke his balls, feeling the root of his cock inserted into her rear muscles. The bag contracted forcefully and the man on her groaned. The flood of liquid into her guts and the frenzied motion on his finger in her cunt caused her to respond and her entire body constricted in sympathetic orgasm, made more pleasurable because she had found him the gentlest lover she had ever had, except for Ocho and the nun.

He rose from her finally, and there was respect in his voice, something that had never been there before. "We should charge a fortune for her!" he whispered as one of his men took his place. He longed to stop the brute from destroying this lovely flower, but knew it to be impossible. Instead he crouched over the couple, seeing to it that the man did not damage her, cursing in a deep whisper when the man became too rough.

Though the second and third men were hardly as gentle or as perfect as the first, Momoe found herself responding to them in much the same way. Her ass muscles were somewhat sore, and she badly needed some time alone to evacuate her bowels, but nontheless found herself responding to their male gushings with orgasms of her own.

Okiku was breathing heavily by the time the third man had finished. Her finger's were covered by her own juices and her body was trembling with the tension of unrelieved sexual energy. Though she liked to masturbate, she much prefered to have a man in her, and she did not care in which orifice, preferably in all of them. She wondered whether she should drop from the roof and proposition or assault some male passerby, or whether to hurry home to Jiro . . . The thought of his massive frame driving his cock deep into her caused her insides to peak. She almost groaned with relief as the first waves of pleasure flooded over her, and the drops of dew that ran down the insides of her thighs were a hidden counterpoint to the spasms that rocked Momoe for the third time down below.

They all rested quietly. The men allowed her to rise and retire to the corner for evacuation and a wash. They gave her a sip from the bottle of sake that had been a present from Wasa. Presently there was a dry whisper from the side of the storehouse. The men tensed. The leader shushed them and slipped to the wall. There was a whispered consultation and the clink of something metallic. The leader returned.

"Here y'are. Now scram."

Above them, Okiku breathed a sigh of relief: Now she would be able to get to the real source.

The other two hefted the chinking oblong silver coins, rose to their feet and slipped out into the dark. From her perch above Okiku saw them disappear one after the other into the dark alleys of the city. They would be easy to find and she watched their departure with no regret. A shadow grew into the image of a man. He was hooded and dressed simply in a dark gown, but bore the two swords of a

157

samurai stuck into his sash. He gave an order to the burly kidnapper, who hoisted Momoe quickly to his shoulders. The girl tried to protest but was slapped into silence.

The odd procession moved through the predawn dark. Burly kidnapper and victim, hooded samurai and, well behind them, dark-clad woman who darted from shadow to shadow. They worked their way rapidly to the slopes of Arashiyama, then around the periphery of the city. Suddenly Okiku realized that they were in back of the Ito mansion. The kidnap party slipped inside. Okiku crept closer and almost stumbled over the kidnapper as he let himself out through a crack in the wall. By the time the man had left, there was no sign of a kidnapping boss and victim. But at least she was one step ahead.

Again Momoe found herself lying in an old *kura* storeroom. This one however was better appointed. At least there was a quilt on the floor for her convenience. Or actually her kidnapper's. As soon as the stocky man had left, the samurai began exploring her body thoroughly, stripping her as he did so. Notwithstanding her tiredness and her previous experiences, Momoe found herself responding with alacrity.

He pulled her roughly to him. His hands digging into the soft mounds of her ass. Then he lowered his head and she found her mouth invaded by his hot questing tongue. She fought him with her own oral digit for awhile and then the pleasure his tongue evoked made her join in a duet. His cock continued plunging into her soft womanhood, diving deep. His balls slapped against her straining buttocks, and she was conscious of the tension in them. Then he raised her slightly and his finger, liberally bedewed with her cunt juices, was twiddling at her rear passage. The previous entry of the three kidnappers had loosened her there and she felt the gradual insertion of his questing finger with great pleasure. She clutched at his muscular stringy back, aware that finally she was being fucked in each of her available orifices. Randily she surrendered to the sensations, not even conscious of the moans and gasps she emitted that were muffled by his mouth. She started bucking roughly at him as a triple orgasm shook her. He waited for a moment, enjoying the sensation of her coming, then joined her, squirming about rapidly and forcefully on her clutching sweat-bedecked body.

Hori stepped out of the *kura* and tiredly made his way through the short passageway into the Ito garden. A shimmering figure made him start and reach for his sword.

"Well?" a cold female voice asked.

He relaxed and said acidly, "Don't startle me like that again."

"Don't give me all that nonsense, elder brother. Do you have some merchandise or not?"

"Of course I do," Hori said pacifically. He had never admitted it, not even to himself, but he was somewhat afraid of his younger sister. Adopted while still young into another family, she had grown into a cold beauty with a penchant for luxurious vice which even her husband's wealth could not satisfy. Her idea of finding and selling concubines at high prices to provincial lords with special tastes was a good one. But her cold-bloodedness exceeded even his own.

"We will dispose of her in three days. I believe there is someone in Tosa who is interested. Don't come to the villa now. Uemura is there."

"Aren't you through with that puppy? He was a good messenger but having him around the house. . . . Ito might have suspected. He was beginning to suspect *me*! It was a mistake supplying him with that girl before he was killed . . ."

"Shut up," Haruko said without turning around. Then she froze. "What do you mean Ito suspected?"

"He called me in to ask what had happened to the girl and where she came from."

"And what did you tell him?"

Hori, as if realizing he had said too much, did not answer. He glared back into her eyes, then turned and retraced his steps out of the garden. Haruko stared after him thoughtfully.

† † †

Matsudaira Konnosuke looked haggard, and Muto wondered whether it was the crime wave they were experiencing, or some private problem. Matsudaira thought of Rosamund. She had slipped out again and as usual, her maid had no idea where she had gone. She always came back, but Matsudaira knew that there was a depth of feeling against the pale Southern Barbarians that often blazed into violence. Masterless *ronin* samurai, unemployed since the end of the wars some years before, were particularly prone to taking out their frustrations violently on any passerby. A Southern Barbarian was a prime target.

Muto discussed the previous night's police events, then added, "I have heard a rumor, something worth checking . . ." he stopped, not sure Matsudaira was attentive, not wishing to break into his thoughts.

His lord signalled him to proceed, his attention drawn away from his errant mistress.

The retainer read from a paper stamped with a police agent's sigil. "At Sanjusangendo, yesterday afternoon. After the attempt by the archer Wasa Senri to shoot five thousand arrows at a target. A well-dressed man in Honganji livery carrying a matchlock demonstrated exceptional skill. At a great distance he shot off the branch of a tree. At the same time I noticed Sanbonkichi, known to me as a dip reaching into the robe of . . . The rest is not relevant, Muto said. I only received the report this morning. Could it be our murderer, I wonder?"

"Entirely possible." The young magistrate-governor stroked his chin. "But then why would he display his skill so prominently?"

Muto said thoughtfully, "Some men have an urge to boast. Perhaps this is one such."

Matsudaira nodded. "Perhaps. Institute some quiet inquiries and alert your men. I will also have someone look into it. Now, what about this murderous samurai friend of ours . . ."

"No news so far," Muto answered after consulting his papers. "We are still looking."

"I think you may not find anything then." He grinned, mentally thanking Jiro for prompt and decisive action.

Muto said nothing, speculating on the giant samurai himself.

The crowds around the Ito mansion were thicker than the usual throng of passersby in that quarter of the city. Everyone knew that a juicy and interesting murder had occurred, and everyone was speculating on precisely *what* had happened.

Rosamund wandered through the crowd, her large hat pulled low on her face, the lower part of which was obscured by a hood. She could not understand how his office occupied Goemon's time, but she was interested in trying to understand. But the constables guarding the mansion and the paper seals on the doors limited access to all onlookers. Still, the feeling of freedom was wonderful.

It was hot, towards noon, and she decided she needed a rest. She feared her foreign appearance would be obvious at a public eating place. Instead she walked slowly towards the shade of the mountain behind the villa. Here too the area was roped off and constables were minutely examining the ground behind the villa. Rosamund made a wide circle around the constables and climbed into the cool pine-clad hill. Through the trees she could see the city of Miyako spread below her, spots of grey tile and yellow thatched roofs amidst the enclosing green.

Climbing higher into the mountain she eventually found herself alone. She walked until the sound of a tiny mountain rill attracted her attention, then suddenly remembered she was thirsty. She drank the cool sweet water then ate the pounded toasted rice cakes she had brought with her from the kitchen. By the time she had finished she was drowsy. She dozed, but the sweat on her body was discomforting. Finally she rose and stripped, then doused herself with the fresh cool water.

She fell asleep on her robes, not bothering to dress. Her dreams turned violently erotic. Heavy cocks were forcing their way painfully and delightfully into her waiting cunt. Hard hands were bruising her skin and she revelled in their touch. She struggled awake, dream becoming reality. Something heavy was suddenly pressing her down and rough fingers were searching between her legs. She tried to struggle erect. A smooth-shaven man with a handsome aristocratic face was holding her down. He wore a doublet of bear fur and nothing else.

He grinned at her. "I have never seen anything as beautiful and desirable as you. You must be a heavenly messenger, and though I know I will be cursed forever, I will have you."

His accent was thick and almost incomprehensible to her, but she grinned at him savagely. "If you want me, you will have to fight for it,'' and struck him hard in the ribs while twisting her hips sideways. Surprised at her ferocity, Isei was unseated and he flew over. Rosamund rose and pounced on him, her blonde hair flying, her full jugs bouncing heavily. She was aroused now and her blows rained down on him without mercy. Her weight and skill surprised him and he tried to fight back, then tried to avoid her blows. He was on his back now, her pale form crouched over him. Desperately he struck at her exposed cunt with his open palm. His hand grasped a fistful of pale golden curls and a wet handful of delicious flesh. She shrieked at the sudden pain of the blow at her sex, then fought back wildly. Isei's hand contracted in a grip as he fended her off. His fingers clutched at the insides of her cunt and her tight asshole, penetrating deeply. She shrieked again and reached for his semi-erect cock. He fended her off and shook her above him. Her full breasts jiggled in his face, practically blinding him. Isei knew that she would reach his manhood and rip it off unless he did something quickly. He pulled her soft rounded body to his, searching for his hand with the tip of his cock. Without releasing his grip he inserted the crown of his shaft and thrust upwards with all his might.

To Rosamund the first few seconds of the fight were reflexive. The pain of his attack merged with her own rage and frustration and her bloodlust rose when she felt her own victory. The sudden pain of his blow in her loins fanned the ever-present embers there into a blaze, and the continued pain of his hard fingers clutching at her brought a rush of delight to her brain. She felt the sudden insertion of his cock with satisfaction. Thrusting her hips down she sought to ensure the continuation of the contact. His clutching fingers did not relax their hold and she swayed, grateful for the delicious pain. Her hips automatically adhered to his while she fought his torso, intent on inflicting as much damage as possible. Isei brought a new weapon into play and bit deeply at one full breast. She pulled back and slapped his face twice. He hit wildly at her, connecting as often as not with the full soft bags of her breasts. His cock was massively thrusting into her tight soft cunt. The movements of the lower halves of their bodies contradicted the violence of their upper torsos. Rosamund felt herself melting, her juices flowing heavily to wet his clutching fingers and rapidly probing cock. Lust overcame her violence and she leaned forward, capturing his face with her hands. He tried to fend off her mouth and was surprised to find her lips sucking hungrily at him, her tongue probing his mouth demandingly but with no intent to punish. His hips, completely out of control now, pushed deeply into her demanding cunt. Her remarkable vaginal muscles went into operation and Isei almost screamed with relief as he felt his cock being milked, sucked into a vortex of her inner being.

"Harder," the golden-headed vision murmured into his mouth as he tried to extricate his hands. "Harder. Hurt me. Push in!" He obeyed, nonplussed but cognizant now of the nun's strictures. She groaned and his hand was covered with the evidence of her pleasure just as his cock spurted his load again and again into her interior.

She rolled off him, breathing heavily. There were purple welts on both their bodies and he leaned over her full breasts, licking them in apology.

"There is some salve in my pouch," he said. "It will take away the marks."

She nodded, stretching her glorious form and smiling radiantly. Though she had come only once, Rosamund felt as if she had known this man's body and pleasured herself on it forever. Or just as long as necessary. There was an animal magnetism about him combined with a sophisticated shyness and response to her needs. He brought her the salve, was about to speak, then raised his head like a hart testing the winds. He reached for his clothes hurriedly and dressed himself.

"I will find you," he said, then vanished into the forest.

She too could now hear the sound of men calling to one another below her, towards the city. Not anxious to be found there, she dressed hurriedly and climbed higher up the mountain. She always carried a document from Matsudaira which ordered her brought before him, but this insurance was precisely what she did not want in her present mood.

CHAPTER 22

P ALE WHITE LIGHT WAS WASHING THROUGH THE *SHOJI* PAPER when Okiku awoke. The small house was eerily quiet. She felt incredibly horny and wondered if Jiro had returned. He had not been in when she had returned before dawn. She called for him, then when there was no response, called for Otsu, her plump maid, to no avail. Finally in exasperation she rose. Her hand was no good outlet for her current needs. Dressed in a casually tied *vukata* robe she wandered out to the back, hoping to find Jiro at his practice in the small clearing among the bamboos. What she saw there sent her hurrying desperately to the grove.

Jiro was seated on his knees in *seiza* on the small platform in the clearing that was used occasionally for tea. His robe was about his waist, sleeves tucked under his knees. The blade of his short sword, wrapped in a single sheet of plain white paper, was lying before him. Three inches of steel protruded from the paper. As Okiku rushed towards him he reached for the blade and poised it before his stomach.

Okiku knew it was futile to argue with him. She knew her mate was as stubborn as a mule once his mind was made up. Something terrible must have caused him to want to die thus, in privacy, without even proper ceremony or a helping second. She bent as she ran, then swiftly cast with all the skill learned and practiced in her twenty years as the descendant of *shinobi* family: experts in trickery and camouflage, ambush and murder. The short wood post, one of those used to line the path between the bamboos, ran true as a javelin. It thudded heavily into Jiro's fist, twisting the blade from his grasp. The giant leaped to his feet, reaching in berserk rage for the great *katana* that rested by his seat. Okiku rose in one desperate leap. The side of her foot connected squarely with Jiro's neck and he collapsed as if poleaxed.

Okiku stood over her man. Tears welled from her eyes. This was the first time she had ever cried in her memory. Even when she had found her entire family murdered in the mountains, she had not let tears drop. That time she had only sworn revenge and laid plans to kill the perpetrators. Now there was no one to kill. She dropped to her knees beside the man who had completed her revenge and then her life and wondered what she was to do. Jiro would recover soon, and stubborn as he was, he would try *seppuku* again. She buried her face in her hands, then scratched her naked breasts in frustration. Finally a possible, almost incredible solution occurred to her.

Jiro returned to consciousness with a pain in his head and a dark sense of defeat in his mind. He realized now that he was not a man. Even the honorable way of atoning for his failure was not available to him. Without opening his eyes he wondered drearily what it would have been like to be dead. He had a confused image of Okiku running towards him, then everything was a blank. He thought of his stomach, it was not painful, then noted that another organ, somewhat below it, was. The powerful sensations of his erect prick suddenly flooded his brain and surprised, he opened his eyes.

Okiku was staring down at him fiercely. "You tried to kill yourself and leave me!" she said accusingly. "That is unforgivable." She squeezed his silky column with all her might. He was conscious that she had tied his sword cord around the base of the column. His erection was violent and painful.

"I failed," he said dully. "Sugiyama beat me in a duel."

"You're still alive!" she said.

"I shouldn't be!" he shouted back. "A samurai should emerge victorious or not at all from a battle."

"Stupid!" she screamed back. "Stupid, stupid. Do you really believe that? Do you think people are like that? They merely pick up the pieces and start again. Until they succeed. *I* did that."

"You're a *heimin,* a commoner. What would you know of samurai dignity?"

"And you're a half-caste barbarian. What would you?" Okiku emphasized her words by squeezing his pulsing hot column of flesh.

"I was raised a samurai!"

"So then kill me too!" she said in a quiet voice. "I would not live without you, and it is my shame too."

Involuntarily he searched for his sword, then realized that the platform was bare. Not only that, but both he and Okiku were bare as well.

"Kill me with this," she urged, tugging at his inflamed fleshy sword and kneeling passively before him.

He tried to resist, but she pulled harder. "Come on samurai. Do it. Strike! Kill with one cut."

He rose behind her angrily and stabbed at her waiting cunt with a stiff finger. It was dry and his insertion obviously painful, but she endured it without a murmur. He wanted to humiliate her, to hit back for the hurt he had endured. His big hands slapped at her smooth golden buttocks viciously. Okiku still crouched there like an obedient mistress, no emotion showing in her body or her face. He poked his finger out again, and she did not respond, except for opening her legs to facilitate entry. A second finger joined the first, stabbing into the tight tiny ring of her anus. He knew she liked being fucked there, but her own sexual demands needed to be met usually. This time she was entirely passive, allowing him to satisfy himself without any attempt to demand her own pleasure.

Jiro's humiliation and pain were not assuaged by her surrender. He rose over her, cresting like a giant wave. The head of his giant cock swayed before him, aimed unerringly at her waiting cunt, then tore through her dry channel until it was buried to the root. She cried out uncharacteristically in pain and shock, but even the full weight of his body failed to buckle her legs. Jiro rammed into her, not caring of her comfort, intent only on rending and stabbing, the thought of his humiliation at the hands of the small quick Sugiyama upmost in his mind. As he fucked Okiku brutally some of the tension left him and he found himself detached, examining the fight with great deliberation, seeking for Sugiyama's flaws. He found none, instead he found a flaw in himself. Not having known defeat for many years, he had become overconfident. Okiku had taught him that defeat had its own virtues. If one survived it, one came out strengthened. She was a good teacher, as good as . . . reality crashed into him. Okiku was there below him, suffering his thoughtless use of her body. A great wave of tenderness swelled in him. He almost pulled out of her, then realized that was not the way to thank her for what she had done.

Okiku felt the change in Jiro. His thrusts became slower, less brutal, more loving. She allowed herself a small ray of hope which grew as he began touching her body in the ways he knew she liked. She sighed lightly and allowed her own moistures to descend, easing the passage of his prick. His timing of movements into her cunt lengthened and he paused at the entrance to her vagina, twiddling the head of his cock against her small delicate nether lips before thrusting home again. She smiled shyly and looked over her shoulder. His eyes were closed and tears were running down his cheeks. She held her breath and prayed.

Jiro pulled out of Okiku's slim sweet body and rolled her over on her back gently. His lips came down on her moistened cunt. Using plenty of his own saliva he began licking and sucking the delicate flower between her legs. He stabbed his tongue several times into her honey pot, then slipped his lips the length of her own slick ones. He found the tiny pearl at the upper entrance and nibbled at it with his lips. She responded by raising her hips and clutching happily at his head, drawing him with growing force into herself.

She urged him up. His salty-sour–tasting lips clenched at her mouth, his tongue slipped in to join with her own. She guided his rampant cock into her waiting sopping cunt and they moved together to a delicious orgasm, their juices mixing, the fragrance carried about the grove by the slight breeze.

Jiro rolled off Okiku and lay panting by her side. He was utterly drained. She stroked his heaving chest, wincing slightly as she moved. His last lunges had been brutal, though she had enjoyed them. She hid the motion from him.

The passion that had driven him to attempt suicide seemed washed away. Jiro even found he could secretly laugh at himself. Far away in the back of his mind Jiro heard a voice say in English, "Commit suicide because you lost boy? Fookin' stupid! Yer alive boy, go back and kill the bastards!" In his imagination he conjured up the ghost of his father. The old English sea-rover seemed to grimace in approval as Jiro mentally abandoned the idea of suicide.

"Now what?" he asked Okiku lazily, stroking his wife's slick sweat-streaked skin.

"Sharpen your sword and try again. And again, if necessary."

"Sounds like something my old man would have said."

"Smart man, the old barbarian," she grinned.

"And what about this sword?" he joked, pointing to his limp, glistening cock. It lay on his thigh, as exhausted as himself.

"It too can be sharpened," she laughed.

"Not right now it can't," he teased her.

"Would you like to bet? A new obi for me?"

"All right," he agreed, curious to see what she would do.

"Get up and come with me. We'll find Otsu."

"Hey, not fair . . ."

"You haven't had her plump ass in some time. I bet that would do you a world of good."

Holding their clothes and his swords, they walked back to the house.

CHAPTER 23

"WELL, WHAT HAVE WE HERE?" THE SHARP CRUEL VOICE pierced through Momoe's dreams. She tried to rise, blinking, only to find a heavy weight pushing down on her chest. The pressure was being exerted by a dainty foot encased in a white *tabi* sock. A woman's face loomed over her. It was coldly beautiful with a towering, expensive hairdo. "A present for me, I imagine. Get up girl, let's have a look at you."

Momoe rose slowly to her feet, conscious of her grubby looks and inadequate covering. Cutting her bonds on a carelessly exposed hinge, she had managed to escape the old warehouse. By then, exhausted and cold, she had cared for nothing but some shelter. In the light of the dawn she had managed to creep unnoticed into the villa, looking for some food. A plate of stale bean-jam cakes had satisfied her hunger and she had curled up in a large closet full of musty bedding, hoping dreamily that she would not be discovered by the owners. She had found a large workman's sark with which to cover herself, but not a sash. The woman slapped her hands away from the front of the large man's shirt and dropped the covering to the floor of the closet.

"Umm. Lovely." She looked Momoe up and down and slowly licked her lips. Behind her a door slid open and a young woman with smooth brown hair knelt at the opening. "Mistress . . ."

"Why do you have to interfere . . ." the imperious woman began. Then she saw the figure of the young samurai behind the kneeling maid and said in the same breath, "Oh, it's you."

Uemura smiled at his mistress, then noticed the naked girl in the closet. His eyebrows rose in surprise.

"A new playmate?"

Haruko looked at him over her shoulder for a minute, wanting perhaps to object, then she smiled tightly and said, "Yes. We can have some fun."

Momoe tried to back away but was held by the closet. Haruko noted the movement out of the corner of her eye. She spun to face Momoe and slapped her hard, once on either cheek. "You'll not move, girl. Do what you're told. You realize I could have you arrested for theft? Who gave you permission to enter this house?"

Momoe fell to her knees and started babbling an explanation.

"Shut up!" said Haruko fiercely. "Or I'll have this samurai kill you for insulting his presence."

Momoe buried her face in the mat, shivering with fear. She knew the woman was right: *kirisute gomen,* cut-and-go was the normal samurai response to any rudeness from a commoner.

A male hand stroked her back and a male finger penetrated the length of her ass-crack.

"If you behave," the young man said, "We'll let you go later without harm. And perhaps a reward. Do you understand?"

Helplessly Momoe nodded, shivering.

"Bring her to the bedroom. And you Midori, come with us."

Haruko preceded them into the room she used for sleeping. Midori and Uemura dragged the unwilling Momoe with them. A quilt, still disarrayed from the sleepers' presence, dominated the room. The quilt was of the highest quality workmanship, Momoe noticed, while the woman and the man examined her. The maidservant knelt passively at their side. They ran their hands over her body, slapping her hands aside when she tried uneasily to stop them from examining her hidden parts. Momoe noted dully that her asshole was still somewhat sore from the penetration of the previous night, but otherwise she was unchanged. A tingling started invading her body. She trembled and her breasts jiggled on her chest.

Haruko forced Momoe down onto the quilt. Uemura held her legs apart, gripping her ankles. She raised her head to see what they were about to do to her.

"Midori, come here!" Haruko demanded.

The brown-haired maid glided towards her mistress. Uemura examined her lustfully. He had his own plans for her.

"Prepare this whore for us," Haruko said.

Without a word Midori knelt besides Momoe's hips. She inserted a delicate knowing finger into the young weaver's cunt, touching her tiny clitoris delicately with a saliva-moistened finger. She spread the delicate lips with both hands, then kissed the long lips passionately. Momoe, her eyes closed, raised her knees to facilitate Midori's work. Haruko looked on. Seeing Uemura's anticipatory glances at Midori's bent form, she ordered him to rise. She kissed her paramour deeply.

"Undress me!" she commanded. He untied the silk sash which slithered to the floor, then the under kerchief. Her rich robes, three layers of them, parted. His hands slipped automatically to fondle her thin form, though his eyes were on the couple on the floor.

Midori's expert tongue was raising great waves of passion in Momoe. Her hips were jerking upwards uncontrollably and she clutched the soft brown hair, bringing the tongue deeper into her. "I want to touch you too," she murmured, her eyes closed. Midori ignored her. Momoe twisted on the futon, disarranging it still further, intent only on the delicious tongue that was exciting her to the first in a series of climaxes. She opened her eyes to see the cruel samurai lady and her man crouching over her. Both were stark naked. The man's hand was dug deep into the woman's cunt, which he was rubbing furiously. The woman's lustful panting increased. She grabbed Momoe's small chin with iron-strong fingers.

"You'll do precisely as I say!" she commanded. Momoe nodded, scared but expectant.

Haruko saw the glint of lust in Uemura's eyes. Her control of him in the last few days had become precarious. She would have to re-establish her dominance, first by honey, later. . . .

"We'll have them together," she muttered.

Uemura, entranced by the spectacle, nodded.

"Undress the maid while I attend to something. Position her over the whore's mouth."

Nothing loth, Uemura stripped Midori rapidly. Her slim body called out to him. He stroked his hand against her soft-haired mound and she urged him on by moving her hips, then he inserted two fingers into her eager cunt. She did not pause at her labors, merely moving her hips in time to his strokes. His cock was almost painfully erect and he longed to plunge into her waiting femaleness.

Haruko returned and directed him to place Midori over the other girl's head. She carried a lacquered box decorated with peonies out of which she withdrew a double ivory *harigata*. Two ivory cocks were joined cunningly at their bases, forming an acute angle which was flexible at the join. She inserted one end of cock into herself, her face beatific at the feel, then knelt beside's Midori's head.

Momoe saw the most delicate cunt she had ever seen poised over her face. The hairs were soft and brown, the lips delicate and pink, exuding an aroma she could not ignore. Unbidden she pulled at Midori's hips. The perfect cunt descended to her mouth and she joyfully greeted it with a kiss that turned to a long passionate suck of the delicate scented membranes. Midori reciprocated by drawing lovingly at Momoe's cunt. The downy black hairs tickled her nostrils and she buried her face as deep as she could in the new girl's pussy.

Haruko and Uemura looked on with satisfaction. Haruko squatted before Midori's face and roughly shoved it aside. Momoe's juicy, saliva-wettened cunt was exposed. Momoe clutched fitfully, searching for Midori's face to no avail. Instead the ivory prick was presented at the opening of her cunt and thrust well inside, propelled by Haruko's strong belly muscles. Momoe grunted but her sounds were muffled as the man squatted over her face and presented a long shaft to the brown-haired girl's delicate cunt. For the first time she watched, fascinated, as a long shaft disappeared into a cunt in front of her eyes. The skin marked by prominent veins bunched at the entrance to the slit, then slid inside reluctantly but inexorably. The tiny hole widened to accept the pole that seemed too large to ever find its way in. At the end of the shaft the large hair-covered scrotum, wrinkled and moving, rolled across her forehead and rested on her mouth. Her own juices rose as Haruko inserted a stiff prick deeply into her own waiting cunt.

172

"Suck me!" the man above her commanded, and when she did not comply instantly he jogged his balls over her lips.

"Lick me!" Haruko commanded, and Midori was swift to obey, searching for Haruko's clit which was pushed up and made prominent by the insertion of the back end of the double dildo.

The two young girls used their mouths energetically as the other two began moving above them. Midori alternated her attention between the two prominently displayed clitorises. They mashed together, sandwiching her tongue between them, and with each motion she could feel both women coming closer to their climax. Her own cunt was filled by Uemura's lustful, rapidly moving cock. She could feel Midori's hot breath on her own clit, and occasionally the girl would hastily suck at Midori's lower lips and cunt, absorbing the juices that flowed from her.

Haruko embraced Uemura passionately. He returned her embrace, tasting and touching her breasts, her face, her neck and shoulders. He used one hand to feel Midori's breasts, marveling at the contrast between hers and Haruko's, then doing the same to the anonymous girl who was lowest on the pile. He reached a pitch of excitement from which he could not retreat. Liquid boiled out of his balls and overflowed from Midori's soft cunt. Momoe hastily sucked up the delicious liquor and was rewarded with tremors of delight from Momoe, who quivered deliciously above her. Instead of withdrawing Uemura continued shafting into Midori's willing cunt. This time he was slower at reaching his climax. Haruko rammed her cunt furiously into Momoe's and closed her eyes as shudders of pleasure reached her. She continued moving, delighting in the compliance of those around her. Uemura came again, small dribblets of exhausted juice running down Midori's thighs again and being absorbed by a willing Momoe unconsciously. Her own body was clutching haplessly at Haruko's hips, drawing her in as deeply as she could, gulping with her mouth for breath and with her cunt for more cock. Midori lapped quickly against her exposed cunt and Momoe rose in a passionate orgasm that almost unseated the entire pile.

They fell apart, Uemura rolling tiredly onto his back, staring breathlessly at Haruko, who was rearranging the other two women to her satisfaction. She crouched over the two girls, forcing Momoe to tongue her wet cunt while Midori inserted a tongue into her waiting asshole. Haruko's eyes were closed and she forced the two women to her pleasure. She varied the posture, kneeling over Momoe's face and rubbing herself furiously to a climax over the tired but willing stranger.

Midori tilted her head. "There is someone at the entrance, mistress."

Haruko, still sunk into her pleasure, said, "Let one of the servants answer."

"Most of them have fled, mistress." Midori persisted.

"Go and answer then."

Midori rose and slipped her robe on with practiced hands. "Please wait a moment," she called in a high-pitched voice, rushing through the empty mansion. "Ah, Muto-san from the magistrates," she called out gaily and bowed.

In the inner room Haruko heard the words and frowned. She could not understand why the police were there.

Uemura heard the words too and rose with alacrity. "It would be better if he were not to find me here," he said.

"But your sword?" she asked.

"I did not leave it at the entrance rack," he said with satisfaction. This unwonted caution, and his obvious reluctance to meet someone from the magistrate's office, gave Haruko some new food for thought. She pushed it into the back of her mind however. There was a more immediate concern.

"Help me with this bitch," she said.

They bundled Momoe, still stark naked, her cunt wet with their discharges, through a series of dark unused rooms to the entrance to a storehouse and into a large chest, slipping a peg into the hasp. She crouched there miserably in the dark as she heard Uemura and Haruko moving purposely and rapidly about the room. The sounds faded and did not return. Momoe's thoughts turned to extricating herself from her own predicament. Like most commoners, she was reluctant to face officials from the magistrate's office. She would make her way alone, if possible. She regretted only that she had not gotten to know the brown-haired maid any better. She battered at the chest lid, then turned in the narrow space and kicked with all her might. The box started to splinter.

A final kick managed to crack the linchpin of the simple lock. A thrust, and Momoe found herself sprawling on the *tatami*. She rose quickly and looked around her. Piles of clothes and bedding lay in the unused storehouse. She found something to her liking: not too rich, but good material, and dressed herself, then slipped outside. Looking around frenziedly she saw a well-kept garden and beyond it the pitched roof of a temple. She trembled violently for a second, then made her way through the garden at a run. Her feet were bruised by the round pebbles of the walk and she feared being noticed, but there was no one about in the garden or in the rooms looking onto it.

A convenient rock by the tile-topped wall offered her a height from which she managed to scramble to the top. From there she was able to drop into the unkempt space around the temple. She breathed deeply. Freedom at last. The temple appeared to have been abandoned, or at least decrepit for a great many years, but there were signs now of renewed activity. Lumber lay about, cut and mortised for joining. Wood shavings gave rise to the smell she associated with Saburo, and tears came to her eyes as she made her way through the materials, in search of shelter in the temple.

She heard gruff male voices above her on the raised platform of the building. Not wishing to meet any more males for the night, she slipped quickly through a worn lattice between the building pillars and into the space beneath the temple. The earth was cold and she made her way further in, hoping for some warmth. In the dark she bumped her nose against a wooden wall. Exhausted, she huddled against the wooden barrier.

Suddenly her life in the past few days came back to her. She started crying, imagining Saburo the traitor, Saburo the cause of her trouble, then imagining him comforting her with his strong arms. Lost in her reverie, her hand stroking herself between her legs, she imagined she could hear his voice.

The voice persisted long after her dream began to fade. She leaned back against the wooden barrier and heard it again. Suddenly she realized that it was not all a dream, that the voice was somewhere here beside her. There were several other male voices, but Saburo's was the most prominent. She crawled along the length of the wooden barrier, scratching at the wood until she found a tiny crack. Peering through it, she cried out in surprise.

A group of artisans was crouched around a series of worktables in a bare hall under the temple. Some were working at wood, others were gilding images, others engaged in lacquerware. His profile to her, Saburo was working on joining the parts of a large black-and-gilt cabinet for the temple's altar. Momoe scrabbled in her clothes, in the dirt around her, looking for something to attract his attention. There was an intensity and a thinness about him that indicated he was in some sort of trouble, and she did not know if the other men were with him or against him. The only thing she could find were some small pebbles and slivers of wood she managed to break from the barrier. She smoothed the slivers laboriously with a pebble, then inserted one of the slivers between her lips.

The first puff was too weak and the sliver of wood fell short. The second struck at Saburo's apron, and he brushed it off unconsciously. The third hit his neck. He looked around in annoyance but all the other men were engaged in their work. Saburo frowned and Momoe's heart leaped at the sight of the dear boyish face. She tried again, and Saburo clenched his lips and raised his eyes angrily. He caught sight of the obi hem Momoe inserted through the crack. He blinked once, then looked around carefully. When he looked back the piece of cloth was gone.

Saburo stretched casually and made his way to the wall as if needing the short stroll to clear his muscles.

"Hey you, Saburo, get back to work!" The owner of the harsh voice was not visible from Momoe's vantage point.

Saburo turned and gave some pacific reply, then squatted at the barrier below Momoe and went through the motions of looking for some object.

"Who are you?" he asked in an undertone.

"Saburo-chan, it's me, Momoe. It's me, dear. What happened to you?" Momoe could not forebear to cry out.

He shushed her without raising his head. "Quiet! They

will hear you. Momoe dear, how did you find me? No matter. You must help me get out.''

"How can I do it? And what is going on?''

"Later!'' he hissed.

Eventually the workmen were allowed to rest from their labors and eat a supper of simple gruel and pickles. The candles were extinguished and they disposed themselves for sleep. Saburo laid himself down by the crack. When the noises of sleepy men had been replaced by snores, he whispered at the crack.

"Momoe-chan, you are there?''

"Yes dear,'' she answered with alacrity. Her heart warmed at his use of the diminutive which only parents or lovers used.

"They take away all our tools,'' he whispered urgently. "The doors are guarded, but I have noticed the guards are often absent. You must slip into the temple and undo the lock, or whatever it is at the door.'' He gave her precise instructions.

Heart in her mouth, Momoe crept towards the inconspicuous door in the temple that led towards the basement.

Two monks were sprawled before the door. She waited in the shadows while they laughed and talked in low voices, their weapons—long *naginata* halberds—clinking.

One of them rose and stretched. "I'm for a piss. Coming?''

The other looked at the door reluctantly, then reassuring himself that it could not be opened from the inside, rose and joined his companion. They stomped outside towards the privies.

Momoe slipped from her hiding place and approached the door. She struggled with the heavy bars, encouraged by Saburo's whispered instructions. Easing them to the floor, she pulled at the reluctant massive barrier.

Saburo was suddenly in her arms. They clutched at one another for a brief moment, then he turned to replace the bars.

"Otherwise they will start hunting us immediately. Some of the men inside rat on the others,'' he whispered.

They started towards the temple exit, then heard the sound of returning footsteps. The monks were returning, and apparently there were others with them. Twisting aside,

Saburo led her deeper into the temple, then higher up over the temporary wooden and bamboo structures, searching for a hiding place high up near the eaves.

They huddled together in the tiny niche, warming one another with their bodies. Momoe felt the rise of desire at the nearness of his hard muscles. She snuggled close to him as he stroked her hair.

"Poor Momoe. How did you find me?"

"I searched and searched and searched," she said, only half truthfully. "It was terribly difficult, but you know I would do anything for you." All her difficulties were forgotten, moved to the back of her mind in the warmth of his embrace.

His hand descended to the small of her back and she was conscious of the hardening between his legs that pushed against her belly.

He bent his head and kissed her deeply. Momoe responded eagerly, her hands leading his, without conscious volition, to the folds of her kimono.

He rolled her over on her back and nibbled at her ear. "Dear Momoe. I am sorry, you must be very tired. But I have not held you for so long . . ."

"No, it's all right dear. Do it, do it . . ."

He pushed his way between her legs. "It won't hurt like last time, I promise you . . ."

"Are you sure?" she asked tremulously, simulating innocence while a hint of laughter threatened to break through. She knew what she had to do, and shrank from him slightly. Saburo kissed her breasts and spread the lips of her cunt gently, barely inserting the tip of his member. "I'm sure, Momoe-chan. It will be a great pleasure to you now."

"If you're sure . . ." She spread her legs as wide as she could in the narrow corner and he pushed forward carefully. He was biting his lips and she knew he was trying to control his entry, the lust of his womanless time boiling strongly in his egg sack. The long warm pole glided up the length of her cunt. In seconds, it seemed, his seed was spurting out of his swollen balls, along the tube of his cock. Saburo felt his woman responding with delighted writhings of her hips, her own lust, pent up as long as his, finally finding release.

She cried out, muffling the sound in his shoulder. Her juices welled out and flooded the joined hairs between their bellies. Unconscious almost with the happiness of finding him, she clutched his muscular frame to her delicate body. Her hips rocked back and forth as her exploding lust tried to force him deeper into her. The incredible spasms subsided and she slowly regained her senses. She looked up at him in the dark, stroking his sweating face with the satisfaction of love consummated.

CHAPTER 24

HE HAD CLIMBED INTO THE TREE-CLAD HILLS BEHIND MIYAKO after wandering through the large and confusing city the better part of the day. The noise and the constant bustle annoyed him, and he knew that he would soon have to lash out. Instead he had wandered away, past the Golden Pavilion built by a shogun long since gone. The tree-shaded slopes soothed him and he had time to think, something he had not done since setting his mind on getting to Miyako. For the first time he needed to consider what to do with himself. The age of glorious deeds on the battlefield was long since gone. The clerks and the cautious old men ruled now.

He paused beside a mountain stream that ran down to the city below, perhaps to be captured in the garden of a temple or villa, perhaps to be lost forever in the narrow alleyways where the common people lived.

''What are you doing here?'' a harsh voice broke into his reverie.

Sugiyama raised his eyes slowly. A constable dressed in the uniform of his trade—pale blue trousers and a checked kimono tucked into his sash—and carrying the badge and weapon of his office—a *jutte* baton—was standing peering at him. Recognizing he was facing a samurai, he mediated his tone somewhat. ''You are?'' he asked politely.

Sugiyama did not answer. He was unreasonably tired of the city people and their silky ways. He slid forward. The constable, recognizing the sudden menace, raised his *jutte* to chest level. Sugiyama's pose relaxed. The constable, misinterpreting Sugiyama's relaxed fighting pose as non-aggression, started to say ''I arrest . . .''

Sugiyama's perfect draw cut off the constable's head at the neck. Without pausing in his stride or looking back at the headless body spraying the trees, Sugiyama cleaned his sword and resheathed it. His dark figure receded into the darkness of the trees as setting sun and drying blood conspired to paint the forest crimson.

Before him a giant figure suddenly loomed. Sugiyama drew to a halt in a small clearing. He recognized the features and grinned broadly.

"You again! How did you enjoy your swim? Clean already?"

The large samurai regarded him patiently, then just as patiently drew his sword. There was something different about the draw this time, and Sugiyama realized that things had changed. The samurai looked different, his draw held signs of hidden strength and determination. He was now a dangerous man indeed. Sugiyama's jeers died on his lips and he silently prepared himself for battle.

A glimmer of motion caught their eyes. Each of the two warriors turned his head slightly. A man carrying a gun had emerged from the trees behind them. He kept to cover, tracing something on the ground. Raising his eyes he saw the two samurai and stopped. He blinked once, otherwise he was as still as the ground on which he stood.

Isei had come upon the headless body on his way back into the town. The nun had left him to his contemplations, but had extracted a promise that he would return and meet her. Curious and a bit apprehensive he followed the tracks in the forest mold. He did not want to have anything to do with murder, but did not want to be ambushed either. The *ninja*'s attempts to kill him were still fresh in his mind. He was so intent on his tracking, and the two warriors in the clearing were so still, that for the first time in his life he came upon prey completely unaware of its presence. He wanted to turn and fade into the forest, but found he had passed by a large rock that barred his way. Warily he watched the others, noting the drawn swords. The Isei of several days before would have made some pacific gesture, smiled ingratiatingly and faded away as a mountain outcaste should. The new Isei merely stood his ground, waiting to see what would develop.

The three men faced each other in the clearing, none daring to make a move. Isei's eyes shifted quickly from one to the other of the samurai facing him. Samurai meant trouble, and these were obviously out for it. Isei gnawed his lips fearfully. The bigger man would obviously not be easy prey for his own short *nata* hatchet as the samurai near the lake had been. The other one . . . Perhaps. But there was a look in the slimmer man's eye that bode evil for any one foolish enough to come close to him. Isei began a judicious retreat only to find himself blocked by the bole of a massive cedar.

Sugiyama watched the two hunters warily. The musket was a problem, but the lowlife was obviously fearful of him. So the only problem was this pesky *ronin* who seemed to have some grudge against him. He watched the big man carefully. The fact that he had managed to survive an attack was in itself remarkable.

Jiro considered his options carefully. He had no idea who this ragged *sanka* was, but he seemed interested in being part of the fight. In any case, he was obviously not retreating. And he seemed fearful of the samurai presence, yet determined too.

Jiro shifted his weight. Sugiyama acted. He slid forward in a glide that carried him over the rotten leaves like a shadow. His left arm flashed and a tiny glittering *kozuka* knife flew from his scabbard to Isei's eye. Then Sugiyama turned and struck at Jiro. Without moving anything more than his hands, Isei twisted the barrel of his matchlock and fired. The kozuka shattered and in the smoke of the black powder, he himself had scrambled through the bushes to his side and up the slope.

Jiro deflected Sugiyama's rush. Their blades rang together and they stepped apart. Sugiyama readied himself for the giant samurai's counter. Instead Jiro called out in surprise, "The gunner! The murderer!" and then he too was gone, crashing through the woods after Isei, leaving a puzzled Sugiyama far behind.

The samurai bent and examined his *kozuka*. It had been a fine piece of metal. Well tempered and balanced. The lead ball had hit it squarely, shattering the steel into splinters of lead-streaked worthless metal. "Lucky bastard," Sugiyama said slowly. But somewhere, deep within him, he had the uncomfortable feeling that luck was not at all the case. He glared about him one last time, then grinned and sheathed his sword. This was the second time the giant samurai had run. Dead twice in all but the spilling of his blood, and still moving: A coward with luck.

It was turning dark and Sugiyama descended unwillingly towards the city. It attracted and repelled him in equal measures. A figure moved below, loomed out of the dark on a path converging to his own. Closer up he saw it was a woman. A nun, to be precise, her face hidden behind a cowl, but her body nonetheless female for that. The heat in his loins, which he had ignored till now, burst into flame again. He caught up to her, grasped her shoulder and spun her around.

She turned and raked her clawed hand at his face without a word.

Sugiyama glared through the dark at the woman before him. He had come on her providentially. His need for a woman was great, and he did not care if she were a nun. It was sufficient that she was a woman.

She pushed away his grasping hand impatiently, hurrying to some unknown destination in the forest.

"Get out of my way and depart," she said in a thick unknown accent, trying to glide away. "Don't you see who I am?"

"I've had nuns before, and I'll have you," he snarled. His failure to kill the giant ronin still smarted. She made a movement and he slipped aside, barely in time to avoid the swing of the weighted chain she had procured from her sleeve. He drew his sheathed short sword and the chain wrapped itself around the sheath in its next swing. Sugiyama stepped forward suddenly and sank his fist into the soft midriff. The nun dropped the chain and doubled over. Sugiyama spun her around and raised her skirts. She was still sobbing for breath as he plunged his erection deep between her buttocks.

The delightful sharp pain tore through Rosamund's anus as he missed his target. She screamed loudly and he pulled her to him forcefully, disregarding her cries, concerned only with the tight warm dryness of her channel. Holding her hip firmly with one hand he resettled his *shuto* in his sash, then set out to enjoy her fully. She was still bent almost double, though much of her breath had returned. Sugiyama tugged violently at her tits, noticing that they were the largest and finest he had ever felt. The nipples were prominent and the full bags jiggled pleasurably under his hands. He heard the sounds of his belly smacking against her full ass with pleasure, and he explored her loins with a free hand while the other controlled the speed of his motions in her tight hole. He discovered her prominent clitoris and played with it, then found, without much surprise or concern, that he was in her backside, rather than her cunt.

She twisted in his grasp and he noted with growing surprise that she was forcing herself on him, rather than the reverse. His motions did not slacken, but his confidence did as she called out to him to hurry, to drive into her.

His over-full balls exploded a stream of gluey sperm into the depths of her belly. She let out a disappointed howl and turned her furious face to his. In the dark he could not make out her features, but her anger was plain to see.

"You cockless bastard," she sneered. "You aren't able to content a woman you accost."

Taken aback by the charge, Sugiyama tried to drive his shrivelling cock deeper into her, to no avail. She taunted him with his unmanliness and he lost all control, hitting out with his hands and biting at the clothes on her back with his strong teeth. She wriggled and struggled again, but it was plain she expected that and more from him, and moreover, she was enjoying it. Breathing heavily he managed to control himself. He armored himself with the disdain he normally had for the lower orders and sought to withdraw. Sensing his intentions Rosamund tightened her anal muscles. For the first time in his lifetime, Sugiyama yelped in pain as his cock was squeezed by a smooth corrugated muscular vise. He hit her brutally on her buttocks, but the pain only caused her to cry in obvious pleasure. She backed up suddenly and, intent only on his own escape, he found himself sprawled on the ground with the nun's figure towering over his loins. She ground herself forcefully into him, her ass muscles squeezing him for all he was worth. His cock stiffened in her nether orifice and she began bouncing quickly, shafting herself to pleasure. Bemused and somewhat frightened, Sugiyama was powerless to do anything but watch, completely detached from the action. He felt her hands on his balls and again the fear washed over him. But rather than emasculating him, she merely toyed with the bags until he felt the remains of his semen squeezed upwards into her willing and demanding body.

Rosamund rose from the anonymous samurai's body and wiped herself with the skirts of his loose trousers. She pulled down her robes, then walked into the forest without a backwards glance.

Sugiyama studied the camellia blossom intently. It offended his senses. Though perfect now, he knew that it would soon wilt and fade, die sickly like an old man. Quicker than thought his sword was cutting through the fragile stem. The tree did not move, as if a tribute to his skill while the blossom fell to the ground. He felt at peace for the first time since he had had the courtesan. The foreign woman gave him the same sense of peace, and he tried to understand how she was different from any other woman he had known.

CHAPTER 25

SABURO AND MOMOE CREPT DOWN THE STAIRS HAND IN hand. The light was dim. Boards and various carpenter's paraphernalia lay about the large structure. Momoe sniffed the fresh cut wood appreciatively. It was a smell she associated with Saburo, and the feel of his large warm hand in hers was a comfort.

The seated figure of a man loomed suddenly at them out of the dark as they turned a corner. Momoe barely suppressed a cry. Saburo peered fearfully about, then grinned at her. She could see the flash of his white teeth in the dusk.

"Only statues," he whispered. He pointed here and there. There were other statues sitting quietly on their dais, most of them unfinished. Saburo suddenly froze in place. "I thought . . . yes . . . there is a noise there."

Some of the statues suddenly leaped to their feet. Saburo ran, pulling Momoe's hand. She slipped and rolled on some loose lumber. He turned to see two large monks bearing down on him and took to his heels. Momoe found herself raised to her feet by rough hands.

"What are you doing here? Come here quick! A spy!" The last was not for her as out of the gloom several of the statues resolved themselves into stern-visaged monks.

One of her captors lit a candle, another holding her roughly by her arm. They moved aside as a short rotund monk in silk robes, his sash elaborate with gold, pushed his way through the monks, some of whom seemed armed in an unmonkish fashion.

"And what do we have here, eh?" The plump cleric peered at her in the candlelight. "A spy is it?"

"Oh no sir, no sir," the frightened girl protested. "I merely came into the temple to seek shelter for the night."

"I see. And didn't you know the temple is closed for repairs?"

"No sir, I didn't. I found out and a kind workman said he would show me the way out, then there was shouting. . . ." She started to cry.

The abbot patted her shoulder softly. "Don't cry my daughter. This temple is going to be the most magnificent in Miyako, in the whole of the country. Yakushi Nyorai himself has commanded it." His face was glowing with the sweat of emotion and Momoe found something frightening in the cleric's intensity.

"Here, someone fetch the girl a cup of tea. One of the workmen, did you say?"

"Yes," she sobbed. She grasped unsteadily for the cup someone shoved her way. Through lowered lids she saw the round monk signal to some of the others who rapidly disappeared into the gloom.

"Did he tell you his name my dear? We should reward his helpfulness."

"No," she shook her head, hoping Saburo had made his escape. "No. He was a carpenter I think."

There was a sudden shout from the direction of the exit. The burlier of the monks hurried that way. The chief monk stayed with her, as did two of his stronger henchmen.

"What will we do with her?" One of the men whispered to the abbot.

"Hold her in the meanwhile," he muttered. "I must know what she has found out. In any case, the neighborhood is full of the magistrate's men, and we cannot afford to draw attention to ourselves."

One of the monks who had been dispatched to the underground hall where the workmen were kept hurried back. "One of them has escaped!" he said urgently.

The abbot's plump face firmed. "Find him. Immediately. Take her and put her somewhere. I will decide what to do about her later." He chewed his lips anxiously.

"Should we run?" asked one of the monks, his eyes darting uneasily around.

"Fool!" the abbot snarled. "Yakushi Nyorai Dai Bosatsu will not abandon us. I will go to divine the escapee's whereabouts. You two guard the girl." He motioned Momoe's two guards and they roughly hauled her to her feet. "I am so sorry, my girl," the abbot said sweetly to Momoe. "There is a necessity on us however, for the greater glory of the Dai Bosatsu. Follow these brothers please. They will see to your welfare."

Submissively, Momoe followed the two black-and-white-clad shaven monks across the fresh wood of the floor. They took her to a tiny cell deep in the interior of the temple. There was no door but bolts of cloth showed that it was used for storing the great banners that were to be used for decorating the interior of the building. The two monks sat, staring eerily at her through the gloom. While maintaining a cowed expression, Momoe's mind was racing, looking for ways out. The two men were armed with short curved *naginata*: sword blades attached to long poles. They looked too alert to be fooled by anything, or to fall asleep on guard. She moved restlessly and she noted that one of the guard's eyes were focused on the space between the hems of her kimono. Her hand moved to close the gap between the sides, and then a plan of escape occurred to her. Instead, she ran her hands around the base of her throat as if hot, and managed to expose her chest to the tops of her breasts. In the candlelight she could see the guard's eyes riveted to the V of her cleavage. She moved again, uncomfortably, and this time the other monk's eyes drew to her figure.

Inwardly she smiled. Perhaps she could get them interested in her. And after all, they were not ill-favored, though shaven. She lay back on a pile of rough woven cloth and closed her eyes. She was conscious of stealthy movement, then felt a large hard hand on her ankle. She opened heavy lids slowly and raised her knee slighty, affording the monk a better view of her cunt.

Momoe opened her eyes fully in time to see the form of the monk crawl onto her. He held his stiff stander for her inspection, and she smiled ingratiatingly. His strong teeth flashed in the dimness and he set the knob at the entrance to her pleasure hole, then pressed inwards. Her thighs rose to encompass his rough-clad back. He hammered his spike home to the root, grunting and licking with effort. His lust increased as he exposed her breasts, mauling them unthinkingly with his hands, squeezing the nipples in his lust.

She turned her head from the sweating face of the monk and smiled at the other one who was squatting beside them enjoying the show. She clutched with her legs at the man's bobbing ass while her hand searched the clothes of the other one. She found his erect fleshy pole and pulled slightly. He followed her lead and the pole of the *naginata* fell beside him as he knelt on all fours over her face. Like a calf come to its mother she sucked in the length of the monk's cock, laving it with her tongue and soft lips.

The suction and thrust of her loins did the job. Her mouth flooded soon with the second monk's discharge, and the first one to approach followed soon after, filling her willing vagina with his white discharge. Momoe did not want to give the men time to rest from their labors. She reversed herself rapidly, forcing her mouth onto the shrivelling penis of the one who had been in her cunt. She could taste the mixture of his milk and her honey, and her efforts were soon rewarded. The monk exclaimed in admiration as his member came fully erect. Momoe's hands had been busy with the other holy man. He rose onto her and she inserted his penis into her hungry vagina. The two bonzes grunted in double effort as they rammed the willing body of their woman captive. Momoe's reward was not far in coming. She swallowed the poor offering of the man in her mouth, and rubbing furiously against the shaft with her hand, brought the other to a climax.

† † †

Saburo knew he must get away for help. His and Momoe's only chance lay in that. A wall loomed before him, topped with tile. He leaped and gained the top, then leaped again without looking to find himself in a well-kept garden. Before him a villa lay in darkness. Unthinking he rushed in the direction of the building, wanting to ask the residents for some help. He ran around to the front, seeking an entry, battering at the shutters. Behind him one of the wooden shutters shifted silently. A naked figure slipped out. A heavy bag was raised and came crashing down on his head. Darkness filled his thoughts.

Saburo came to in an opulent room well lit by several candles. A woman knelt at his side, examining him carefully. Another woman, simply dressed, sat in a corner. He noticed suddenly that he was naked.

"I wonder what we have here," he heard her say to herself.

Saburo looked up at her cruel cold face and wondered what it was about. He turned his head then groaned as the pain in his head was accelerated by the motion.

"Why, the darling is awake. What were you doing, thief?"

"I was trying to ask for help . . ."

"In your nakedness?" she asked mockingly. Then she regarded the length of his muscular body thoughtfully. "You know, I have never had a male at my mercy like this before." She grasped the root of Saburo's cock. "I could have you killed, you know?"

"Please mistress," he gasped, "I am not a thief. I am merely asking for help. For me . . . for me and a friend. A woman, like you. Please . . ." he sobbed.

"I love it when they beg," Haruko looked pleased. "I have no interest in your woman friend."

He was panting slightly. "Please. There is a great crime being committed. Kidnapping! And worse!"

Her hand, holding a bright hairpin, was suddenly at his throat. "A crime, you said? Tell me!" Her cruel playfulness was suddenly transformed into an icy commanding presence.

"The abbot," Saburo whispered. "The abbot of Saionji has been kidnapping workmen to build the temple. He cannot afford to pay them. Also. . . ." Saburo's voice sank. "He has been counterfeiting gold *koban* coins! He has the workmen coat lead forms with gold."

Haruko's relieved laughter caused his eyes to snap back to her face. "Is that all? Old purse-mouth is a counterfeiter and kidnapper." She laughed with a high tinkling laughter that brought shudders to both Midori and Saburo. "So that's why the area is infested with magistracy runners. And I thought . . . well, no matter what I thought. Now, I think I'll keep you for my own amusement for a while." Another use for this young man occurred to her as well. If things *were* falling apart, she might need a fallback position, and old holy fat-jowls might just provide it. "Get me some sashes, from that chest in the corner, then go away." Midori wordlessly handed her the sashes and departed. Haruko gagged the helpless Saburo, then tied him into a bow, ankles and wrists together. His muscular chest was taut with strain, and his loins projected provocatively.

Haruko stood back and laughed at the sight. "You are too feeble, master. Hmm, I should have kept Midori here for the mundane details. Well, no matter, I will do it myself."

She pulled impatiently at his cock which not unnaturally refused to stiffen. "Bastard," she said. Then again furiously, with her hands while biting his prominent pectorals. His cock started to swell at the touch of her naked body on his. She eyed the roll of limp male flesh with disfavor, then bent and sucked it into her warm wet mouth.

Saburo jerked in surprise, notwithstanding his awkward position. His cock rose to stiffness in her demanding mouth. Her teeth nipped him painfully, then scraped over the shaft and crown. They both examined the result. His cock was dark and pulsing, shining with the moisture of her mouth. She laughed at the sight and he, bemused by the situation and oddly excited by it, laughed too. She rolled him onto his back and the pole projected over his tightly muscled belly. She amused herself by slapping the swaying fleshy branch from side to side. Notwithstanding the initial pain, Saburo got into the spirit of things and swayed his belly backwards and forwards, avoiding her hands to the best of his ability.

She tired of her game, rose, and crouched over his head. He knew what was wanted though he had never done it before. She rubbed herself against his face and his uneducated tongue did its best to keep up with her rapidly moving hairy slit. His tongue was tiring when he felt his face flooded in the warm sour darkness with drops of moisture which covered his face with a glistening mask. She reversed her position and skewered herself onto his erect member. She loosened his bonds sufficiently to allow him some freedom of motion, but not enough to allow him escape. Her cunt was looser than Momoe's, the friction lesser, but she used it to a good advantage, churning her hips when she descended, twiddling the tip of his cock against her entrance when she rose. Her movements grew faster, her breathing and the bites and sucks of her mouth more urgent. Suddenly she rolled them both over so that they lay side by side, one of her thighs under, the other over his hips. Her ankles clutched at his ass, and her fingers dug in. She closed her eyes and moaned freely as she came for the second time. He tried to speed up the thrusts of his own hips so as to match hers. She scowled, recognizing his needs, and hit his chest resoundingly. "Not until I've had enough of you!" she commanded.

Rolling him back, she crouched over him. Her hand grasped the dew-slickened member and fed it between her thighs. He found her much tighter, much dryer now. She sank down the entire length of his cock. Her knees rose up and he could see the entire hairy purse and the female hole which she was opening with her fingers, strumming and tickling. She had inserted him into her anus, a practice he had heard about but never experienced. Haruko bounced on him wildly. Her fingers turned to a blur in the candlelight. Her hips trembled violently as she forced herself into the throes of another wild orgasm. The tightness of her anus drove him near to the peak, but again she frustrated his desire, pulling away from him and slapping the shaft painfully to cause him to desist.

She impaled herself on his cock again, then rolled them over so that he was riding on her. His hands were still tied behind his back though she had released his ankles. "Fuck me now. Fuck with all your might. Now." She dug her nails deeply into his ass. Saburo's loins were on fire. He knew he had to come to a climax or die. His toes dug into the futon and he jerked his way into her complaisant cunt with as much energy as he could muster. She encouraged him, whispering "fuck, fuck, cunt, fuck, ass," into his ears, stroking his head, tugging at his ears. Her heels beat a tattoo on his back and her teeth scored his chest and sucked at his willing mouth. The heat began rising in his balls, and he found he could no longer control his movements. She felt it as well and her trained body responded with a rising orgasm of its own.

Saburo exploded into the noblewoman's thirsty cunt. All his pent-up lust burst like a dam swollen by rains. He could feel the sperm thundering through his penis, shaking his frame with electric discharges from head to foot. The spraying of his hose seemed endless, his muscles jerking in spasm after spasm of wonderful release. He was barely conscious of the woman bearing down upon him, lost as he was in the pleasure of her own contractions.

They subsided together and she rested on his chest. He was panting heavily, moving about uncomfortably. Haruko rose off the craftman's exhausted penis. She crouched again over his face. "Clean me," she said. He tried to move his head in negation. His own sperm? She was flooded with it, large pearly drops hanging from her lower beard and streaks hidden in the folds of her cunt. She forced herself down on his face and grabbed his flaccid penis with an iron hand. He understood the threat. His tongue searched out the recesses of her cunt, collecting the mixed flavors of his own milk and her honey. He was conscious of the tremors that rocked her frame as he did so, and learned to enjoy the work because of the obvious pleasure it gave her. She rose from his face eventually. There was a glint of something like appreciation in her face as she looked down at him.

"Can you untie me now, mistress? Let me go to call the constables? My friend is in great danger . . ." He pleaded with her.

The look of appreciation and satiety disappeared from Haruko's thin features. She smiled maliciously.

"Oh no my dear. I'm going to turn you over to the abbot. I need something from him too, and you are an excellent bargaining chip."

"Let him go!" a sharp female voice interrupted from the entryway. Saburo's sight was obscured by Haruko's pale thighs. She stood up suddenly and Saburo could see that the commanding tone came from the serving girl who had been sitting in the corner of the room.

"You little chit, how dare you speak to me in that tone!" Haruko said furiously.

"Let him go, or else."

"Or else what, you slut? I'll have you thrown back into the street." Haruko's voice was barely controlled. Saburo peeked behind her legs and saw the young woman with waist-long, curiously soft-brown hair standing firmly at the entrance to the room. She was dressed in a plain kimono over which she had put a darker coat.

Haruko took a step towards her. Suddenly Midori slid naturally into a curious stance, her weight seeming to rest fully on one leg, the other extended before her. One hand, fingers open, was raised before her forehead, the other was held palm down at waist level.

Haruko's mouth dropped open, then snapped shut. She looked wildly around, but she was as naked as Saburo. Fearlessly, still not believing that Midori was anything else than a meek servant girl, she charged forward. Midori met the other woman's charge with both hands extended. Her right pulled at Haruko's neck, her left between her legs and she shifted the position of her hips. Haruko cartwheeled to the floor. The fight would have ended then and there but for the slickness of Haruko's cum-slathered cunt. Midori's left hand fulcrum slipped and Haruko fell half to her side and rolled away from the arm hold Midori tried to use.

The older woman rose to her feet and looked at her erstwhile maid with some degree of respect. "Who are you?" she gasped.

"Osei, a woman of Gion," Midori answered in a deep and confident voice completely different from her previous meekness. "I work for Matsudaira Konnosuke-sama."

"A spy," Haruko gasped. "A spy for the magistrate." For once in her existence she was completely rattled. "You've been telling him about our kidnapping scheme!" She screamed with rage and threw herself at the slighter girl. "I'll kill you!"

Midori had only a split second to digest that startling information and worry about its import. Suddenly she was grappling with a slick naked woman who seemed just as well versed in fighting as she. She twisted her hips and straightened her arms. Haruko was hurled away, unable to stop herself.

She crashed through the shoji. Another shadow loomed beside her. She squealed and rolled away. The dark-clad figure ignored her and dashed through the remains of the sliding paper-glazed frame. Haruko crawled away, then rose and ran towards the back of the garden. There was a chance of escape still if she made the forest behind the mansion. The abbot would be no use to her now: The magistrate's spy had probably overheard that stupid workman's babblings, and the abbot would be next on their list.

Okiku slammed full tilt into Midori, who was recovering from her throw and just about to give chase after Haruko. She narrowly avoided spitting the young courtesan on her dagger blade.

"Where are they?" she asked urgently, recognizing Midori more by her body scent than by sight.

"She got away!" Midori called.

"She? Aren't there any others?"

"No, no. Only she. And this poor young man here."

Okiku looked down at the floor as she wiped her face. She smiled. "Why Midori . . ."

Midori, still gasping for breath, but more familiar with Okiku than she had been, tried to chuckle. "No, no. Ito Haruko had him. But he has a very interesting story to tell. I'll release him. The Ito woman is important."

Okiku shrugged and said, "Why should we care about her? What was this about anyway?"

They released Saburo while listening to his story. Okiku hissed angrily between her teeth. "This is a serious business. And Go . . . Lord Matsudaira has withdrawn the watch from around the villa. But why did Ito's wife run like that? Anyway, I will go to the temple. You two run and call the magistrate's men. Go quickly now, there is someone coming. Hurry."

The three of them slid into the night as heavy footsteps approached.

CHAPTER 26

THE TWO MONKS NESTLED ON EITHER SIDE OF MOMOE FELL
soon into a deep sleep. Carefully as a mouse, Momoe
crept out from between their snoring forms. There seemed
to be much movement in the depths of the temple, and she
glided as silently as she could on her bare feet from one
dark corner to another.

The knife which pressed against her neck came as a
complete surprise. She froze, not daring to breath as her
body was explored quietly and impersonally.

"Who are you, sneaking about the temple at this hour?"
a female voice, somewhat familiar, asked in a whisper.

"Momoe, that is I, . . ."

"What are you doing here?" there was a quiet, confident menace in the voice. "Do not make a sound to alert
the guards . . ."

Momoe decided the voice was to be obeyed, and anyone
working against the temple monks . . . "My name is
Momoe, of Gion," she hurriedly explained. "The monks
were holding my man prisoner . . ."

Her head was tilted suddenly back and studied in the
faint light.

"Yes, tell me more."

Momoe gave a censored version of her recent adven-
tures, concentrating on her arrival and incarceration in the
temple.

"Where are the craftsmen kept? Lead me to them."

Notwithstanding her fear, Momoe obediently led the
way. The other followed behind her like a shadow, slipping noiselessly from one pool of darkness to another.
Momoe pointed to the door leading to the cellar. Five
monks stood guard there, and this time they were very
alert indeed.

"I must get in to see what they are doing," the voice whispered in her ear. "Is there any other way?"

"Not that I know," Momoe said.

"We must find a way to distract them," the shadow said. "Wait for five minutes then make a noise . . ."

"Only some of them would follow you," Momoe objected. She thought a moment, then gathering her courage said, "I think there is another way. Go and hide at a point where you can enter quickly."

The five monks were alert, their eyes constantly searching the dark corners of the hall before them. Other monks had returned to their cells or were busy beating the bushes around the temple in search of the fugitive. One of them saw a glimmer of white. He rose to investigate, and his surprised cry brought the others.

Momoe was leaning against a pillar. Her hair and clothes were disarranged. She giggled shyly as she guards approached. Her robe fell open displaying a pink-tipped plump breast. She was crooking her fingers at the first guard as the others came up.

"Hello dearie," she said. "Such a pretty . . . hic . . . bald head you've got . . ." She staggered forward and her robe flipped back, exposing a length of golden thigh.

One of the monks looked at her and muttered, "She's drunk."

She overheard him. "Only a wee drinkie. Do you have something to offer me, little bonze of mine?" She staggered forward and fell into the nearest monk's arms. He dropped his pole arm and reached for her. Somehow her robe dropped from her shoulders to her waist, exposing both high full breasts.

"Kiss my nipples?" she whispered in his ear, nibbling the lobe.

The monk looked back at his companions then lowered her to the floor, raising his knee-length skirt.

"No," Momoe pouted. "One of you beautiful fellows is not enough. Bet I can take on all of you at once."

"We'll just do you one at a time sweetie," the oldest of the monks said.

"Just for that I won't give you my mouth. You'll have to make do with my hand. Here, you're younger and probably much more fun." She motioned to a scar-faced monk and he grinned foolishly. The monks crowded around her. The oldest among them cast one look back at the door they were guarding. It was about twenty feet away. If anyone tried to leave he would be sure to hear it. Even in the arms of this delightfully randy drunk night wanderer.

The others were crouched around Momoe, lust in their eyes. She was undoing them one after another, exposing erect and semi-erect cocks out of their loincloths. She examined each cock with care. Scarface had a short, very thick member gnarled with prominent veins. The old man the others called Uncle had a thin rod which, notwithstanding her previous strictures, she knew she was going to put to her mouth. Jibei and Hachio were heavy-set fellows and their cocks seemed almost perfectly alike. The last was nicknamed Gaptooth. One of his canines had been knocked out and his face was lopsided from some ancient wound. His cock rose like a bent bow before him, jerking eagerly.

She surveyed the forest of members critically. Rough hands reached for her and she giggled, falling back on her robe as they removed her loose sash. Scarface and Jibei possessed themselves of her breasts. In their eagerness they knocked their shaved pates together. Momoe and the others laughed and she consoled both monks by rubbing their stubbles tenderly. Uncle, perhaps to expiate his former doubts, attached himself like a leech to her inviting pussy. He fought off all attempts by Gaptooth to insert his curved cock in the desirable little hole. Momoe laughed at their fighting and consoled the loser by stroking his peculiar member, an attention he received eagerly. Her own lust began rising and Momoe no longer had to dissemble her desire. Uncle's lips and tongue were drawing her juices and she hugged him with her thighs, urging him on. Two of the monks presented their cocks for her inspection and she seized them eagerly, kissing first one and then the other, licking and sucking at the presented members. Someone unseen by her started rubbing his cock against her breasts. At the juncture of her legs Uncle was a driving fire that possessed all of her. Gaptooth, frustrated in his attempt to reach her cunt, was rubbing his curved cock against the arch of one foot while he nibbled and sucked at the toes of other.

Momoe shivered as the sensations of their lust coursed

through her. She pulled at the nearest monk and at her unspoken bidding he lay on the floor. She crouched over him, her dangling breasts tweaked and squeezed by several hands. A perverse notion occurred to her and she reversed herself so as to present him with a sight of her glorious smooth buns. She parted the moons with her hands and the erect cock nuzzled at the ring of her anus. Slowly she let herself down. She could feel the wide flanges of the cock head parting her muscles, and then the easing as the shaft sank slowly into her depths. The monk breathed heavily but none of the men made any move. Momoe adjusted her position, leaning back onto the monk's broad chest. She parted the hairs in her cunt. Uncle could see the sweet pink hole. Below the length of the slit he could see the thick male member protruding between the two moons of the buttocks. The stretched ring of muscle was almost invisible. She motioned to Scarface. He knelt between her legs presenting the head of his knobbed cock to her entrance. He pushed in, applying counter pressure to Hachio whose cock was distending Momoe's rectum. The two monks' balls met against the soft mat of Momoe's dark moss. She pulled Uncle to her. His long thin cock was guided to her lips. Delighted, he knelt on her breasts before Scarface's eyes and inserted his cock deeply into the waiting mouth. Momoe's tongue flicked against the sensitive spot at the bottom surface of his member and the elderly monk shivered with delight. Momoe reached for Jibei and directed him to her armpit. He knelt by her side and his cock ground into her flesh while he competed with other rough hands for possession of her breasts, her thighs, her cheeks and neck. They moved together, Momoe delighting in the pricks that were doing her bidding, raising her to delights she had experienced separately before, but never together and never at her command.

Okiku watched from the shadows as the weaver girl she had recognized from Gion attracted the randy monks to her. A line from a poem flitted through her head as she quickly slipped to the door. "A bonze fucks as he drinks/ too much/and without care for the fragility of the vessel." She watched the tangle of five men and a woman as she rapidly raised the two horizontal bars and slipped through the door. It was the work of a moment to return the bars to their place using the tool and thread she had prepared.

She slipped carefully down the stairs, attendant to possible traps. The underground part of the temple was divided into several areas by partitions. Okiku prowled around the identified various work areas: carpenters, metalworkers, and finally, gilders. None of the raw material was to be found and Okiku wondered where it was stored. She examined the benches, which looked perfectly normal. And yet, Okiku thought, there was something peculiar. Then it struck her. With all the activity going on, there had to be another way to get materials and finished products in and out of the workshop area. She directed her eyes upwards and soon found what she was looking for: a faintly deliniated rectangle in the ceiling. It was the work of a moment to put on the bear-claw climbing hooks, walk up a pillar and along a beam to where she could examine the bottom of the trapdoor.

It was impossible to open from below, she concluded. Encouraged by the find itself, she searched the ceiling and the corner of the room, clinging like a fly to the wooden beams. She came finally upon an inconspicuous panel set flush with the wall in one of the upper corners. Anchoring herself with some more of her hooks, she pried about the panel until it opened with a quiet snick. She smelt the air. Someone had been there recently by the smell of burning wax. She listened carefully. No sound. Good, the owner was away. She slipped through quietly. Her head brushed a cobweb. Instantly a silk netting studded with hooks fell from the ceiling, entangling her in its folds. Okiku cursed and started to struggle, then realizing it was doing more harm then good, reached for one of the innumerable tools she carried. It was going to be a long job, and she was glad the owner was gone.

A statue, barely visible in the dark, stirred and came to life. It lit a candle with flint and steel. The yellow light disclosed the benovolent plump face of Abbot Saishiden.

The abbot smiled at his captive and produced a large hexagonal-sectioned iron bar. "If you struggle," he said mildly, "I shall have to brain you. Have a good look around. I want to ask you some questions."

Okiku looked at the small low-ceilinged room. It must

be hidden by the multi-level structure of the temple she decided. Then she drew a deep breath. Most of the items were of gold. Gold statues, panels, lotus decorations. And several boxes filled with neat rows of paper-wrapped palm-size ovals: boxes of *ryo* coins.

"Attractive, isn't it?" the abbot inquired. Then he sighed and smiled angelically. "Unfortunately, all fake," he looked sadly at the glittering treasure. "You are not a thief I take it? No, of course not. I rather expect an undercover agent of the magistrate's."

"You don't have a chance," Okiku spoke her first words.

"Ah, a female spy! Of course not. I am fully aware and fearful of the might of the law. No, I shall slip away and start again somewhere. You see, the temple *must* be built, and the people of our great land *must* be brought to the right path, the proper worship of the only true Buddha, Yakushi Nyorai." He smiled gently, but there was a hint of steely fanaticism in his voice.

"But we of these blessed isles have always worshipped a multitude of kami and buddhas," Okiku objected, more to keep the conversation going than for any desire to engage in theological debate.

"Wrongly, very wrongly. I learned this from the Spanish friars years ago. Of course they, being benighted barbarians, worship some rude god or other. But at least they realize that only one supreme deity counts, and demands all our adoration. No matter. My monks will fearlessly protect this place until I am well away with some of this stuff. I merely await my porters. You I am afraid, well, . . . I shall be leaving you here."

A thought occurred suddenly to Okiku. "Why did you kill Ito Shinichi?"

The abbot stopped in his preparations and smiled quizzically. "You are more perspicacious than I thought, and definitely an agent of the magistrate's. He was becoming a menace, my dear. Just as you are. Is there anything you want? Before you die I mean? My means here are limited. I can offer you some water to drink, a morsel of rice. Some sexual relief perhaps. My needs are few."

"You mean you're going to rape me?" Okiku squealed

in pretended distress. At the moment she could do nothing, but in time. . . .

"Of course not," he said in genuine surprise. "My needs are few, as I've said. But being a woman I imagine coitus is your main concern and I will satisfy your lust if necessary to ease your passage. As for me, I have not engaged in sexual congress for at least forty years."

He said it so simply and forthrightly that Okiku was compelled to believe him. The abbot, she thought, was indeed a holy man, driven by motives that were well beyond those she was familiar with, and doubly dangerous for that.

"I think I would like that," Okiku said, spreading her legs.

"Do you prefer my mouth, my fingers, or my penis?" he inquired. "Please do not be hesitant at stating your preferences. I will do my humble best."

"All three," she said.

He examined her carefully, then bent and removed her pants. His soft delicate fingers applied themselves to her pink slit, tracing each fold methodically and thoroughly, raising her juices in imperceptible degrees.

Above them the monks were nearing exhaustion. Momoe's feet were covered with sperm as the pedophilic Gaptooth spurted again and again against her delicate arches. Her cunt was overflowing with milky sperm, as were her asshole and the valleys between her breasts and her armpits. At last they fell off her, and their heavy panting turned slowly into tired snores. After all, they could see the door they guarded from their resting place. Momoe rose, still naked, and dragging her robe behind her went in search of the washing trough, then slipped into the night.

CHAPTER 27

EVENTS WERE MOVING TOO FAST FOR ISEI. IT WAS TIME TO leave, but not before he had accomplished the objective of his visit. From the slope of the mountain he had noticed the roofs of a temple someone had pointed out to him as dedicated to the Yakushi Nyorai. It was there he had to go to settle his accounts with the *daibutsu*. He crept carefully down the mountain, perching on a small slope to observe the temple below.

After escaping from the wild samurai, Rosamund had needed to think. She had two alternatives. She could escape the sometimes cloying existence in Goemon's House of Women and escape into the wild world, or she could acquiesce and make the best she could of her existence. There were advantages and disadvantages to each course: freedom against security; the love and support of loyal friends against the cruelty of the outside world; familiarity against strangeness. She had no illusions about her fate in the Japans: she would be found out, her body worked for the pleasure of whomever found her. Her traitorous skin tingled at the thought. On the other hand, she enjoyed despotic control of Goemon's House of Women, and for that matter, of the governor himself. She was so sunk in her meditations, and the passing figure was so silent, that she did not notice the man squatting down before her and peering down through a bush until it had actually happened. Her mind was suddenly made up for her. She recognized the figure of the man with the matchlock who had had her before. Her loins blazed in excitement. He was her salvation, he was a possible support in lieu of Goemon and the others of her friends. With thought came action and she slid across the tiny clearing, her hands out to grasp.

Isei spun around at the sound behind him. Not fast enough. A sudden weight pinned him to the ground, a skillful hand searched in his pants and gripped his penis.

"Don't struggle!" a voice hissed in his ears, and then a demanding full mouth was applied to his. He dropped his ready matchlock and cupped the two full breasts that were pressed into his chest. The nun again. Not his, but the one who had come after.

"I have found you," she said contentedly, rolling on to her back and pulling him deeply into her. They struggled out of their clothes, their organs deeply joined, moving in a rhythm of their own.

Isei pushed at her lovingly. His teeth nipped at her soft parts, his hands explored her bulges and hollows, urged on by her whispered instructions, finally doing all that needed to be done by wordless empathy. He knew that he had to satisfy her for his own satisfaction, and moreover, knew how to do it. Her body was a sculpture he was building out of instinct and passion as his father was wont to carve the beautiful wood of the deep forest. Hands, lips, tongue, chest, penis. All his body was concerned with was the pleasing of the vision beneath, then above him, then lying by his side.

The strange, pale-faced, golden-haired woman was now moving with him, matching each of his thrusts with one of her own. Her strange round eyes were open, looking deeply into his. He pinched her ass mounds hoping to cause some pain but she only wriggled gratefully. The words of the nun came back to him. The pain brought pleasure to this golden vision and he struggled to meet her demands. She began shuddering in an orgasm that continued and continued beyond anything he had ever witnessed. Still he did not cease his explorations and his efforts, turning every nerve ending in her milk-white skin to a blazing pinpoint of pleasure.

The pain and the delight mixed in Rosamund's belly to a volcano that spewed an unquenchable fire. She barely moved an exterior muscle, but her vaginal tissues stroked and milked the man's perfect penis with knowledge and love. He approached orgasm many times and each time she managed, without effort and without making him withdraw, using only her vaginal skill, to stop the progress before he reached the crest. She knew that for him, as for her, this was the ultimate bodily delight. She thought she actually was him, taking delight and pleasure in her own body, and her own continuing orgasm, like a phoenix feeding on its own flames, grew even higher. Her mind and body completely uncoupled, and from a point of view high above the two bodies on the ground she floated in a cloud of pleasure.

Isei's eyes darted suddenly from Rose's beatific face to a space between two trees. Sugiyama was standing there looking at them, an evil grin on his face. He started pulling out of Rosamund and her loins clutched at him. He knew that she was nearing her final climax. The tie between them was so intense that he knew every nerve end of her body was singing. She was in complete harmony with him. His matchlock was barely out of reach. The need for defense, and the imperative need to complete this act to its final glorious climax warred in him. Rational thought won out and he chose to engage in that which was so rare the sages dared not talk about it. Detached, Isei's mind watched life and death unfold. Rosamund cried out. A sweet, high piercing unhuman sound of pure exaltation. All her physical muscles contracted at the same moment, merging her completely with Isei's body. His penis became a part of her, the interaction between it and her vagina the center of the world. Her spirit finally, for one glorious and eternal moment, found itself and centered perfectly in the universe. Then reality rushed in once again and her body slackened back into the normal shuddering, demanding clay. Events started taking place again.

The sword blade whistled down, shining bright lightning aimed at the space where Isei's broad back had been a moment before. Rosamund's mounded breasts, slightly flattened over her rib cage rose towards the blade. Isei rolled swiftly away and his matchlock leaped to his hand.

Time stopped for all three of them there in the small glade. The wind in the pines paused. Birds and other life forms froze in their place. Sugiyama brought his sword down in a blow that would cut both torsos in two. Even his death would not stop the cut. He knew it better than he had known any blow to be true before. This, now, here, was the ultimate stroke. Not as he had expected it, in battle, but the true stroke nonetheless. In the timeless moment of the sword's movement he wondered why this would be so, striking at an unprotected back, then the unresisting front of a beautiful strange woman. No expert against which to test his skill, and yet the feel of reaching the climax of his skill against the most deadly of opponents.

The sword descended in a moment that was eternity. Isei reached the matchlock. For the briefest spark of a second he smiled at himself, knowing the end of his life was here. Casually, not really aiming, in the briefest of seconds that lasted an entire age, he shot.

Lead slug, dull and almost ungainly, travelling fast, intercepted the shiny polished slab of worked steel. Layer after layer of welded steel and iron, thousands and hundreds of thousands of them accepted the stress of the lead's energy, and when they could not do so anymore, flew off at a tangent.

Rosamund had barely recovered from her orgasm, her insides still heaving, when the man ripped himself from between her legs. She had time to see that her horizon was filled with the image of the rough samurai who had raped her before. His face was frozen into a mask of calm divinity, as if he had seen his god face to face. She heard the bang, saw the sword fly from the samurai's hand as its blade shivered into fragments. She rose with horror in time to see the sudden twitch of movement as the samurai's short-sword buried itself almost to the hilt in her new-found lover's neck. He was kneeling motionless, his matchlock held loosely at his hip, slight smile on his face. Then Isei the Forester toppled over. A last scion of the Taira brought to ground near the city of the glory of his ancestors.

Sugiyama froze after the throw. Suddenly he knew why he had felt the imminence of his own death. He stared incredulously at the dead gunner, then at the woman the gunner had saved. He looked at the lead-stained blade fragments of his *katana* for one last moment, back at the man who had mastered him, then turned his back and stumbled into the forest. Rosamund gently cradled her nameless lover's dead head. No tears would fall. He had died as he wanted to, and only he and she knew that he had given her more than any lover before.

Uemura had seen Haruko hurtle out of the *shoji* and knew that pursuit was not far behind. A glow of romantic chivalry suffused his breast. He grinned self-deprecatingly in the dark. She was the perfect mistress, something the gallant was always ready to lay down his life for. Reality emulated art, and here was the final art, the final reality of death. His petty robberies, his poesy, his languid ways were no longer of any account. Here, tonight, he would write the final poem. He moved to interpose himself before the moving white figure that loomed out of the dark. It slipped aside, and just as he was about to follow he noted a more immediate threat facing him. The giant samurai dressed in plain grey clothes looked back impassively. Uemura grinned. He knew himself to be a master swordsman. That was the reason Ito and Haruko had both found him fascinating in the first place. The big samurai, bulky as he may be, did not seem to move with any of the proper gestures of a true fencer.

Uemura bowed properly. "Uemura Sonzaemon, at your service."

The big samurai grunted. "Miura Jiro."

"Never heard of you," Uemura yawned.

"Good," the giant said firmly. Then he added in a language Uemura did not know, "Time to go puppy."

Uemura drew his sword properly, holding it in the formal *chudan kamae* posture, sword hilt at waist level, blade up at an angle. Miura drew his own, holding the blade loosely before him with one hand.

Uemura smiled to himself, then shifted his feet minutely, toes pointing inwards for what was called the "crow step" maneuver. The big samurai did not respond properly, and Uemura's smile broadened. His blade flicked up and to his right in a gambit that should have brought the giant's sword up to meet his own blade. His remis, bind, and *morote-uchi* two-handed thrust were all ready in his mind. Instead he found the giant's chest pressed close to his and an excruciating pain in his bowels. He confusedly looked down at the shiny mess of entrails that was pouring down to the ground, wondering vaguely if they were his own. His body gave up the struggle and fell. The giant stepped to Uemura's left, his *katana* held at waist level, back of the blade supported by his left palm.

Jiro stepped over the still-twitching body and wiped his blade. He looked at the darkened mansion and scratched his chin thoughtfully. Now where had Goemon gone to? And where was Okiku whose message had brought him here?

† † †

Hori cowered in the dark mansion. The servants had fled. He was panting heavily. Had the woman Momoe seen his face? In any case it did not matter. The other, Midori, had proven to be a spy of the magistrate's. There could only be one reason to plant a spy here. His activites were known. He licked his lips nervously, then started scrabbling through the chests in Haruko's room. He knew she was the murderess. Perhaps if he found some evidence . . . Maybe he could trade it for his life. He kept his ears cocked for the sounds of movement outside, his mood fluctuating between slight relief and abject terror.

A shadow fell over him. A *shoji* slid silently open and Hori turned. A figure dressed in white kimono and bearing two white-corded swords in his sash stood there looking at him fiercely.

"Hori Narimitsu-san?"

Hori fell back. "Who are you?"

"Matsudaira Konnosuke, Magistrate of Miyako," Goemon responded stepping fully into the light. "I will arrest you. For the murder of Ito Shinichi."

"No. No, I did not do it. She did. The bitch. Ito Haruko. . . ."

"And for the rape and kidnapping of peaceful citizens of the Empire."

Panting heavily, Hori stared at his nemesis.

"How do you know? The woman, your spy is it?" He rose to his feet slowly cocking his head, and a crafty look came and went in his face.

"So you came with your minions to arrest me, eh?"

"Only myself," Matsudaira said mildly.

Hori grinned triumphantly. "Kill him! Kill him!" Hori called out loud. The panels of the *fusuma* burst open and the three members of his gang appeared through them. Two brandished swords and the third carried a massive wooden pole. They interposed themselves between their master and his pursuer. The pole whistled down in a great overhead blow at Matsudaira's elegantly topknotted head. He slipped aside and drew his own sword. The blade flashed in the light. He blocked the thrust of the bulky kidnapper and cut at his face, then reversed the blow and cut *kesa giri*—crosswise from shoulder to hip—at the second man beside him. The sledge came up again as Matsudaira drew his short sword, reversed, with his left and hammered the pommel into the sledge wielder's throat. The man squeaked and dropped his weapon. Matsudaira took a step forward and stabbed both his blades, crossing them in front of his chest. The burly kidnapper gurgled and a gush of blood appeared at the corners of his mouth. The one cut across the chest clutched at his spilling guts and barely noticed the short blade embedded in his kidney. Matsudaira pulled out both blades smoothly and spun around. The burly kidnapper fell to his knees then to his face as his heart pumped blood out in a fountain from the deep stab to the great artery that led to his heart.

The pole wielder stopped scrabbling for his weapon and drew a knife instead. He clasped it to his hip, blade forward, supported by both hands and charged forward. Matsudaira's blades whistled and cut an X-shaped cut across the man's belly. Matsudaira slipped aside and his last attacker tripped on his spilling greyish-bloody guts and fell to the floor. The knife blade dug into the resistant tatami.

Matsudaira spun around again and faced Hori. His white robe was still immaculate, and only his sword blades dripped blood. He raised a quizzical eyebrow and advanced. Hori raised his own blade and tried a feeble salute. He thrust hopelessly in *chudan morote uchi,* both hands on the hilt. Matsudaira parried the thrust with a stop thrust of his longer blade. He continued to thrust in a circular bind and lift which twitched the blade from Hori's nervous fingers. The tip of his *katan* stopped an inch from Hori's belly. "I shall not do it," he said. "You shall!"

Hori fell to his knees, his face white with terror.

Matsudaira looked at the disarmed samurai. "Your interrogation would be a lengthy affair," he said. "Painful, too. For you and for those who had come under your hand and whom we will have to make official inquiries for. The end would be the same.''

Hori licked his lips, then straightened his back. He was, after all, a samurai. ''May I ask you to be my second?'' he asked politely.

''No.'' Matsudaira shook his head. ''I cannot countenance you escaping justice. Before anything, I want a full confession, including the names of the recipients of your . . . services. We may be able to recover them quietly.''

Hori nodded, his head barely shaking. He knelt in place among the dead as Matsudaira watched. Matsudaira found writing implements in the room and Hori, his hand steady, wrote for a long time in his precise clerk's hand, sealing each sheet with his red seal. He was finished.

Matsudaira read the confession. ''You do not confess to your master's murder,'' he noted.

''It was not I,'' Hori insisted. Matsudaira merely nodded.

Hori bared his torso and tucked the sleeves of his kimono under his knees. He looked at the short sword in his hands. His lips firmed and he positioned the point on the left side of his abdomen. His eyes unfocused as his grip on the blade firmed. He pushed the point deeply in with a grunt, then moved it in a horizontal cut across his stomach. Grunting sounds came from his mouth mingled with blood. His eyes stared, incredulous at the pain though his iron will kept his hand steady. Matsudaira looked on impassively. There was a sudden blur of motion. Jiro's large blade whispered soundly through the air and struck at Hori's neck. His head rolled from his shoulder in a gout of blood while his torso fell forward and the short blade hit the tatami.

''I could not let him die like that, pig though he was.'' Jiro mumbled.

''I heard you moving outside. Did you find the woman?''

''No. She has disappeared. I was delayed by the puppy.''

''Ah,'' Matsudaira smiled. ''Uemura? That too would have been an odd business. He was involved in a number of robberies we think. Thank you. Embarrassing having warriors engaged in illicit activities. It makes the commoners think we are no different than themselves. We must find the woman though.'' He collected his papers and both men left the room. Behind them, blood dripped steadily and wet the foundations of the building.

† † †

Rose wearily pulled on her clothes and left the glade. She stood for a while, looking at the forester's peaceful face. She would have to bury him. The samurai was nowhere to be seen. He would like that, she thought, being buried on the slopes of Arashiyama, below a spreading pine. A movement caught her eye. The samurai returning? Then she saw it was the figure of a woman, hurrying in panic through the forest. Rosamund gripped her sash, the only weapon remaining, and hid behind the bole of a tree. She stepped out as the figure passed, slipped her sash over the woman's neck and pulled. The woman gurgled and fell to the ground whimpering. Rose leaped on her and twisted the other woman's hands behind her back.

"Let me go, let me go. I am Ito Haruko. My husband is rich, he will repay you. . . ." she babbled.

Rosamund turned her over and got a good look at the face in the early light. It fitted the description she had heard.

"You. Have. Caused. Me. A. Great. Deal. Of. Trouble." She emphasized each word with a slap. For the first time she allowed her resentment of Goemon's attention to his work to surface before another human being. Haruko had no idea of the source of this resentment. "And where are you hurrying to?" she asked maliciously. "And why are you dressed, or rather undressed, as you are?"

"Away, away," whimpered Haruko.

"Well, you've caused me a great deal of trouble," said Rosamund ominously while Haruko goggled at her without comprehension. "Now you'll help me. Get up."

Haruko tried to object, but Rosamund slapped her twice, hard, and the older woman quieted. She baulked again as Rosamund ordered her to dig in the moist earth. Without a word Rosamund seized a nearby branch and beat her back and buttocks. Haruko tried to run and Rosamund, her magnificent body exposed in her open kimono, slipped a loop of her sash around Haruko's legs.

"You'll do what I *say*!" she said fiercely.

At last Haruko capitulated and the two elegant women

211

dug a shallow grave for the mountain man in the thick moist humus, laying him down in it, his precious matchlock across his breast, his *nata* sheathed by his side.

† † †

The abbot was unskilled in sex perhaps, but he was thorough and meticulous. His lips followed, delicately tracing the lines of Okiku's slipper folds. He was patient and he was willing and Okiku wondered how such a saintly man could also be such a fanatic. Finally, at her request, he knelt between her legs and presented an unremarkable cock to her sopping entrance. He thrust into her, looking at her face to judge the effect, and when he saw her lids close sensuously and her hips jerk, nodded in satisfaction. He fingered a steel rosary. As her orgasm arrived, he would use it. At least she would die in pleasure, perhaps to be reborn in the afterlife as a man or a cow or some other higher being.

Okiku raised her naked legs to allow the abbot more access to her cunt. He worked well at her and she felt minor tremors of the initial orgasms. She had heard the chink of the metal beads and knew what he intended. Both her hands were now free of the cords he had tied around her wrists. She felt the first tremors of her orgasm flood her interior. Before he could identify them and act she had slipped the thin steel blade extracted from her sleeve sheath between his ribs and into his heart.

The abbot groaned. His control over his penis slackened and a small spurt of sperm escaped. He pulled himself slowly out her, his eyes glazing, lacking the strength to strike her temple with the steel beads as he'd intended. He fell backwards onto a box of oval coins.

"I am dying," he said. "So sad, so sad. Millions will not be saved because they do not know Yakushi Nyorai's grace. That is what I did it all for . . ."

"Including Ito's murder?"

He nodded weakly. "I did not have the resources for a properly glorious and attractive temple. My craftsmen showed me the way. We made statues, artifacts, decorations of gilding. Why not then coins as well? It would have been glorious, a shining temple dedicated to the one true god. I tried to cultivate Ito's friendship. Gave him gifts. Of course, I couldn't afford the sort of antique armor he fancied and so I had one of my craftsmen make up a fake one and gild it cheaply. Didn't think Ito would notice.'' He gasped. His lips were turning blue and he supported his side with his hand. ''I . . . I couldn't afford to hire craftsmen. But that did not matter. I had them brought to me . . . by my monks. *I* could not reward them, but the work for the *daibutsu* should be reward enough.'' He coughed pinkly.

''And Ito?'' She prompted.

''He hinted to me that he knew. Some days ago. I had my craftsman make the sword then.''

''Sword?'' Okiku asked.

Saishiden laughed, then coughed as blood welled out of his mouth. ''You mean your smart magistrate hasn't figured it out yet? Or you? Fumijiri, that's the artisan, was a genius! A pity he was such a drunkard too. I had to have him killed as well when he ran off to have a drink. There's a spring-operated piston in the hilt. I knew Ito's habits you see. Every man holds a sword in a particular way. Ito loved playing a part and he *always* held his swords the same way and went through the same motions. He triggered his own death. Once he raised the sword, the tiny cover slipped open. When he grasped the hilt with his left he triggered the mechanism.''

''And the fire on his clothes?''

''Simple. We had to add a small powder charge. The spring wasn't powerful enough.''

''But why kill him?''

''He became suspicious. He examined the armor, don't you understand? He hinted he was suspicious when he gave me a Senno Rikkyu tea bowl. I saw him later—by then I'd put a watch on him from the eaves—examine the armor carefully.''

''Why give him the armor?''

The abbot sighed and his face twisted with pain again. ''I made a mistake. I'd hoped to rally him to my cause. To build the most magnificent temple to the worship of the Daibtsu. I failed. *I failed!!*'' He wailed the last and his chubby body arced off the floor. A flood of blood gushed from his mouth. The body relaxed. He was dead.

CHAPTER 28

MOMOE SLIPPED OUT OF THE TEMPLE GROUNDS AND PAUSED only to secure her clothes around her. A moment later she was grateful she had done so. A rough hand descended on her arm and she spun around in a panic only to throw herself gratefully into Saburo's arms.

"Were you caught?" she asked. "Are you all right?" She ran trembling hands over his dear face to reassure herself.

"I was caught," he said, forebearing to add details. He knew little about women, but telling the tale of his captivity would probably not go well with an innocent girl like Momoe. He mentally reviewed the past few hours and decided that *some* of the things were worth remembering. He would introduce Momoe to them in due time, her essential innocence would recoil from performing some of the things Haruko's actions had kindled in his mind. "Are you all right? They didn't harm you, did they?"

Momoe smiled through her tears, her arms tight around him. "No. They were rough but kind. I managed to escape." She decided against telling him the details of the night. Or, for that matter, the previous week. For all that he had managed to pry open her virginity, he was essentially a straightforward and simple man, and the desires and appetites that had awakened in herself would have to wait until she could educate him to her taste.

"Should we go to the magistrate's?" she asked anxiously.

"No." He shook his head decisively. "The magistrate means nothing but trouble for us common people. We have survived. That is enough. Let us go home and tell your parents we are married."

She smiled shyly up at him as they hurried through the brightening streets of Miyako.

214

Goemon was full of the events of the night. Followed by Jiro, Midori, and Okiku he entered his private apartments in the governor's mansion.

"That was quite satisfactory," he said, taking his place on the cushion. Okiku looked gratified. "We got them all except for the Ito woman, and the whole tangle is undone. The constables caught most of the monks.

He examined the murder weapon critically. "Odd that I had it under my care all this time." Once the secret was undone, Okiku could easily operate the mechanism. The heavy gilt of the sword hilt served to disguise the bulky mechanism inside. "Let's hope there are no more of these around."

"Probably not," Okiku said. "The abbot told me he had another murder committed. The craftsman who made the sword. I don't know the details."

Matsudaira brightened "Of course! The elderly man from the canal! Very well indeed. The only loose end is Ito's wife. I wonder what happened to her. We can't really prove anything against her. Her brother and her lover protected her too well, but from the chance utterance you overheard, Midori, I am convinced she helped the murderer and was also part of the slave trade."

"We'll probably never find her, so why worry? We stopped the thing flat." Jiro said pontifically.

Goemon nodded, then sighed and his square shoulders slumped.

"Still worried about Rosamund?" Okiku asked gently.

He nodded wordlessly and Jiro looked on sympathetically. Okiku leaned forward and stroked Matsudaira's cheek. Jiro smiled. Okiku was displaying depths of tact and warmth he had never seen before. First with him, now with Goemon. Midori, at first shocked by Okiku's familiarity with the Governor of Miyako, looked on with interest.

"She'll be back, once she gets over her snit," Okiku said. "You can be sure about that."

"I am concerned about her," Goemon admitted unwillingly. "There are dangers out there. Something could happen . . . Maybe I shoudn't have beaten her . . ."

"Maybe you should have beaten her more," a bright, foreign sounding voice uttered behind them as the paper *shoji* door slid aside. "Look what I've got for us."

Goemon spun around. Rosamund stood at the doorway. She wore a pale kimono decorated with a pattern of *susuki* grass and sparrows in flight. She moved aside to display her captive. As instructed by her captress, Haruko knelt, her face to the floor, in abject apology. Her hair was made up in a simple knot. She was completely naked.

"Why don't you join us?" Rosamund asked composedly. "This is my new maid."

"Ohei will be extremely jealous," Okiku cautioned.

"All the better. Then she will beat this witch as she deserves." Midori looked on approvingly. "Don't you want to examine her? Thoroughly?" Rosamund prodded her friends.

"I'm going to examine *you*," said Goemon with a pointed look.

"That too. Later," she answered composedly. "Just now she owes, us, particularly Midori, a few things . . ."

Midori licked her lips then shook her head. "No," she said composedly with a confidence she had never before displayed in their presence. "I take delight only in those who take delight in me. But I would be quite content to see her punished by others. Particularly if they know their business," she added as an afterthought.

Rosamund looked at her and glowed gratefully. She knelt by Haruko's side and spread her ass as wide as she could. "Look at her. Lovely ass hole. Nice slit, and the entrance is a bright pink. The hair that frames it is pleasurably soft. Who wants to bid for a first try at this brand new concubine?"

Haruko moved uneasily at the words and Rosamund slapped her resoundingly on one smooth pale bun, then again, harder, on the other. "Shall I investigate her for you?"

Drawn as if by strings the two men and Okiku sat themselves down, ready to enjoy the show.

Rosamund inserted a moistened finger into Haruko's cunt, then another, she frigged the entrance roughly and Haruko complained, only to be slapped to silence by Rosamund. The blonde removed her fingers and Haruko breathed more easily until she felt them probe again at her asshole. The barbarian woman's fingers were now liberally coated with Haruko's internal juices and the muscles slid apart easily.

"Roll over!" Rosamund commanded. Haruko did as she was bid. The slick muscles of her rear entrance slid around Rosamund's finger and she found herself with one leg high in the air, supported by the blonde's shoulder. The finger popped out of her and Rosamund regarded her thin figure with disfavor.

"You are too bony to satisfy me. We will have to fatten you up. Go and undress my friends."

Haruko's lips firmed. For one moment her pride as the cossetted wife of a prominent nobleman surfaced. She started to open her lips as she came to her feet. A stinging blow on her thin buttocks brought her back to reality. She tried to escape a second blow, but was caught by Okiku's strong grip. The second blow landed. Her skin jerked in pain and outrage.

"I will have to discipline her. You had better undress, you lot." The two men hastened to comply while Rosamund wielded the thin willow branch taken from the flower arrangement in the *tokonoma*. Okiku smiled and held Haruko still on her knees. She toyed with Haruko's form freely while Rosamund wielded the switch.

"Enough, oh please enough!" Haruko wailed. Her bottom was a fiery red, striped with light weals.

"Enough? What do you mean enough?" Rosamund snorted, smacking again with the flexible switch.

"Mistress, please stop. I beg of you." Something snapped in Haruko. She was no longer the wielder of discipline, no longer the owner of whims but subject to them. She stopped struggling against Okiku's hold, offering whatever part of her the slim girl wanted to fondle meekly for use. Okiku nodded at Rosamund who stopped the beating. The two men were ready. Rosamund led Haruko to them. Following instructions, the erstwhile noblewoman accepted the rampant pricks into her mouth. They spewed their juices into her moving sucking cavern and she swallowed the effluvia with complete detachment, licking the tip of each cock hungrily until not a drop remained. To her delight and surprise she found that both men maintained their erections even after they had come for the first time. She knelt then before Okiku and repeatedly laved her sweet-smelling cunt with her tongue. Okiku held her head, urging the untutored digit deeper into herself. Uninstructed Haruko found the slim woman's clitoris and sucked at the tiny pearly button hungrily until her mouth was flooded with Okiku's juice and the naked *shinobi* danced on the tip of the noblewoman's tongue. Rosamund replaced Okiku. Her smell was stronger, more animal-like. The hair at the juncture of her legs was a dark golden cloud. Haruko paused before she sunk herself into the waiting cunt. The beautiful pink lips were decorated with an exquisitely done rose. Bright red, it grew out of the demanding heavy-scented hole of her mistress to flower to glory on her thigh. Rosamund allowed her a brief glimpse, and then her large claw-like clitoris was shoved between her new servant's lips.

Haruko's mouth was flooded with the essence of her future life, and she sucked obediently at the delicate demanding morsel while the others crowded around her subservient body, ready to make use of it as they would.

† † †

A lone monk paused on the road going north out of Miyako. To his right, Hiei-san topped by Enryakuji temple guarded the sleeping city from the supernatural perils of the Northeast. To the south the city lights twinkled dimly. The monk looked back at the city of dreams for one last look. He intoned a last prayer for the soul of the boddhisatva saint he had met in life, then turned resolutely away. His head was newly shaven and his robes, hastily acquired, did not yet show the dust of the road. He was not yet ready, not yet set firmly on the path. It would come in time. Then he would return to glorify the saint, the only one who had been his equal, yet had turned away and shown him the path.

The lonely monk who had once been Sugiyama Tamasaburo followed his road to the deep north. Behind him a female pilgrim stared thoughtfully at his stride, then followed with a peculiar smile on her face.

Selected Blue Moon Backlist Titles

J. Gonzo Smith
SIGN OF THE
SCORPION
Clara Reeve's amateur
sleuthing to find her sister
catapults her into a thrill-
seeking world, and a
labyrinth of sexuality.
#161 $7.95

Patrick Henden
BEATRICE
An aura of eroticism
surrounds Beatrice, as well
as her equally attractive
sister, Caroline, who is ld
into the strange fulfillments
of their desires. #81 $7.95

Daniel Vian
SABINE
A beautiful but naive demi-
mondaine travels from
France to South America
with her rich patron, who
tells her upon their return
that he has no money for
her. #29 $7.95

**David (Sunset)
Carson**
LAMENT
Carson's western is, in the
words of Hubert Selby Jr.,
"bawdy, bizarre, satirical,
Rabelaisian, iconclastic,
and zany. It is also
gruesome, and funny as
hell." #153 $7.95

Akahige Namban
WOMEN OF GION
When a respectable
councillor is murdered in
old Miyako while enjoying
his new concubine, there
are a plentitude of suspects,
including the councillor's

wife, her ambitious lover, the beautiful blonde Rosamund and even the governor of Miyako.
#36 $7.95

Richard Manton
LA VIE
PARISIENNE
These extracts represent the cream of banned fiction from La Vie Parisienne: from the shuttered rooms of lesbian "amorettes" and passionate nymphs in exclusive finishing schools to whip-wielding jealousies of circus girls.
#9 $5.95

Pauline Réage
STORY OF O
This sado-masochistic tale is considered a classic, worthy to stand besides the best writing of the Marquis de Sade.
#130 $7.95

To Order a Complete Backlist Catalog Write to:

Blue Moon Books, Inc.
61 Fourth Avenue
New York, NY 10003
fax (212) 673-1039
e-mail: bluoff@aol.com